How had Cyn wound up on Santa's knee?

Even worse, Amanda crawled onto his other knee and swung a sprig of mistletoe above his head.

"You gotta kiss Mommy!" Amanda exclaimed.

"A quick peck won't kill you," Cyn whispered. *Why did I say that?*

Santa's brow arched. "To please Amanda?"

"Only Amanda," Cyn shot back. "I assure you."

But instead of kissing her cheek, the man's tongue plunged between her lips! Cyn's insides turned to jelly, and her lips started swelling like a prizefighter's. *Oh, no!* Anton Santa even kissed like the thief who'd betrayed her four years ago.... Cyn wrenched away.

"Good," Amanda pronounced.

What an understatement, Cyn thought numbly.

Santa winked at Cyn. "So glad to oblige, Amanda," he drawled.

Dear Reader,

You're about to step under the mistletoe with one of our four hunky heroes this month in our CHRISTMAS KISSES holiday promotion!

Jule McBride sends this holiday message:

"I'll always remember my childhood winter holidays. We would skate on West Virginia's frozen creeks, warm our toes over the heater vents, then scald our tongues on too much hot chocolate.... Then I grew up and moved to Manhattan—where snow makes the city streets glitter more than all the diamonds in Tiffany's. At Christmastime, shoppers rush, horse-drawn carriages circle Central Park and artists fashion angels from ice outside the Plaza Hotel. As different as the city seems, Christmases remain as warm as those of my youth. After all, Christmas is really about kids and excitement, second chances and the healing power of love. I hope you're warmed by *The Baby & the Bodyguard*."

Jule McBride and all of us at Harlequin wish you a joyous holiday filled with CHRISTMAS KISSES!

Debra Matteucci
Senior Editor and Editorial Coordinator
Harlequin Books
300 E. 42nd Street
New York, New York 10017

JULE McBRIDE

THE BABY & THE
BODYGUARD

Harlequin Books

TORONTO • NEW YORK • LONDON
AMSTERDAM • PARIS • SYDNEY • HAMBURG
STOCKHOLM • ATHENS • TOKYO • MILAN
MADRID • WARSAW • BUDAPEST • AUCKLAND

For Debra Matteucci, Alice Orr, and Corinne Meyer—
three very special women who've made
my every day a Christmas

ISBN 0-373-16562-5

THE BABY & THE BODYGUARD

Prologue

"So, how are my three busiest elves this morning?" Analise Sweet smoothed the skirt of her green wool Chanel suit, tapped a perfectly manicured red nail on top of a file folder, then ensconced herself at the head of her laquered boardroom table.

Evan Morrissey merely grunted. The numbers cruncher for Too Sweet Toys' retail division was already seated. His eyes remained riveted on rows of figures that indicated holiday sales trends. Judging from his expression, they weren't good.

"My, my, I do believe Evan is the Grinch himself," Analise teased. Standard protocol dictated that her meetings begin with friendly joking, but the Wall Street transplant had never really adjusted.

Bob Bingley had. The thirty-something man chuckled, ran a hand over his shock of white-blond hair, then sprawled in the leather swivel chair nearest Analise. "It's three weeks till the day, and this particular elf is tired of working 'round the clock." He tweaked his mustache. "I'm ready for the parties, if you want the truth."

"Did I ask for the truth, darling?" Analise smiled at her favorite office prankster. When their eyes met, Analise decided he was almost perfect for her daughter. Unfortunately Bob was a womanizer, and Cynthia had already been played for a fool. The last man had left her a single mother—and worse. "Clayton?"

As usual, elderly Clayton Woods, devoted family friend and head buyer, was positioned in front of the boardroom's wall-to-wall window. He didn't respond, but leaned on his cane and glared across the Rockefeller Center complex through a pair of binoculars. *Poor Clayton. He's taken my separation from Paxton nearly as hard as I have.*

Outside, couples skated on the Rockefeller ice rink. Analise could see their foggy breaths and catch bright snatches of their bobbing hats and blowing scarves. The twinkling bulbs on the center's huge blue spruce lit up the cloudy winter day, making her feel wistful for Christmases past.

After all, she'd been married thirty-five years ago, on Christmas day, 1959. Then four Christmases past, she'd discovered her daughter Cynthia had fallen in love with a man named Jake Jackson. On Christmas Eve, when Analise and Paxton had been away, Cynthia had caught the jewel thief and his two cohorts stealing the Sweet family heirlooms, including Analise's lucky Christmas necklace. Although two men had gone to prison, one had absconded with the jewelry.

The necklace had been of ruby and emerald links, and Analise's husband had added a new link every Christmas since their marriage. Now the necklace was gone. Not that Analise would have received her thirty-fifth link this year. Last December twenty-fifth she'd walked out on Paxton.

"There's Paxton!" Clayton clutched the binoculars. "Eileen's bringing him coffee."

At the mention of her husband's assistant, Analise tried not to bristle. "Of course Paxton's in his office. He works there."

In response to her censuring tone, Clayton placed the binoculars aside and hobbled toward the table. "Ever since he left, this company's been a mess," Clayton said defensively. "I'm worried, if for no other reason than I own such a large share of the stocks. We're in a ridiculous situation, with him and Cynthia handling marketing, while we—who are right across the ice rink—handle the toy store."

"And never the twain do meet." Bob sighed, eyeing the building opposite. "Unless Cynthia and I—" he glanced at Analise "—running the gauntlet between you and Paxton counts as communication."

"Now, now, Too Sweet is fine," Analise said soothingly.

"Why doesn't he just come back?" Clayton groused. "This split has caused rumors of takeover, you know."

Analise forced herself to smile. Paxton hadn't returned because she'd walked out on him, not the other way around. But that was too personal to divulge to her executives. "May we please get into the holiday spirit?"

"Oh, but we are, Analise." Bob's blue eyes twinkled naughtily. "I have the perfect plan. We'll punish Paxton for leaving, by hitting him where it will hurt him most."

"And just where might that be, Bob?" Analise noted that even Grinchlike Evan was now perking up.

"Well—" Bob leaned forward conspiratorially "—we'll steal the central, key element in the biggest marketing campaign he's ever launched."

Evan chuckled. "You are thoroughly incorrigible."

"Ah—" Clayton leaned back and steepled his fingers. "So we cutthroats would steal the star baby? The three-year-old spokesperson, mascot and figurehead of our own beloved toy company, Little Amanda? That *would* ruin Paxton's special promotion!"

"If it hit the tabloids," Bob added reasonably, "it would increase our holiday sales."

"Why, you know how people are drawn to a good tragedy," Evan said, picking up the thread.

"And once Little Amanda was returned," Clayton continued, "sales would absolutely skyrocket."

Bob sighed with satisfaction. "Why, it would look more like the Fourth of July than Christmas."

Analise's lipsticked mouth dropped open in feigned terror. She playfully scrutinized Bob, Evan and Clayton, in turn. "Now, gentlemen." Her voice lowered to a stage whisper. "Do you honestly think I should kidnap my very own granddaughter?"

The members of the group maintained a long, wicked silence, while contemplating the ludicrous suggestion. Then, suddenly, everyone burst into merry laughter. Or *almost* everyone . . .

TWELVE DAYS TILL CHRISTMAS...

Chapter One

"Little Amanda needs a bodyguard." Paxton Sweet sounded furious. He shook Anton Santa's hand, then draped the bodyguard's garment bag over a chair. "I'm sorry about interrupting your Caribbean vacation, and I want to thank you for stopping by in the evening." Paxton gestured wildly around his office. "During the Christmas season we work nonstop."

Santa grunted and glanced around. Dolls tumbled from an overful box beside the door, inflatable Teenage Mutant Ninja Turtles bobbed on cabinet tops. Windup beetles, yo-yos, and gum banks littered Paxton's desk. And on the windowsill, next to a Barney doll with a torn ear, was a framed picture of Cynthia Sweet. Just looking at it made Santa feel vaguely murderous.

He had no intention of taking this job, although he almost wished it was Cynthia who needed protection. Then he'd take it...and kill her, himself. No, his reasons for entering the office, once he'd realized the address led to Too Sweet Toys, had nothing to do with Little Amanda, whoever she was. "Well, Mr. Sweet," Santa finally returned tersely, with a hint of a drawl from his long-lost Southern roots, "sunning myself in the Caribbean is less of a vacation, and more my everyday life-style. At least, when I'm between jobs."

"Call me Paxton."

"Paxton," Santa repeated, feeling his chest constrict. Was he really in the office of the man he'd once hoped would become his father-in-law? "You can call me Santa."

Paxton scrutinized him, clearly liking what he saw. "You *look* like a bodyguard," he said, sounding pleased with himself.

Feeling edgy, Santa rubbed the razor-thin scar on his jaw. "I *am* a bodyguard."

"I've been looking all over the place for you! Everybody says you're the absolute best in the business. Top of the line."

"The most expensive, too," Santa added dryly, making Paxton smile. Santa blew out a sigh as Cyn Sweet's father dug a file folder from a locked cabinet, then began to remove the toys from his desk, so he could better display whatever it was he meant to display.

While he did so, Santa studied him. Paxton had never seen him. Nor had he seen Paxton. But Santa recognized him from an oil painting above the piano in the Sweet family's living room. The last time he'd seen the sixtyish man with the thick silver hair, Anton Santa—along with Matthew Lewis and an unidentified man who remained at large—had been stealing the Sweet family blind.

If the man only knew. Santa stared into the wintry darkness, through the window, which was decorated with paper snowflakes, thinking that he hated Christmas. Christmas in Manhattan was worse. And Christmas anywhere near the Sweet family would be like slow death.

"Will there be anything else this evening, Paxton?"

Santa glanced in the direction of the voice. A fiftyish brunette in a blue flannel suit hovered in the doorway.

"Yes, Eileen." Paxton smiled. "Go paint the town red *and* green."

The woman chuckled lustily. "I'll get right on it, boss."

As soon as she left, Paxton finished cleaning his desk and arranging the materials. "What you've got to understand," he said, "is that our three-year-old Amanda is no ordinary child."

Santa fought not to roll his eyes. Kids were kids, weren't they? "How's that, Mr.—er—Paxton?"

"Well, this year we're running a special promotion, all surrounding a ghostwritten book, called *Little Amanda's Perfect Christmas.*"

"Well now, that sounds real special." Santa hadn't meant to sound so cynical, but the past four years had left him bitter.

"Yes!" Paxton clearly hadn't caught Santa's irony. "The story's about a little girl who's been so bad all year that she only has the twelve days until Christmas to atone for it. She needs to be extra nice, so that Santa will bring her toys."

Santa forced himself to look interested.

"She helps her friends decorate a tree, then takes them to *The Nutcracker* ballet. She goes caroling at a shelter for homeless children, too. So, Little Amanda—the real Amanda—will be involved in such activities over the next twelve days, just like in the story!" Paxton's rising excitement suddenly fell flat. "And now we get these."

Curiosity got the better of him. Santa rose lithely from his chair, crossed to the desk, then stared down. There were three notes, composed of sharply cut red and green letters, probably taken from magazine pages with an X-Acto blade. All three said, "Take Amanda off the Promotion or She Will be Kidnapped!"

"So these are the notes," Santa drawled noncommittally. "They're a bit juvenile." He hadn't seen anything so nonthreatening since the notes left by The Grinch Gang, the jewel thief ring of which he'd been a part. The college boys had seduced security information from young heiresses at New York University, like Cynthia Sweet. Then, they'd stolen family valuables during the Christmas holidays, pawned them during spring break and used the cash to tide them over in high style, during the longer summer vacations. At every theft, they'd left a bottle of good champagne and a note to the victims, wishing them a happier new year. Four years ago the Sweet family had received no champagne, of course, since The Grinch Gang had been interrupted in the act, thanks to Cynthia.

"I knew you'd be as worried as I am when you saw them," Paxton finally said.

Something in the man's voice actually made Santa want to take the job. But he couldn't. Not that he'd see Cyn. Last he'd heard she was married to a man named Harry Stevens and living in Alabama. Even if she saw him, she wouldn't recognize him. He was a master of disguises. As the chameleon par excellence, he bore no resemblance to the young man she'd once said she loved.

"Look—" Santa suddenly decided to soften the blow. "I protect senators, stalked movie stars, star witnesses with mob contracts on their heads—"

"That's exactly why I requested you!"

I'm a bodyguard, not a babyguard. "Usually, there's a lot of danger involved—"

Paxton's Adam's apple bobbed up and down when he gulped. "Have you ever taken a bullet for anyone?"

Your damn daughter, who left me for dead. "On occasion."

Paxton paced the length of his window, which overlooked the Rockefeller tree, making the paper snowflakes flap in his wake. He pivoted and stared at Santa. "You have to take the job! I—I'll pay double."

Santa chuckled. "You already were, because of the holidays."

"I mean double the double!"

"Sorry, Mr. Sweet. I can't—"

"Granddaddy!" a little girl squealed.

When Santa turned, his whole body tensed. The child who flew past him was nothing more than a blur. Because Cynthia Sweet herself was standing in the doorway. A thick, luxurious *faux* fur coat was wrapped around her fabulous figure, and her lush blond hair hung free, just past her shoulders. Shopping bags dangled from both her wrists until she gracefully set them down.

When her coat fell open, he caught a glimpse of her suit. The skirt was short and her long, perfect legs went on for miles, all the way down to her trademark spiked heels. She was exactly as he'd remember: Rectangular face. Wide, full lips. A body to die for. *One I very nearly did die for,* he mentally corrected. Now she seemed even more beautiful than the last night he'd spent with her, the one and only night they'd ever made love.

For an instant, he was sure—maybe even hoped—she'd recognize him, but she didn't. In her eyes, which were still as bright, shiny and green as Christmas lights, he read nothing more than surprise at seeing a stranger. Of course, she'd never expect to find him in her father's office, and when it came to identifying people, context played a larger part than most people assumed.

"I picked up the elf outfits from the seamstress, Daddy," Cyn finally said. "Then Amanda and I went out for dinner."

She's still a daddy's girl. Santa realized he'd been holding his breath and slowly exhaled.

"Mr. Santa," Paxton said, "I'd like you to meet Amanda."

Only years of masking his personal responses and reactions gave him the power to turn away from Cyn. He did so just as Amanda leapt on top of Paxton's desk. From the back, the little girl's head was a mass of blond waves. When she whirled around, her eyes were the same bewitching green as Cyn's.

Then he noticed the tiny cute mole beside her pouty upper lip. His grandfather had had it. His father had had it. He'd had it, too, until a doctor had insisted on removing it.

For the first time in his life, Anton Santa couldn't move. The plush red carpet seemed to take flight beneath his feet, like a reindeer-driven sleigh. He felt downright woozy. Was he really being hired to protect a baby he and Cyn Sweet had made four long years ago...a daughter he'd never known he had?

TIME STOOD STILL. Cyn Sweet held her breath and clutched her shopping bags as if she were drowning in rough seas and they were her only lifeline. How had she been able to speak? A thousand unwanted impressions were still flashing through her mind.

First, it was crazy, but she could swear Jake Jackson was in her father's office. He wasn't, though. The strange sensations sweeping over her could have nothing to do with the man who *was* there, either.

She summed him up in a heartbeat. An aura of self-containment clung to him like a second skin. He was clean shaven and tanned a deep bronze, even though it was winter. The medium-brown eyes weren't special, and his too-short, slicked-back hair was also an unremarkable dark brown. Given his tailored brown wool suit, he was possibly rich. Still, the jacket hung so loosely that she'd barely recognized it as a Valentino Uomo original.

The expression was aloof, distanced and unreadable, something she'd learned to hate in a man. Very definitely, she was falling in distrust at first sight, but that may have had nothing to do with the stranger, specifically. Cyn knew better than to trust men, categorically.

In the next heartbeat, images of Jake Jackson flew through her head. Fury had shaded her memories of Jackson, the thief who'd loved her then betrayed her. Where once she'd thought him the most handsome man alive, she now remembered his long blond hair as scraggly and obviously dyed. He'd had a scruffy, unbecoming beard and a mustache that had almost covered a mole beside his lip. Four years ago, the mole had seemed sexy, of course. Now she mentally added a hair that grew from the center of it, just to remind herself that she hated him. He'd been overly pale, reed thin, and had usually worn sunglasses with his leather jackets.

No, the man in her father's office in no way resembled Jake Jackson. In fact, the two were as different as night and day. This man was all business. The other had been a hellion and a rebel, just the sort an overly protected, well-to-do college girl might use for her one brief fling with danger. Was the stranger wearing Jake's brand of cologne? *Eau de Bad boy.*

She realized Paxton was staring from face to face with a perplexed expression, as if sensing strange energy in the room. "Amanda, Cyn," he finally repeated, "this is Anton Santa."

Amanda's giggles cut through the tension. "You're Mr. Santa, so is Santa Claus your daddy?"

The man's brown eyes narrowed, as if he'd heard enough Santa jokes to last him a lifetime.

"Now, Amanda," Cyn said quickly, "please don't tease Mr. Santa."

As soon as she'd spoken, she was sorry. The man shot her a look that made her feel as hot as fire, then as cold as ice. He turned to Amanda, with a grimace that Cyn supposed was his best attempt at a smile. "Maybe I am related, sweetheart," he said gruffly.

The faint Southern accent gave Cyn pause, but she bit back a smile, nonetheless. The man—probably a manufacturing VP, she decided—clearly didn't have much experience with kids. In spite of that, Amanda was charming the Uomo trousers off him.

In her twenty-eight years, no man had done more than play Cyn for a fool, but give Amanda ten seconds, and she'd wrap even the toughest cases right around her pinkie. Anton Santa, with his panther-about-to-kill posture and blank expression, was very clearly a tough case.

Amanda reached up and squeezed the poor man's biceps. "Are you my new bodyguard, Mr. Santa Claus?"

"You didn't!" As soon as Cyn imagined Anton Santa as a personal sidekick, he became a lot less "medium." Had her initial, very strange reaction to him really been attraction? "You didn't hire—"

"Yes." Paxton glared at her pointedly. "I intend to ensure that you and Amanda are safe."

Cyn gulped. Between the Christmas promotion, shopping and running the gauntlet between her parents, her next two weeks were going to be busy enough. She couldn't have a tall, gruff bodyguard shadowing her, too! Especially not one who made her feel so oddly uncomfortable. "No offence, Mr. Santa—"

"Just Santa." His voice was both rough and unsettling.

"Sorry—er—Santa, but we really don't need a bodyguard." Her eyes shot to Paxton's. "I talked to Bob Bingley. He said kidnapping Amanda was a joke cooked up during one of Mother's meetings. We simply can't involve—" She glanced at the man. His eyes now seemed hazel, hard to define. Changeable and arresting. Were they dark or golden? "A third party in our family infighting," she finished in a rush.

"Some joke." Paxton sniffed.

Cyn stared him down. Her father didn't take the warnings any more seriously than she did. He'd merely followed through with his own threat to hire the best, most expensive protection money could buy. His game plan was to make her mother feel like an idiot.

"I think I need a bodyguard!" Amanda sounded more excited about Anton Santa than about the Santa who came down the chimney. "People are gonna kidnap me and lock me up and everything!"

Was it her imagination, or could she feel the bodyguard scrutinizing her? Cyn glanced his way and caught his gaze roving over her face. He shoved his hands deep into his trouser pockets, then leaned idly against a file cabinet. It was strange, but she could swear she saw coldhearted fury in his eyes, in spite of his relaxed body language. She turned away and almost glared at Paxton.

"You know how they are about office pranks." She felt Mr. Calm, Cool and Collected's eyes drop from her face to her stocking-clad legs, and wished she'd worn a longer skirt. "Sometimes their jokes go too far. Bob probably sent the notes himself. He just won't admit it now because of all the ruckus you've caused."

Her eyes narrowed when they landed on her father's sleeves. He was missing both cuff links, as usual. When her mother left, it had become clear who'd been dressing him all those years.

"Well—" Paxton smiled wanly. "Mr. Santa was just saying he won't take the job."

Cyn sighed in relief. "Then things are—"

"I do believe I've changed my mind," Santa said.

Paxton began wringing his hands. "You said the threats seemed juvenile!"

Santa shook his head. "True, but I've been around a long time...."

Santa's voice had changed! Previously it was so gruff that Cyn was convinced he ate gravel for breakfast. Now it sounded silkily persuasive and as clear as a bell!

"Long enough to know that even the most ridiculous threats can be very real." His casual shrug suggested that even death couldn't faze him. "Better safe than sorry."

"Daddy, everything's fine," Cyn insisted, wishing Santa wouldn't encourage her father. "It was a practical joke taken—"

"Too far," her father finished, not looking convinced.

Cyn sighed. It wasn't the first time her father had gone overboard. He'd told lies on her own behalf that had left her a pampered widow, when she wasn't one, for instance. Paxton had a warm heart and good intentions, but his childish streak was a mile wide. It was why he'd started a toy company.

"You're a single mother!" Paxton exclaimed urgently. "I simply can't leave you and Amanda unprotected. If this is a false alarm, fine. If it's not, you'll have someone to watch over you."

"You live alone, then?"

Cyn's gaze shot to Santa's. The question was simple—just the sort a bodyguard might ask—but something in the man's eyes seemed almost suggestive. Cyn was so taken aback that words failed her. She felt her knees go a little weak.

"She was widowed over three years ago," Paxton explained.

"Her husband died?" Santa prodded.

"Very unfortunate." Paxton shook his head. "A car wreck."

"Please, Mommy!" Amanda piped in, seemingly unconcerned about her father's death. "I really want him!" The way she said it, Santa could have been a Ken doll.

Cyn shot her father a quelling glance. "I live alone," she said. "I like it that way. And I *can* take care of myself." She put her hands on her hips. "I can answer for myself, too."

"Such a talented woman," Santa remarked, making her mouth drop open in astonishment. The man's lips curled in what might have been a smile. He turned to Paxton. "Yes," he said softly, "I can certainly see why you'd want to keep two such charming ladies safe."

It was obvious he didn't find her at all charming. He was railroading her father and talking about her as if she weren't there, too. "I said I don't need—"

"You're gonna be bodyguarding me?" Amanda interrupted. She bounced on the desk, her dimpled cheeks bright with barely contained pleasure.

"He is." Paxton sounded decisive.

"Yeah." Santa nodded as Amanda jumped off the desk.

If she really put her foot down, Cyn knew she could dissuade her father. Instead, she found herself wondering what being guarded entailed, and wishing she wasn't so inclined to indulge Paxton since her mother had left him. Fortunately, her father's whims always ended as quickly as they began. Santa wouldn't be around long.

"So, I'm your boss," Amanda said precociously. "Right?"

"Guess you could say that."

Santa's voice sent a sudden shiver down Cyn's spine. It had turned gravelly again. Like his brown hair and eyes and suit, it should have been unremarkable. It was an ordinary baritone, touched with the slightest hint of a drawl. And yet, it was as changeably sexy as his eyes. The man was hardly nondescript, but there was something fluid about him. It was as if she kept reaching for him but couldn't quite grasp him.

"I'm the boss and you gotta carry me." Amanda's arms shot into the air.

An awkward moment passed. Santa's face tightened, looking more unreadable than ever. Cyn felt sure he was going to deny the request.

"Well, Amanda. I guess I do."

Cyn watched in surprise as the man lifted Amanda into his arms. "Wait a minute!" Maybe one last protest would put an end to this! "We're not in danger. Between the doormen, elevator operators and lobby attendants, my building's as secure as Fort Knox. I can't have a strange man underfoot during the day. I've work to do, both here and at home." She stared at her father, looking for support, and got none.

"I'll be there day *and* night." Santa glanced over his shoulder but kept walking.

Amanda yelled, "Stop at the door!"

Santa halted and shifted Amanda on his hip. While she swooped down to lift a doll from the overflowing box, Santa's eyes remained fixed on Cyn's.

"Okay, you can go again, Santa Claus," Amanda said, cradling the doll against his chest.

Santa chuckled. "Why, you little thief." He glanced quickly at Amanda with seeming approval, then looked at Cyn again.

"Day and night?" Cyn echoed.

"I always move in with my clients." His leisurely gaze dropped down the length of her body, then slowly traveled upward again. "Sometimes I consider it a perk of the job."

The way he'd just looked at her made Cyn want to kill him. "And do you in this particular instance?" she asked tartly.

"Probably not," he said. Then he breezed over the threshold without a backward glance.

"WHAT HAS MY FATHER gotten me into?" Cyn fumed under her breath. The new bodyguard, still carrying Amanda, had the audacity to precede her through the outer door to her building. Worse, the doormen were nowhere to be seen and she'd somehow gotten stuck hauling Santa's heavy garment bag and a camel coat that was every bit as tasteful as his suit. Just as the door swung shut in her face, she nearly yelled, "You're a real gentleman, Mr. Santa."

He smirked, kicked the door partially open with his foot, then kept walking. She swung his garment bag, wedged it in the crack, then nudged through, using her shoulder. "Thank you so very much."

"You're so very welcome," he drawled. He glanced over his shoulder, then looked pointedly downward, at where his bag touched the floor. "Watch the bag. It's a Louis Vuitton, and I'd sure hate to see it soiled."

Her eyes narrowed as he turned away and began walking down the corridor. Jennifer, the lobby attendant, flashed her a quick smile of sympathy. "If you didn't want it *soiled*, then perhaps you should have carried it yourself." Cyn sped her steps, hoping to keep pace with him. "What's in it? Lead?"

He was far ahead now, but she heard his infuriating chuckle. She also realized that her initial estimation of him as average had been dead wrong. Outside, temperatures were hovering somewhere around subzero and the man hadn't even bothered with his coat. He hadn't shivered, either.

Now, still holding Amanda, he somehow managed to shrug out of his suit jacket. His shoulders were broad, accentuated by stylish thin suspenders. They tapered to a narrow waist, a perfect behind and long, lean-looking legs. Handcuffs were affixed to an unused belt loop. Beneath that loose-fitting suit, his body was very definitely not medium.

And then she saw the holster. "I will not have a gun in my apartment!"

"Maybe not," he called, without turning around. "But you sure need something. Your place is wide open. Where are all those doormen you were talking about?"

She forced herself to keep moving. Her high heels were skittering across the polished tile floor, and the exertion of dealing with him and carrying his luggage was making her short-winded. "I don't know—" He was a good ten feet in front of her now, so she had to raise her huffy voice. "They're usually right—"

"Which floor, Amanda?" His voice was soft, but it carried. Every time he addressed Amanda, rather than her, his tone became as sweet as honey. Cyn had never felt so annoyed in her life.

"Penthouse," Amanda and the elevator operator said simultaneously.

Apparently, the operator hadn't seen Cyn. The mirrored elevator doors slid shut just as she reached them. She scrutinized her reflection. She was well coiffed. Her green suit was tasteful and flattering. When her gaze dropped to the man's luggage, she jabbed the up button so hard she nearly broke a nail. "Once I get upstairs," she muttered, "you're history."

And then she smiled. Amanda was too young to carry keys, which meant the bodyguard was locked out.

WITHIN MERE MINUTES, Santa would feel prepared to see her again. It was enough time that he could wrap his invisible shield tightly around himself. He quickly cased the apartment, ignoring the wreath on the door, the lighted, ornamented tree in the living room, the red stockings hanging from the mantel, and the profusion of other homey Christmas decorations, all of which made him feel vaguely uncomfortable.

The front door, he found, opened onto the overly Christmassy living room, which led to an unsecured terrace. The dining room, kitchen, den and study were on one side of a hallway. Four bedrooms were on the other. Cyn had bad locks, one fire escape, no window bars, and in this case, "penthouse" only meant one of two top-floor apartments in a brownstone that would be easy to scale. Santa could do it with his eyes shut.

"Given her experience with thieves," he muttered as he began to pace, "you'd think she'd buy a decent dead bolt."

"Where's Amanda?"

He was walking the perimeter of the living room, mentally listing the new items he'd need, since he intended to secure the place, whether Amanda was really in danger or not. He turned around easily and smiled in Cyn's general direction.

"Your daughter—" Santa let the phrase hang in the air, as if to point out that she might be his, too. "Said she had to go change, in order to model her favorite nightgown for me."

Cyn gasped. "Do you mind telling me how you got in here?"

He shrugged. "I picked the locks."

"There were three of them!"

He seated himself gracefully on her cream velvet sofa. "I *did* leave the door open for you."

She remained in the doorway, with his bag in one hand and his coat in the other, her chest heaving. Her skin was flushed, more from fury than exertion, he thought.

"Why do you keep looking at me that way?" She sounded almost as curious as she did angry.

Because we used to be lovers. "What way?"

She sniffed, then kicked the front door shut with one of her high heels. "Like you hate my guts," she returned haughtily, as if the fact that he might didn't bother her in the least.

"I don't hate you," he said, even though the thought had entered his mind at least a thousand times. Did he? he wondered. He sure wanted to rail at her . . . right after he tasted her sweet-smelling skin again. He even wanted to tell her the truth.

But as near as he could tell, Cyn Sweet had kept a few secrets of her own. Namely, Amanda. "Nice spread," he finally said. It was an understatement. Her uptown penthouse would appraise at over a million.

She sighed. "Would you mind telling me what you've got against me?"

Where do I begin? The list is as long as your legs. "Not a thing," he said lightly. Looking at her, he realized that he'd have to attempt civility. Otherwise, she really would throw him out. He knew the dynamics between Paxton and Cyn well enough to know that she'd get her way if she really wanted it. So why hadn't she done so earlier, in her father's office?

"Do I look like a doormat?" She stared pointedly at his belongings, which were in her hands.

He couldn't help it. He looked her up and down, then tilted his head as if considering. "Well, you sure don't have *welcome* written on you." So much for being civil.

She dropped his bag with a thud, tossed his coat on top of it, then stared at him, looking thoroughly puzzled. Cyn Sweet—with her cheerleader good looks and helpful personality—was definitely not used to having people dislike her on sight.

Why was he torturing himself this way? When he'd seen Amanda, he'd been sure she was his. Now he was beginning to wonder. In the elevator he'd gotten Amanda's birthday, and the timing was right. Still, she could belong to Harry Stevens, Cyn's husband. Santa had to know, but staying here might actually jeopardize his secret investigation.

Maybe he wanted to stay, since the situation was so strangely coincidental. But then, Santa didn't believe in fate. He still wanted Cyn, of course, but his fantasies were so ravenously vengeful that *how* he wanted her could hardly be called lovemaking. Finally, being in Cyn's apartment when she didn't recognize him made him feel as if he had power over her. Wielding it, he felt he was delivering the punishment she deserved. She hadn't given him the benefit of the doubt. She'd married someone else, and possibly to give Santa's own child a name.

"Are you going to apologize or not?" she asked impatiently.

He told himself he was staying merely because Paxton Sweet was paying him a bundle. "I'm sorry." There was nothing he hated more than groveling, but he had no choice. "Guess you just rubbed me the wrong way."

"I didn't rub you at all," she said levelly, making it clear she wasn't going to, either.

He nodded, as if agreeing to a hands-off policy.

"I love my father," she continued. "And if he thinks you should be here, I'm willing to let you stay. I figure this whim will pass. Until then—" she pointed "—your room is the first on the right, nearest the front door." Her lips suddenly twitched into a near smile. "That way, if any kidnappers come, maybe they'll take you first."

He almost smiled back. "Do you really think they'd mistake me for Amanda?"

"If I'm lucky."

Cyn was as high-handed and imperious as she'd ever been. And yet there was something in her eyes . . . a sadness that hadn't been there before. He sure hoped he'd caused it. "I'll stay wherever you like."

He only half listened as she ran down a list of house rules, which included him wearing a robe. She told him to help himself to anything in the kitchen, and that she worked at the office part-time but didn't keep regular hours. The prepackaged speech reminded him that Cyn had grown up with maids, housekeepers and chauffeurs.

"First thing tomorrow, I'll install a new security system," he said, when she'd finished.

"My security is fine."

At that, he almost chuckled. "Well, Ms. Sweet—"

"I guess you can call me Cyn."

He stretched his legs over her carpet. "Well, Cyn, you never know when unwanted elements might penetrate—" he swept his arm over his own lap "—into your very living room."

"You say that almost as if you're such an element," she remarked with a smile.

"Maybe I am."

"No maybe about it," she said lightly.

Amanda pranced into the room and whirled in a circle, showing off her long white gown. Then she lunged into Santa's lap. "I'm the boss and you have to put me to bed!"

Santa rose without bothering to gauge Cyn's reaction. Was the little girl in his arms really his? "Sure, sweetheart, point the way."

Cyn's spoiled her rotten. Amanda had more toys than were offered for sale at Too Sweet. Her walls were pink, the canopied bed lacy and ruffled. Just looking at the room, and feeling Amanda snuggle against him, he suddenly felt as if his heart might break. Whether it was because he'd never had a childhood himself, or because he may have missed part of his own daughter's, he didn't know.

As he pulled back Amanda's covers and leaned to slide her beneath them, he felt Cyn's eyes on his back. His sixth sense told him she was directly behind him, in the doorway. He even knew that her arms were crossed over her chest.

"Now you gotta kiss me," Amanda whispered. "Okay?"

He clamped his jaw shut, since his face felt quivery. Amanda was so beautiful. Was that why he now doubted she was his? Could rough-and-tumble Anton Santa have helped make someone so perfect? Her green eyes were twinkling, and her blond hair, which was as fine as silk, now spread across her pillow. He suddenly realized he'd never kissed a kid before.

"You don't gotta, not if you don't want, Mr. Santa Claus."

Santa just wished Cyn wasn't standing behind him. He had few vulnerabilities, but he meant to keep the chosen few hidden from her. He leaned slowly and kissed Amanda's cheek. Her skin was smooth and cool, like fine china. His throat felt as dry as dust. "Night, Amanda."

"You're gonna shoot 'em when they come here. Right?" Amanda murmured excitedly. "Like on a cop show."

"Yeah," he said softly.

Amanda's blond brows crinkled. "You don't gotta go home for Christmas, do you?"

He shook his head. "No."

"You're gonna get in big trouble from your mom and dad."

"They're dead." The look of surprise and sorrow on the little girl's face made him want to double over. How could he have been so insensitive? Amanda was just a kid.

"It's okay," he quickly added. "It was a long time ago."

"Oh, Mr. Santa!" she exclaimed in a soft, breathy voice. She sat up, hugged him tight and pressed kisses against his shirt.

"Night," he managed to say, turning away.

He didn't look at Cyn when he passed her. He just couldn't bear to, somehow. He was nearly out of earshot, when he heard Amanda say, "Please, can I call him daddy? Please, Mommy?"

He cocked his head, listening for Cyn's response. He heard none.

"I need a daddy and I don't got one! And he doesn't got a mom *or* dad."

He heard whispers and hushed rustling. After a moment, Amanda's voice rose. "I'm gonna tell him your secret!"

"Fine, then," Cyn said.

Santa's jaw dropped open in astonishment. What was Amanda using for blackmail? And was she really his daughter? The Santa mole was a possible giveaway, but Amanda also happily engaged in doll theft and now blackmail. Definite proof of the Santa genes, he thought dryly.

"I'm turning off your light now, honey," Cyn said.

Santa quickly gathered his bag and coat and headed for the room Cyn had indicated. It was early, but he didn't want to see her again. Not tonight.

"I wouldn't have imagined you'd go to bed at seven-thirty."

It was Cyn. He turned in his doorway. Their eyes met and held. "I need to sleep," he said gruffly. "I've been traveling a long time."

For a moment his last words hung in the air, as if they meant something special. He wondered if he would tell her his true identity, or if she would discover it. Would he then tell her about those four long years of traveling?

"Somehow," she said softly, "I imagine you have."

Santa breathed in sharply, feeling sure she'd recognized him after all.

"ON THE FIRST DAY of Christmas my true love gave to me..." Cyn sang along with the CD. She'd meant to finish wrapping copies of *Little Amanda's Perfect Christmas*, which would be given away tomorrow, during the Christmas tree decoration promotion at the toy store. Instead, she found herself leaning in the living room window, sipping mulled cider. Outside, dry flurries spiraled in the dark air but never landed. It was so cold, the cement of the sidewalk below looked white.

Inside, warm yellow light seeped from beneath the bodyguard's door, which meant he'd lied. He was wide-awake. But why had he been in such a hurry to escape? The man really was as mysterious as the North Pole Santa, she thought wryly. After all, *he* was the one who'd been uncivil.

Seeing him with Amanda, she'd felt herself warming to him. She felt sorry for him because he had no family to visit at Christmastime, too. Maybe a man like Santa—one who kept his cards close to the vest—was better than the more flirtatious type, she decided now, wishing she could quit comparing him to Jake Jackson....

Like Santa, Jake had had no family. At least he'd *said* his father had died in a work-related accident, and that his mother had died of cancer. Unlike Santa, Jake had sure been outward. He'd had a heavy Southern accent, thicker than molasses, but his every word had been nothing more than smooth talk. Only after she'd slept with him had she started to worry about his many small evasions. Only then had she started wondering if they'd added up to him seeing another woman.

That was why, four long Christmases ago, she'd followed him. He'd already kissed her goodbye, since she was supposed to meet her parents in Puerto Rico for a tropical Christmas, but when she'd reached Kennedy, her plane was snowbound. Like a thief in the night, she'd stolen back to Jake's place in the Village and waited for him.

She'd tailed him and another man over perilously icy roads, right to the house she'd just left, the one she'd shared with her parents. At the high wrought-iron gates, they'd met a third man, the one who'd gotten away. He was already wearing a red-and-green ski mask.

That a group called The Grinch Gang had been playing local heiresses for fools was old news, but she was so shocked at finding herself a victim that she'd waited another fifteen minutes before calling the police from her car phone.

No. Admit it, Cyn. You were considering not turning Jake in. Now she turned away from the window, hardly wanting to think about what happened after she'd made the call. She glanced at Santa's door again, just in time to see his light go out. The darkness left her feeling bereft.

"You can't make me feel safe," she whispered. *I doubt you'll make me forget Jake Jackson, either.* "Even if you're the best of the best." After all, there were no locks for the mind. No chains or bars to keep away the fantasies. No cage that could withstand her dreams. And even if there were, her jewel thief was as slippery as Houdini.

Why can't I stop thinking about Jake? Perhaps because it was Christmas again. Or because the bodyguard made her think of danger, and Jake was certainly the most dangerous thing she'd ever known. Anton Santa would never know her secret, but it was her attraction to him and her memories of Jake that had made her decide to let him stay. She could have dissuaded Paxton, and she was positive the notes didn't signify real danger.

But other threats were always real. That Jake would be released from prison and come to claim Amanda, for instance. It was all the more terrifying, since Cyn still found herself wanting to make excuses for him because he hadn't had parents. And yet, it wasn't his background but his lips that had almost made her lie for him. If he ever came back, she was sometimes sure she wouldn't be able to resist....

How could she? No other man had set her nerves on edge in the exact way Jake had—until today. And that was the real reason Anton Santa had to stay.

Because maybe he could make her forget.

ELEVEN DAYS TILL
CHRISTMAS...

Chapter Two

Wednesday, December 14, 1994

"What are you doing to my apartment?" Cyn croaked. She'd hardly forgotten about Anton Santa, but now she wished she'd come into the living room in something other than her red silk robe after she'd checked on Amanda.

The new bodyguard turned away from two jeans-clad workmen who were standing beside her fireplace. "Exactly what I was hired to do," he said calmly. Had his eyes really flickered with contempt? It almost seemed as if he were testing her, or as if he harbored a secret he thought she should know.

As her gaze flitted around the room, her lips parted in horror, then pursed again. The windows were covered with white wrought-iron bars, which weren't entirely unattractive. A complicated-looking, dowel-style lock secured the terrace door, and parts to a keypad alarm system were sprawled over her floor. Her mild annoyance rose to outright anger. "I have no intention of living in a fortress, Mr. Santa!"

"You'll live any way I tell you to," he said simply.

Their eyes met and held, neither wavering. The various parts of him—his short hair, practical dress shoes and nondescript tie—should have made him look like a G-man. But his hooded hazel eyes seemed to smolder with hidden emotion. The slacks to his loosely tailored gray suit—the jacket of which was neatly draped over a chair—hugged and accentuated his slender hips. Thin, narrowly striped suspenders curved over his crisp white shirt, showing off his powerful shoulders.

For the first time she decided he had a little Latin blood. It was in the eyes, which were more heavily lidded than she'd previously thought. He turned back to the workmen, as if satisfied. That gesture, showing a complete lack of regard for her opinions, made her anger rise to the level of pure fury.

"Wait just a minute!" Unfortunately, her voice was too sleep-creaky to carry much authority.

He turned his head to the side, as if she didn't merit so much as direct eye contact.

She tossed her hair over her shoulders with two quick jerks of her head. "By the time I'm dressed, I want those bars off my windows, that mess off the floor, and these men out of here! My father hired you, I didn't! And I can't have you waltzing in and rearranging my life to suit his—and your—whims!"

One moment, he wasn't even looking at her. In the next, he'd crossed the room. He grabbed her elbow firmly, turned her, then began propelling her down the hallway. "Go ahead and install the front door keypad," he said over his shoulder.

"Just who do you think you are?" she sputtered.

"Whoever it is, I'm sure you'd be surprised," he said cryptically.

"Let go!" His chest was flush against her back and he was breathing down her neck, making it tingle. She tried to wrench around and face him.

In a quick reflex he tightened his grip, pulling her even closer. Cyn clutched her robe lapels against the collar of the high-necked gown she wore beneath, feeling exposed. Without her high heels, he was taller than she and when she craned her neck to look at him, her gaze settled on his jaw. She realized a hairline scar ran the length of it.

"You will *not* rearrange my life," she repeated. "And you *cannot* manhandle me from room to room, either!"

In the kitchen, he pulled out a chair and shoved it beneath her behind. He stared at her for an instant, licking his bottom lip as if the gesture might keep him from smiling. "I can't? I believe I just did."

She blinked as if that might somehow make the man vanish. Not that he noticed. The timer on her coffeepot had ensured that coffee would be waiting when she awakened, and Santa was now pouring a cup, without offering her any.

"I see you know where my cups are," she said huffily. "I take it you've already pawed through all my cabinets." When he glanced over his shoulder, his lower lip curled slightly, as if to say she amused him. She sighed. "You wanted to make sure my cups and saucers didn't pose a serious threat to our security, right?"

He turned and leaned against the counter. "No," he said calmly. "I made myself breakfast. Not everyone sleeps until noon."

Somehow she couldn't imagine Anton Santa puttering around a kitchen. She rolled her eyes. "It's only nine."

He glanced at a clock. "Ten after."

Her lips suddenly quivered with impending laughter. What would it take to get a rise out of him? Had any woman ever gotten under his skin? "You seem to have a lot of hidden talents," she said coyly.

"Like knowing how to tell time?" He shot her another trademark Santa glance that was so hard to define. His lips parted slightly, but he didn't really smile. His head tilted to the side, but he didn't quite cock it. His eyes were just about to roll heavenward, but they never did. That look both chastised her for baiting him, and yet it urged her on, since it also said she'd never best him.

"Yeah," she finally said. "Why, the next thing I know, you'll be tying your own shoelaces."

"Only time will tell," he drawled, still sizing her up with his eyes. His own seemed to say that she was playing with fire and she was about to get burned. To her surprise, he placed the cup of coffee, he'd poured, in front of her. His lips twitched. "I had mine at five-thirty."

"This morning?" she couldn't help but ask, appalled.

This time, he did roll his sexy eyes, almost flirtatiously. Or was that just wishful thinking? "No. Five-thirty last night."

Her brows drew up into points. "You really don't like me, do you?" She toyed with the rim of her coffee mug, deciding she would get a rise from this standoffish enigma of a man one way or another. His sudden smirk seemed to say that she was welcome to think whatever she pleased.

"Why?" she prodded, lowering her voice. "Judging by your suits, you do all right for yourself, so it can't be because I'm a spoiled rich kid."

When his eyes dropped from hers to the lapels of her robe, she wondered if it was intentional or accidental. Either way, his gaze lingered on her breasts, as if to point out that she wasn't a kid at all, but a woman. The tips of her breasts constricted and stiffened against her nightgown, and she sucked in an audible breath. His jaw tensed, his facial muscles hardened and his eyes rose again in a leisurely fashion, as if he meant to make no apology for looking. There was an extremely awkward silence.

"You don't really think Amanda's in danger, do you?" she finally managed to ask. His gaze remained so steady that she felt the sudden urge to jump up and tickle him.

"Like I said, I've been around." His voice made her think of tightly coiled metal that was about to spring free. "And no threat should be taken lightly."

But it was Santa she shouldn't take lightly. His strangeness had worn off, and she could see *him* now. The powerful, sensual virility in his gaze and body carried both threats and promises. "And just how long have you—" The back of her throat went dry. Her gaze dropped from his eyes over his rounded, muscular shoulders. "Been around?"

He shot her the trademark Santa look again, and she felt a little silly. Surely she was imagining he desired her. She could bait him all she wanted to but he'd never rise to it. As soon as she blinked, he turned to the refrigerator, took out a carton of half-and-half and placed it beside her mug.

"Now, wait a minute, Santa." She squinted at him. "How do you know I take cream?" Something about his air of suave cool made her smile. "Do you have ESP? Before you became a bodyguard, you were a professional psychic, right? You had a big glass ball in which you could read the future and a book of spells...."

This time he gave her enough of a smile that she could see his polished, gleaming, straight white teeth. There was another difference between him and Jake. Jake had had crooked bottoms.

"I'm sure I'd be good at anything I undertook."

She wasn't certain but thought he was implying he was a good lover. *He probably is.* Her smile faltered. "You're sure about that?" Her voice was raspier than she'd intended.

"Absolutely."

She decided he had to be attracted to her. Their combined physical energy seemed to make the very air vibrate. "So how did you know I take cream?"

He leaned quickly, so his lips were next to her ear. "Because I've been around a lot longer than you think." His breath sent a tingle down to the toes of her bare feet.

"And what else do you *think* you know about me?" She couldn't decide whether his self-containment was making her angry or not.

"Ms. Sweet," he drawled softly. "Before you ask, you should be damn sure you really want to know." With that, he pivoted and strode from her kitchen.

"You're a strange one, Anton Santa. You really are." Cyn was still staring from the carton to the empty doorway when Amanda bounded over the threshold.

"Mommy, Mommy," she said breathlessly. "How can Santa Claus get in now?"

For a second, Cyn didn't know what she was talking about. Then she remembered the bars, dowel and keypad. She chuckled, thinking of Anton Santa. "Amanda," she said, "maybe the real question is whether or not we can get out."

"MORE CHRISTMAS CAROLS," Santa muttered. This time they were Musak. He reclined on the guest room bed, bunched the pillows beneath his head in preparation for a long wait, then coiled the phone cord around his finger. While he patiently waited for one of his old college friends who now worked at the census office to come on the line, he simultaneously listened to "Rudolph the Red-Nosed Reindeer" and the running shower.

He was glad Cyn was performing her morning ablutions, since it was buying him time to make calls, but he wished he could quit imagining how she looked, scrubbing herself beneath those water jets. He could nearly see her long, well-toned arms stretch as she sudsed her hair. Slender, foam-tipped fingers kneaded her scalp. A round water drop glistened on her collarbone. It grew heavier, then slowly snaked toward the dark, hard, beaded tip of one of her breasts. Santa's slacks tightened and he all but squirmed. *Quit torturing yourself. Hell, she's just a woman.* He blew out an annoyed sigh. Their encounter in the kitchen had left him with enough unwanted arousal to last him a week. He hardly needed fantasies.

"Census office," a woman said.

Good. Something to occupy my mind, other than Cyn. "Right. I'm holding for Josh Meyers."

"He'll be right—" The woman didn't even finish before she put him on hold again. Just opposite him was a large mirror in which he could see himself. The room itself was chic and contemporary, done in blue and black, with steel and glass tables. Anyone would have been comfortable in it. Even him, if it weren't for the fact that it was in his ex-lover's apartment.

"Anton? Sorry to keep you on hold."

"No problem. I know you're not really supposed to—"

Josh's chuckle cut him off. "Anything for a buddy."

Santa smiled. "I just wanted to see what you could tell me about a man named Harry Stevens. He used to live in Alabama. I need his marital statistics."

"You sound pressed for time."

Santa mustered a good-old-boy laugh. "Yeah, but I promise to call and converse soon. Maybe I'll even head down to D.C."

"That'd be great," Josh said. "Hold on a minute and let me see what I can give you."

Santa listened as the water was turned off. Now Cyn was stepping from the shower, fully naked, and into a thick woolly towel. He could smell her everywhere, he thought, and hear her steps. Last night she'd nearly driven him crazy, singing along with those sappy Christmas carols. Santa sighed again, thinking he'd really hate her if he found the proof that she'd withheld from him the one thing he'd never really had—a family.

Winter was always tough. His mother and father had both died in winter. Christmas was even worse. During the season, everyone on earth seemed to have somebody. Not that he gave a damn if he didn't, of course, but the impending holiday was why he'd grabbed the New York job. When the referral service that managed his schedule called, he hadn't even asked questions. He liked to keep moving. This time of year, he moved even faster.

But now he'd stopped. And he was reclining on a bed in Cyn Sweet's apartment of all places. After their exchange in the kitchen, he was beginning to think that neither he nor she were particularly likable people. She was as spoiled as ever. He was acting edgy. *But I have every right to, because of Amanda.* Still, he could remember a time when they'd both been open, thoroughly likable and deeply in love.

"Anton?"

"Josh?" The severe cold had been affecting the lines, and the phone suddenly crackled. "You still there, Josh?"

For a moment the two waited for the static to clear.

"Yeah," Josh finally said. "Harrold Stuart Stevens married Cynthia Anna Sweet..." Santa grabbed a notepad and began writing the pertinent dates as Josh talked. "The daughter, Amanda, was born September 17, 1990."

It was a close call, but Amanda could be Harry's. "What do you have for the guy's death date?" Santa felt a little disappointed. He'd gotten this much from Amanda.

"Death date?"

"Yeah," Santa said. "He died in a car wreck."

"Hang on."

"We wish you a merry Christmas, we wish you a merry Christmas..." Santa sang along with the Musak in spite of himself. Then he tilted his head and stared into the mirror, trying to recall the particulars of his Jake Jackson persona. After all, given the palpable, sensual energy coursing between him and Cyn, she was bound to recognize him sooner or later.

He half hoped it was sooner, though he wasn't sure why. Maybe it was simply because high drama and heart-stopping action made him feel so alive. If Cyn recognized him, sparks would surely fly. Especially if Amanda really was his.

He decided he didn't *look* like Amanda's father. The reflection staring back at him was clean shaven, shorthaired and in a suit. It was definitely the no-frills Santa. He sighed, wondering how anyone could have loved Jake Jackson. Especially Cyn. She was a golden girl. Spoiled, no doubt, but made for life's finer pleasures.

Long-haired rebel Jake Jackson could have given her none of them. He'd been as lean and mean as Santa had been back then. A scruffy kid who was out to prove himself. His hair, mustache and beard had been blond and he'd had a penchant for hip leather jackets and motorcycle boots. He'd worn sunglasses so often that Cyn probably couldn't even remember his eye color. Yeah, Jake had been a far cry from the clean-cut straight arrow who was now staring back at Santa. And if Cyn's taste ran to the Jake Jacksons of the world, the real Santa didn't stand a chance.

"Great," he murmured aloud. He tried to tell himself that the last thing he wanted was a second chance at Cyn Sweet. "We Wish You a Merry Christmas" broke into "Deck the Halls."

"You say this guy died in a car wreck?" Josh asked.

Santa sat up. "He didn't?"

Josh chuckled. "According to this, buddy, Harry Stevens is alive and well and still living in Alabama."

After a long moment Santa murmured, "Do you have an address and phone?"

"Sure do."

Santa started scribbling again.

"You visiting family for the holidays?" Josh asked.

"No." Santa thought of Amanda. "Well, I'm not sure yet."

"Well, merry Christmas, Santa."

"You, too, buddy."

He hung up still thinking that Harry Stevens could be Amanda's father. But why would Cynthia and her father take it upon themselves to claim the man was dead?

"AMANDA?" Cartoons played on television, the door was wide open, and all Santa's senses went on alert. He hadn't been on the phone but ten minutes. Now he slipped noiselessly into the living room. Involuntarily his hand slid over his chest toward his holster, and he wished he hadn't removed it in deference to Cyn's wishes.

"You can't catch me!" Amanda shrieked. She shot from behind the Christmas tree, a fast blur of a man on her heels.

Santa easily lunged between Amanda and her attacker. In a second flat, he'd gripped the man's parka and lifted him clean off the floor.

He turned his head slightly to the side. "Go to your room, Amanda," he said with deathly calm.

Amanda wavered uncertainly by the door to the guest room. Her white velvet dress was embroidered with holly berries. Its sash had come untied, her white leggings sagged at the knees, and her little black patent leather shoes gleamed. In spite of the circumstances Santa found himself thinking she looked as pretty as a picture.

"Go."

She streaked down the hall like a bolt of white light.

"Now—" Santa glared at the culprit. He was blond, blue eyed and about five-ten. He looked twenty-five or thirty and scared spitless. "Who are you?"

"Get your hands off me!" he yelled, trying to squirm away from where Santa held his collar. Suddenly he pushed both hands against Santa's chest.

"Oh, brother," Santa muttered as the man bolted for the door. He threw out his foot, catching the other man's ankle. The poor fellow crashed into Cyn's Christmas tree, then leaned forward, in an effort to regain his balance. He tripped over a wrapped present, then went sprawling across the floor.

"Please don't try to get up," Santa said, sounding bored.

The man rolled over, raking his fingers through his hair. It was strewn with strands of silver tinsel.

"What is your problem?" The man sounded furious, but it was clear he didn't intend to fight.

"How did you get in here?"

"I let him in!"

Santa turned toward the hallway. Cyn's hands were on her hips. She was either going to laugh or start shrieking. Amanda peeked out from behind her. "For heaven's sake! He's the delivery man from Bloomingdale's."

"Bloomingdale's?" Santa repeated. For a long moment he and Cyn gawked at each other. She was wearing a red suit today, with another short skirt. She had on high heels, too, the kind that made him want to let her walk all over him. "Never leave the door open," he finally said.

"I had to get my wallet," she protested, still gaping at him.

"Next time, leave him in the outside hall, then lock the door," Santa said, fighting to maintain his cool. "And then you go get your wallet."

"If you hadn't put in that newfangled keypad, perhaps I would have."

"I could sue for this!" The man was clearly trying to salvage some semblance of his destroyed dignity.

"You could." Santa shot him a quelling glance.

"But maybe I won't," the man quickly added. He warily watched Santa as he struggled to his feet.

Amanda giggled. "You still got tinsel in your hair, mister!"

"You were the one who insisted I play tag with you," the man returned tightly.

At that, Santa was glad to see that Amanda had the decency to blush. But then she giggled again. "I was winning!" she squealed.

Cyn's shoulders started to shake with laughter. "I'm so sorry," she said, rushing forward. One of her perfectly manicured hands slid inside her wallet, and she pulled out a hefty-looking number of bills. "So very sorry," she repeated, pressing the money into the man's hands.

The tip seemed to help some. "Merry Christmas" the man said grudgingly, heading for the door. "And have a happy New Year."

Santa shut the door and activated the lock from the inside. Behind him, Cyn's chuckles gave way to full-scale laughter. When he turned around, she was crumpling against the wall, indulging her shoulder-shaking giggles.

"Heavens," she gasped, between fits. "I'm sure glad you're here to protect us."

He decided to let her get it out of her system. It would take more than a barb like that to unman him. Amanda hadn't joined in. She was staring at him, looking as guilty as sin. After a moment she crept uncertainly to his side. She placed her tiny hand in his and squeezed tightly.

"It's okay, Mr. Santa Claus," she said in comfort. "It could have been a robber or a mugger." Her voice rose hopefully. "Maybe next time it will be."

The words sent Cyn into another bout of hysterics. The situation made Santa feel a little ridiculous, but he had to admit it was good to hear Cyn laugh—really laugh—again. She nearly staggered across the room, teetering on her high heels, then collapsed in an armchair, sighing. Watching her cross her long, elegant, black-stocking-clad legs, Santa almost sighed himself.

"I'm gonna go get my coat by myself now, like a good girl," Amanda said, releasing his hand. "Mommy says we've got to go to a promp-tion at the store."

Promp-tion? Oh. Promotion. He glanced down. The little girl barely came to the level of his thighs. He felt a sudden urge to lift her into his arms again.

"I just bet those kidnappers are gonna come to our promp-tion," she crooned, still clearly trying to soothe him.

"Oh," Cyn managed to call out as Amanda flew past her, "but don't you think we should give him the day off, Amanda? After all, he's been working *so* hard this morning." At that, she started laughing so uncontrollably that she actually snorted.

"Very unladylike," Santa muttered under his breath. He tried to tell himself that her hysterics weren't annoying him. He was merely anxious to complete the day's agenda so he could call Harry Stevens and have a nice little chat.

When he could no longer stand it, he said, "You'll need your coat, Ms. Sweet."

His tone sobered her. She opened her mouth, undoubtedly to offer some tart response, then clamped it shut. "Whatever you say, Santa," she finally conceded weakly.

"Right," he said, sounding more agreeable than he actually felt. "I'm glad to see you're getting the picture."

"NOW, AMANDA," Cyn said, "every time someone comes up, you reach in the box and hand them an ornament. Then, when they take the ornaments to the elves, the elves will hand them a copy of your book. Okay?"

Amanda crossed her arms defensively over her sash. "I know what to do."

"I know you do." Cyn smoothed the velvet hem of Amanda's dress, then glanced anxiously around Too Sweet Toys, feeling sure the promotion had drawn in needed customers. All three levels, the glass walls of which faced the Fifth Avenue side of Rockefeller Center, were crowded with shoppers and their children.

The long-needled pine she and Paxton had ordered from upstate rose to the high first-floor ceiling. Ladders had been placed around the tree, and workers in elf costumes—mostly unemployed actors and actresses—were ready to place ornaments on the higher branches. Cyn caught a glimpse of both her father's assistant and her mother on the escalators. Eileen was going up; Analise was headed down. Kids sprawled and squirmed in the many colorful armchairs that had been placed throughout the store for tired shoppers.

Suddenly Cyn's nose came level with a pant leg. She sucked in a quick breath, then slowly raised her gaze. It traveled over the finely woven, expensive fabric, then inadvertently stopped at the apex of the man's thighs. She gulped.

"I'll stick close to Amanda."

Cyn craned her neck and found herself peering into Santa's eyes. They were every bit as powerful looking as his thighs. Realizing that he was towering over her, her mouth went dry and she forced herself to stand. Not that it helped. In her heels, she was nearly his height, and now her gaze met his, dead-on. The way her knees buckled almost made her wish she was staring at his pant leg again. The man was definitely growing on her. In fact, she was beginning to think more about him than Jake Jackson.

"The store's so crowded...." She smiled as kindly as she could, hoping to atone for laughing at him earlier. It had clearly made him furious. "I'm so glad you're here. I really am."

She thought he nodded, but it was hard to tell.

"You're not much for conversation, are you?" she prodded just as the first toddler, a little girl, ran up to her daughter. Amanda handed her a gleaming silver bulb.

"You know—" Cyn felt foolish, but felt compelled to continue. "Like I would say something, and then you would, and then I would." She blew out a quick sigh. "Guess you just don't like to talk."

At that, Santa actually grinned. "Depends on who I'm talking to."

"So the problem's just me?" she asked coyly.

"I'm working."

He sounded more annoyed that he actually was, she decided. Something in his eyes made her sure he was beginning to crack a little. "Well, I'm going to go say hello to my mother." She pointed toward the opposite side of the first floor.

"You're not my client. You don't need to clear your comings and goings with me."

She felt almost as if she'd announced she was going on a date. She arched her brows. "I'm not your client?" If Paxton had hired him, it was as good as if she had.

"No." He glanced down just as Amanda handed a little boy a bright blue origami ornament. "Your daughter is."

Cyn squinted at him, wondering why he always used such an odd intonation when he said "your daughter." She decided there was just no talking to the man, and glanced around the crowded store again. As a mother, she couldn't help but give ear to those occasional stories about mothers who'd lost children in public places. "You'll watch her, won't you?"

"With my life."

He sounded so serious that she gulped. "You would, wouldn't you?"

"It's my job."

It was hard to turn away from him, but she did. Before she'd reached her mother's side, Bob Bingley steered her past an armchair. He pushed her behind a counter, saying, "Sorry, but we need you on register one, Cyn." He wiggled his brows. "Or should I say 'doll face'?"

"If you want to die," Cyn returned playfully. The store was the Sweets' lifeblood, and Cyn easily began ringing up purchases. As she worked, her eyes kept drifting back to her baby and the bodyguard.

They were an odd couple. Santa towered behind Amanda, with an erect posture, his hands held loosely at his sides. Even from where Cyn was, she could feel his eyes sweeping back and forth across the room, in watchful protection. Sometimes, his gaze seemed to want to stop on her, but it never did.

Men had occasionally come on to her like gangbusters. But not this one. Because he was always watching Amanda, talking to him was even more difficult. She found herself wondering how she might arrange to spend some time alone with him. Just to see if he warmed to her....

He's a bodyguard, all right, she thought, as she gift wrapped a Barney doll. Santa's suit was so nondescript as to make him invisible. When she'd first seen him, she hadn't even noticed his good looks. Now the adults in the store barely noticed him at all. But the children did, she realized with surprise. They gravitated toward him somehow, as if sensing he was keeping them safe. Just watching him, noting how good he was at what he did, she felt a chill creep along her spine. *Don't worry. No one will ever take Amanda. Jake Jackson's in jail.*

Her discomfort passed. Once again she was aware of the lively Christmas music. The kids rushed to the elves and pointed toward where they wanted their ornaments hung. Some opted for the lower branches and hung the decorations themselves. In return, each received a wrapped copy of *Little Amanda's Perfect Christmas*.

"Thank you for shopping at Too Sweet!" Cyn smiled brightly and extended the elegantly wrapped Barney doll.

"So far the best day for sales yet!" Bob Bingley called. He raced past her, a ribbon of calculator tape trailing over his shoulder.

"Have you seen your father?" Analise leaned against the counter.

Cyn continued to ring up purchases. "You're looking for Dad?" Were her parents speaking again?

"Looking to avoid him," her mother admitted.

Cyn sighed. If she knew more about her parents' difficulties, maybe she could help fix them. "He's staying on the third level," she said, handing a bag to a customer.

Her mother smiled. "Good. Then I can lean here for the whole of two seconds before Bob requires me again."

"Thank you for shopping at Too Sweet," Cyn said cheerfully to a woman about her age. She lowered her voice as she reached for the next batch of merchandise. "Why are you and Daddy fighting, anyway?"

Analise shrugged. "What I want to discuss is your bodyguard."

Cyn chuckled. "I believe he belongs to Amanda." She glanced in his direction again. Santa was helping Amanda untangle the hanging wires on some of the ornaments. Even from here, it was clear that Amanda's hands were too little and his were too large. Illogically Cyn thought she could almost stretch her arm across the room and fix things for them.

"Well, with that build, I think he might make even a grown-up girl feel safe."

Cyn reached under the counter, groping for more gift boxes. "Or like she's in dangerous trouble," she said to her mother.

"So you like him?"

Cyn shrugged as she punched out the flattened sides of a box. "I don't think he likes me."

"Who wouldn't like my daughter?" Before Cyn could respond, Analise gave her a quick kiss on the cheek. "Bob calls," she said, heading toward the escalators and waving over her shoulder.

A full hour later Cyn felt a tug at her skirt. She glanced down. "Amanda?" When Cyn raised her gaze to Santa's, she realized he looked vaguely embarrassed.

"I gotta go to the potty right now and Santa Claus can't guard me there," Amanda said in a distressed tone.

"Come on. I'll take care of you." She hoisted Amanda to her hip and headed toward the employees' bathroom. Unable to help herself, she glanced over her shoulder and shot Santa her most flirtatious smile. "Coming, Santa Claus?"

"Right behind you."

"You could walk beside us," she offered.

He sped his steps until they were walking side by side, in perfect rhythm. When his hips grazed hers, warmth seemed to infuse all her limbs.

Until Santa leaned against a wall. "Just don't get lost in there, ladies."

"And run the risk of never seeing you again?" Cyn raised her brows and stared boldly into his eyes. "No chance." She playfully slammed the door.

As coy as she was by nature, she couldn't quite believe the way she'd looked at Santa. Even at her age, she wasn't above practicing the proverbial come-on look in her mirror. Her eyes had been beaming out rays of pure lust, and she knew it.

As she helped Amanda, she wondered what he'd say when she came back out. Perhaps he'd actually pick up the thread of the flirtation she'd begun. But to her disappointment he'd vanished. He'd taken up his post by the tree again. Since Amanda ran ahead, there was no real reason for Cyn to follow. Except that she wanted to.

Only after all the ornaments were hung did Cyn come anywhere near Santa again. "Can Mr. Santa please do the star at the top?" Amanda begged.

Cyn could almost feel Santa holding his breath. Christmas clearly wasn't his cup of tea. She looked at him pointedly. "Mr. Santa?"

"Please, please, please!"

He exhaled audibly. "Sure."

Without waiting for him, Amanda marched toward one of the ladders, quickly dispensed with one of the elves, then climbed upward and seated herself on a rung. Her dangling ankles curled around the ladder's sides. She crooked her finger in Santa's direction, then smiled, showing her dimples.

"I do believe your client wants you," Cyn said wryly.

"That she does."

Cyn watched him head for the tree. He took the star, agilely climbed the ladder, then hung it. As he did, all the children in the store applauded. Cyn wasn't positive, but she was fairly sure he would prefer to be back in whatever sunny country he'd just come from.

When he came down, Amanda grabbed his hand. Her face was lit up with pure prideful pleasure. She glanced from Santa, to the tree, then to the other children. When she craned her neck to look at Santa again, her gaze seemed to say she owned him. Cyn felt her shoulders begin to shake. *You poor, poor man,* she thought, as Amanda led him toward the counter.

He gingerly removed a teddy bear from an armchair and eased himself into it. "May I rest now?"

Amanda clasped her hands in front of her and smiled sweetly. "You can do what you want," she said, wriggling onto his lap.

Cyn realized she wasn't the only person getting a juvenile crush on Santa. Her daughter had fallen—head over patent leather heels—in love. Cyn leaned around the arm of the chair and tugged Amanda's elbow. "Why don't you go see Grandmama? Mr. Santa's been standing for a while. He might want a break."

Amanda reached for her, just as a shopper jostled Cyn from behind. Cyn found herself teetering, then turning, and suddenly—without understanding how it happened—she was sitting on Santa's spare knee. An uncharacteristic flush rose to her cheeks.

Amanda giggled. "I already told Santa that I gotta get a daddy for Christmas," she announced.

Everything in her daughter's eyes made clear just which daddy she had in mind.

"But I can't call him 'daddy,' even though you said it's okay. He's not my daddy and I'm not a liar. Now I gotta go." In a flash, Amanda tore toward Analise.

"I—I'm sorry," Cyn managed. Her head was still reeling from her daughter's lengthy speech, and her heart was beating double time. She started to get up, but Santa's hand caught her waist. *This is a definite role reversal. What's he doing?*

"Now, wait a minute, Santa—" She'd meant to sound playful, but failed miserably. She felt unbalanced, even though the thigh that supported her was as hard and steady as a rock. "First you won't even talk to me, and now you're—"

He chuckled. "It's Christmas. I thought everybody wanted to sit on Santa's lap."

This is my fault. I'm the one who was coming on to him. "What?" She was glad her voice wasn't quivering as much as her insides. "Are you going to ask me what I want for Christmas?"

"Now, what could it be?" he drawled. "You've already got your two front teeth."

She relaxed right up until she remembered she was seated on his knee. "The better to bite you with," she returned.

He raised his brows and gazed into her eyes, letting the remark hang in the air. "I didn't mean it like that!" she exclaimed, lightly punching his shoulder.

"Like what?" he asked innocently.

She shot him a smirk. She wasn't about to let him embarrass her into silence. "You know," she said, poking his chest with her index finger. "Like when people kiss and accidentally bite each other."

His lips were twitching all over the place, as if he were fighting not to crack up. "Well, one should watch those slips of the tongue."

She feigned confusion. "I keep all my slips in my drawers." *What am I saying?*

"Funny," he said. "Most women I've known don't tuck them in."

Cyn couldn't help but shake her head. "Sorry, Santa. You lost me on that one." She tried to scoot casually off his lap.

He held her tight. "Drawers as in bloomers," he drawled. "And why are you wiggling away? Not three hours ago, you were desperate to see if I was capable of conversation."

"You call this conversation?" Her cheeks were getting warmer by the second. The undeniable, volatile chemistry cooking between them seemed about to explode. It was no accident that they'd somehow gone from slips to drawers.

"Sure," he said. "You know. I talk, you talk, I talk."

"Whatever it is," she managed to say. "I definitely mean to keep my slips in check." Watching Santa's face, she wondered if she could. The man smelled like clean winter weather, the day of a first snow.

"What a shame," he murmured.

For the first time Cyn realized that shoppers were gawking at them. Nevertheless, she relaxed against his chest, as if his proximity wasn't affecting her in the least. "And I thought you were just wondering what I want for Christmas," she said levelly.

"But, Cyn—" He bent so close his lips touched her ear. "Have you been good this year?"

She leaned back, only to find that his penetrating eyes were judgmental, as if she'd been bad. Her mouth went dry. She felt as guilty as she had when she was a kid on Santa's lap. After all, like most kids, she'd been bad much of the year. She thought about how she'd considered not turning in Jake Jackson. *But that was four years ago!*

"I've been good," she finally protested, feeling suddenly annoyed.

His eyes narrowed, as if he didn't believe her. "Yeah?"

"Yeah." She forced herself to smile. "Better than a man like you would ever deserve," she added tartly.

"Probably true." He chuckled softly, even though his gaze seemed somehow veiled and a little sad now. "Probably true."

"Mommy!"

Cyn turned away from Santa. She felt relieved at the intrusion, until Amanda crawled onto her knee and swung mistletoe above her head.

"Okay, Mr. Santa Claus," Amanda said. "You gotta kiss Mommy. I'm the boss."

Santa grinned. "Where'd you get that?"

"Granddaddy," Amanda squealed.

Good going, Dad. Cyn sucked in a quick breath. Her first impulse was to run. Then she decided to play it cool. After all, she'd been making a play for the man. He'd just shocked her by responding. She raised her brows archly, shot Santa a smile, then jutted her chin forward, offering him her cheek.

"Oh, goody!" Amanda hopped down.

"A quick peck won't kill you," Cyn said.

"To make Amanda happy, of course," he returned.

"And only Amanda," she said. "I do assure you."

When Santa's thumb grazed her chin, white-hot fire seemed to pour into her veins. *He's supposed to kiss my cheek!* Instead, he turned her face, and his lips quickly claimed hers. One instant, she was merely sitting on his knee. The next, she was curled into his shoulder, her chest crushed against his.

It was a full-service kiss, with no preliminaries. She could feel Santa strain against his own desire, every touch of his mouth making clear he wanted more. It was almost as if he'd known and wanted her for a long time, years even. He seemed to be drinking her in...hungry for her.

Suddenly she wrenched away and stared into Santa's eyes. Her breaths came in great gasps. For the second time in two days she could swear Jake Jackson was in the room. Except this time she was sitting in his lap and he'd just kissed her.

"Oh, Mr. Santa Claus," Amanda said breathlessly. "That was just great!"

"Glad to oblige," he said casually.

Jackson slipped from Cyn's mind as quickly as he'd entered it. Hadn't Santa felt anything at all? She managed to shut her gaping mouth and pat his shoulder. "Thank you so much for doing that," she said sweetly, "and all for the sake of my little girl."

Then she stood slowly, brushed her crinkled skirt and sashayed away, as if she had somewhere important to go. She made sure her heels beat a steady, rhythmic tattoo on the tile floor, and hoped she looked thoroughly unaffected.

But her insides quivered like jelly. Her knees wobbled like rubber, and her lips felt as swollen as a prize fighter's. Her heart was soaring, though. Because she'd finally found a man in this world who could kiss as wickedly as Jake. And Anton Santa, thank heavens, was honest in the bargain.

"WONDER WHAT'S GOING ON between those two," one of the Too Sweet executives murmured as he watched Cyn approach. Even from across the room, he'd felt the fireworks. Now, he wondered if this, too, might play into his hands, somehow. Maybe he was about to find out. Cyn was coming at him like a magnet.

He hadn't sent the notes, of course. Still, when they'd arrived, he was sure the story would reach the press. It hadn't, and that had been terribly disappointing to him. After all, he'd researched Too Sweet carefully. The family and company were so intertwined that every time personal tragedy hit, the stocks plummeted, making the place ripe for takeover.

Not that a kidnapping was necessary. Bad press was all he needed, even if he'd prefer not to leak it himself. Nevertheless, he did have enough dirt on the Sweet family to cause a stir. He'd heard the rumors about Cyn's torrid affair with a convict, and about Harry Stevens. And the holidays would be the perfect time to republish materials from The Grinch Gang's trial.

He just wished today's promotion hadn't been so successful; it meant the company was getting stronger by the day, rather than weaker. Suddenly he had a flash of inspiration. *That's what I'll do....*

When Cyn reached his side, he realized her lips were kiss swollen, and that she'd beat a truly hasty retreat across the room. She also looked as if she'd never been happier to see anyone in her life.

"It's good to see a friend, right now," she said.

He smiled. "It sure is."

TEN DAYS TILL
CHRISTMAS . . .

Chapter Three

Santa stepped from the shower onto a bath mat woven with a Santa Claus face, then knotted a woolly red-and-green holiday towel at his waist, wishing Cyn had just left his room alone. He wished he hadn't kissed her, too, since the lingering taste of her lips had kept him awake. Now every cool, dripping-wet inch of him felt singed, as if she'd touched him with burning need.

"But no," he whispered. She either felt sorry for him, or wanted to let him know that his kiss hadn't affected her. She'd employed all her decorative talents, and now his room looked fit for Kriss Kringle. She'd replaced his bathroom water glass with a Frosty mug, switched the previously blue towels to red and green, then hung a wreath of rope pine, complete with red velvet bows on his door. Paper reindeers were now taped above his headboard, flying in the direction of the hallway. And the closest avenue of escape, he thought.

"It's no wonder a man can't sleep around here," he muttered aloud. When he'd opened his eyes at five-thirty, he'd found himself staring into the spray snowflakes on his mirror. He'd read all the morning newspapers, but had forgone his usual police procedurals. Instead, he'd read through Cyn's scrapbooks, yearbooks, and photo albums for two hours while ensconced between Christmas-tree-print bedsheets. The only thing Cyn seemed to have forgotten was to hang some more mistletoe.

He opened the bathroom door and headed toward his closet to choose a suit. Just as he decided on navy, a sheet of lined, ragged-edged paper shot beneath the door and slid across his bare feet. He agilely retrieved it from the carpet, then squinted. "Aw," he said softly. It was a crayon drawing.

He wasn't sure but thought it was of him in a Santa suit, and it was signed with a word that resembled "Amanda," except that the *d* was backward. At the bottom, in Cyn's writing, it said, "Hope you like Amanda's decorations in your room!"

So, it was Amanda's idea, not Cyn's. He should have felt relieved, but he didn't. He'd imagined Cyn riffling through her decorations and thoughtfully deciding where to place them. He'd imagined her breathing in his scent while she'd hung those ridiculous reindeers, too. He'd imagined her *wanting* him.

He sighed, crossed the room and gingerly wedged Amanda's drawing in the bedroom mirror's frame, next to a snowflake. Then he returned to the bed, sat down and glanced around, trying to remind himself that he hated Christmas. But how could he keep hating it when a little girl—maybe his little girl—drew such cute pictures for him? Or when her beautiful mother helped her decorate his room?

"Get ahold of yourself, Anton," he murmured. He grabbed the phone receiver with more force than was necessary, then dialed. *What if she's not my little girl?*

The most annoying thing was that his morning researches had rendered countless photographs of the supposedly deceased Harry Stevens. He'd attended high school with Cyn and they'd clearly been close. Worse—he was far better looking than Santa, at least in Santa's own humble opinion. Fury had coursed through him when he'd realized Cyn had always kept Harry waiting in the wings. Not that he'd found wedding pictures.

But if Harry Stevens had done something terrible—which might be why Cyn had pretended he was dead—then she may have destroyed evidence of their nuptials. *Good.* As it was, Santa had seen more than he'd wanted to. The snapshots of their senior prom had nearly turned his stomach. Santa absently rubbed the scar on the underside of his jaw, as if to remind himself of why he should steer clear of Cyn. Then he glanced at his calf and the circular two-inch scar left by the second bullet.

Harry Stevens didn't pick up until the sixteenth ring.

Santa went directly into his spiel, using his thickest Southern drawl. "Mr. Stevens? Now, you are Mr. Harrold Stevens, aren't you? Well, I'm B. D. Whittacker—talent agent out of Atlanta. Perhaps you've heard of me?"

Santa stopped for a breather and allowed Stevens to say that he'd never heard of him. Instead, Stevens said, "I'm not sure, but I do believe I may have heard that name."

The worst thing was that Stevens was just trying to be polite, and Santa wanted to like him. "Well," he continued, "down here in Atlanta, we've been following the Too Sweet promotion in New York City, and I was hoping to speak with you—and your wife, of course—about using your little Amanda for a commercial. Not a big contract, just a local baby food, mind you, but a start..." Santa paused, almost hating himself for laying it on so thick.

"I'm sorry, you must have the wrong—"

Santa's heart dropped to his feet. Stevens didn't know what he was talking about. Did the man even know Amanda existed? He'd have to, if the census reports were right.

"Oh!" Stevens chuckled. "You mean Amanda?"

"Do you always forget you have a daughter?" Santa returned gruffly.

"It's my ex-wife I try to forget," Stevens said smoothly.

Santa couldn't help but feel a little defensive on Cyn's behalf. Still, he was mad. She'd pretended Stevens was dead. She'd kept the man waiting in a wedding tux, when she'd been seeing Jake. Now it appeared that Amanda was Harry's child. As soon as he hung up, he was going to call Paxton and quit.

"My daughter lives with her mother." Stevens continued so easily that Santa was sure Amanda belonged to him. "Look, I was just leaving, to catch a plane home for the holidays." Santa could almost see the amicable, sandy-haired Harry smiling. "But would you like me to give my ex-wife a call? Or perhaps I could give you the number for Too Sweet Toys."

"Why, that's mighty nice of you." Santa suddenly wished Harry didn't have those sandy-blond blue-eyed good looks. "Just let me get a pen."

He held the receiver in the air and mentally counted to five. It was a shame Stevens was headed out of town. Santa'd had every intention of calling back later—from Puerto Rico, after he quit. He'd play a confused bureaucrat who needed to clarify Stevens's supposed death records. He swung the mouthpiece to his lips again. "Could I possibly have a number where I could reach you? In case I can't find your wife?"

The man was amazing. He actually gave Santa his parents' number in Utah. Stevens had just given the New York area code when thudding steps flew past Santa's door. "Thanks, I've got it," Santa said, sensing that something was wrong. He covered the mouthpiece.

"But I haven't fini—"

"Amanda?" Cynthia called out. "Amanda?"

"Thank you, Mr. Stevens," Santa said curtly, hanging up. Then Cynthia screamed his name.

"WHAT'S WRONG?" Santa asked calmly. Even though he was searching Cyn's eyes, he was aware that her red robe was untied and that she wore a short silk nightie underneath. With relief, he realized Amanda was in the room.

"He was here," Cyn whispered in shock. "The front door was wide open, and this note—" She waved her hand; an envelope and sheet of stationery were pinched between her thumb and finger. "This note..."

He didn't wait to hear the rest. He bolted into the hallway, the thick red carpeting feeling soft beneath his bare feet. He tried the door to the other tenth-floor apartment. Locked. At the elevator, he pressed "down," then ran the length of the hall. The entrance to the roof and metal fire door were locked. *Good in this case, bad in case of a fire.*

Someone chuckled. "Don't tell me you're going down, sir?"

Santa whirled around, hardly needing a reminder that he was clad only in a towel. "Jim." As he jogged toward the elevator operator, he realized a frightened Cyn had shut her door. "Who came up?"

The middle-aged man hit the Stop button, removed his cap and ran his fingers through his thick dark hair. "No one," he finally said.

"Someone must have."

"Toby's the only other person on this shift. He called in sick. So—" The man's jaw dropped. "There was no one to cover me when I, er, had to take a quick break."

"You took one just now?"

"Yes, sir, just now."

"How long?"

"No more than five minutes, tops."

Santa sighed. Cyn's eyes had held pure terror. He could only hope she was overreacting. "No visitors are to come up without calling from the lobby," Santa muttered. "How could anyone have gotten past Jennifer?" He stepped into the elevator. "Take me down."

Jim merely stared at him. "In that, er, outfit, sir?"

Santa glanced down at the red-and-green towel. The words "Merry Christmas" were emblazoned across his privates. He grimaced but nodded.

Unfortunately, the trip to the lobby was a dead end. He accomplished little more than a few raised eyebrows, whispers and chuckles at his expense. Jennifer's phone wasn't working properly, due to the weather, and she was unable to offer a good description of the only person who'd used the elevator. He'd said he was a delivery man going to an apartment on the fourth floor, but she'd been busy talking to repairmen.

"Thanks for waiting, Jim," Santa said gruffly when he returned.

Jim laughed. "You kidding? I got some pointers. You sure know how to create a stir with the ladies." He pointed.

Santa raised an eyebrow. Sure enough, three well-heeled female tenants had stopped to gawk.

"And a very, very Merry Christmas to you, too," one yelled before she doubled in a fit of giggles. There wasn't much mistaking which part of his anatomy had caught her attention.

The last thing he heard, as the door slid shut, was one long, ear-piercing wolf whistle.

WHEN THE DOOR HANDLE jiggled, Cyn put her eye to the peephole. Then she threw open the door. "Did you find him?"

Santa shook his head. "Did you get a look at him?"

"No. I just saw the elevator doors close." Her shoulders slumped, and she leaned against the wall. Only then did her eyes drop from the safe, comforting vision of Santa's face down the rest of his body. It was a good thing the wall supported her; otherwise, her knees would have buckled. She tried to tell herself that worrying about Amanda had left her feeling faint, but she knew the way her heart thudded against her rib cage was due to Santa's attire. The towel rode low and knotted beneath his navel. It rose, just slightly, where it pulled across his hips, too.

Worse, Santa mistook her shocked expression for raw-boned fear. He grasped her shoulder and squeezed with comforting pressure. It was a sweet, soothing masculine gesture. He clearly wanted to force all his own considerable, inner strength into her body. It was working, too. "Everything will be fine," he said in a near whisper.

His voice was so reassuring that she believed him. Out of the corner of her eye, Cyn caught a glimpse of Amanda. She was staring at Santa from the hallway, with her mouth gaping and her eyes popping out of her head. "Run and watch your cartoons, honey," Cyn called weakly. No doubt, she appeared as awestruck as her daughter. Amanda took one long, last look at Santa, then fled as if the hounds of hell were on her heels.

"Guess she's not used to seeing men so scantily clad," Cyn managed to say. Between the frightening circumstances of the morning and Santa, she felt thoroughly unnerved. Blood whirred through her veins so fast that her ears were actually ringing, and her face couldn't have felt warmer if she'd downed a whole jar of red-hot chili peppers.

Santa chuckled softly. "And you are?"

She mustered a weak smile and evaded him by glancing toward her Christmas tree. Then she forced herself to fix her eyes on his again. They looked as darkly smooth and gold as roasted almonds. She gulped. "This is really no time to flirt. I'm scared."

His expression softened. It held so much concern that she was sure she'd misjudged him. Unlike other men—unlike Jake—this one could be trusted. He squeezed her shoulder again. His hand was so warm . . . but it was creeping toward her collarbone! She leaned farther back. Behind her, the wall felt solid and real. It steadied her.

"Just wanted to help straighten you out," he said quietly. She didn't realize her robe had nearly fallen from her shoulders until he lifted her lapels and gently snuggled them against her throat. Ever since he'd kissed her, the man had become a whole lot less standoffish. The role reversal was unnerving her. When she was the aggressor, she'd felt in control.

His fingers grazed her neck. "Thanks," she nearly squealed. She tried to skeddaddle backward, but hit something hard. The wall. So comforting a moment before, it now made her feel trapped.

"I like to think of myself as a full-service bodyguard," he finally returned.

As much as she was trying to fight it, her gaze dropped over his powerful shoulders. His smooth chest was tanned to a delicious bronze, and the dark hairs swirled, then tapered southward, in an ever-narrowing V. She drew in an audible breath and glanced down as he lithely grasped both loose ends of the tie to her robe. Even though Amanda was in the den and the kidnapper's note peeked from her pocket, she half hoped he meant to undress her.

"Wouldn't want you to catch a cold," he drawled as he knotted her robe in front.

How could this man excite her so much in the midst of such horrible circumstances? And how could he make her want to laugh? Why wasn't he attending to the note in her pocket? "If anyone's going to catch cold," she said, regaining her equilibrium, "I do believe it's you, Santa."

Their eyes met and held. His wry half smile made his mouth look lopsided. "So you noticed the outfit?"

The fact that he had tiny laugh lines around his eyes suddenly seemed more important than it should have. "I'm sure it will be the primary order of business at the next tenants meeting."

"When you left it in my room," he drawled softly, "I just assumed it was what you wanted me to wear."

"As a sort of uniform?" She looked him up and down, as if considering, wishing her throat didn't close like a trap every time her gaze landed on his glowing naked skin.

He nodded.

"Well, it is seasonal," she offered, her gaze meeting his again. The fool man wore a towel with the same ease and commanding air he did his suits. "Especially the holiday message."

He glanced down. "A number of people wished me a merry Christmas, in return."

"Why, all you're missing is a bow for your head." She tried not to notice how his fresh-scrubbed skin smelled like a forest full of Christmas trees.

"I'm sure we could round one up."

"But then you'd be so chilly," she countered quickly.

He chuckled. "I *am* feeling the draft," he conceded.

She felt compelled to check him for goose bumps. There weren't any. Actually there were, but they rose on her own arms. A shiver zigzagged down her spine. She had to get him into one of his suits, she thought. Pronto. "Well, I guess you can go change now!" she trilled.

His eyes widened at her voice. She'd meant to sound brightly perky, as if casually conversing with a nearly naked man was her usual morning activity. Instead, due to all her pent-up anxiety and excitement, she'd nearly shrieked.

His eyes crinkled and twinkled. "I should, huh?"

"Well, yes." Her mouth felt so dry she could barely talk. "Don't you have to investigate or something or maybe—"

His smile turned into more of a smirk. It said he knew he'd thrown her off balance. "Don't worry—" His mock gravity almost made her smile back. "I don't intend to run around like this all day."

"That's good." She blew out a shaky sigh, wishing she hadn't sounded so breathless. "It is ten below out there, you know."

"True." Santa wiggled his brows. "And I've got no one to keep me warm on these wretched New York mornings."

"Well—er—oh heavens," she suddenly rambled. Could she possibly recoup some sense of dignity? "I'm sorry, I don't know why I was nearly yelling a minute ago. I was so scared and then, you're—"

His eyes seemed to dare her. "I'm?"

Nothing less than Santa's presence could have taken her mind off that terrible note, she thought. Why couldn't she simply fade into the wood of the door? "You're—well," she managed.

"I *do* feel well this morning."

She was starting to feel a bit hysterical. "Well, I just don't know what's come over me." She tried to clear her throat and nearly choked. "I mean, yelling like that and all."

He merely scrutinized her, and smiled that cryptic Santa smile. "I could make a few guesses," he said pointedly.

She felt herself blush to the bottoms of her Clairol roots.

"But I won't."

"Nothing you could say would bother me in the least," she managed, wishing it were true.

His smile became kindly. Then it vanished by degrees until he looked as serious as he had when he'd said he'd guard Amanda with his life. "Why don't you sit down and relax a minute?" he said softly. "Fix yourself something hot to drink, while I change. Then I'll need to see the note."

Her mouth dropped open in astonishment. His every word, she realized, had been calculated. He'd intentionally offered her a diversion. In the next heartbeat she found herself liking him for it. She did feel calmer now. By the time he was ready, maybe she could look at that note again. She nodded. "Okay."

He swiftly stepped closer, so his rock-hard thigh touched hers. She felt the warmth of his large hand press against the small of her spine. Heat shot right through her back to her stomach, then spread through her whole body. "We'll figure all this out," he said. "Trust me."

For a second she thought he might try to kiss her, but he didn't. "I do trust you," she said in surprise. *And it's been a long time since I trusted a man.*

Sadness seemed to touch his eyes, as it sometimes did. "You should have trusted me always," he said levelly.

"When I first met you, I admit I didn't."

He looked as if he were going to say something more. Instead, he turned and headed for his room. His back was every bit as enticing as the front of him, and though her towels were heavy and thick, they truly left very little to the imagination. When her eyes settled on his legs, she wondered how he'd gotten the scar on his calf. Bullet wound, she decided, just as his door shut.

"I saw Mr. Santa in a towel, Mommy!" Amanda squealed from the hallway sometime later.

Cyn realized she was still staring at Santa's door. "So did I, honey," she said with a sigh. "So did I."

HE DRAPED HIS navy jacket over a kitchen chair. Cyn was seated and gazing wanly through a window. Amanda's cartoons blared from the next room. "You should eat."

She hadn't bothered to change, and her robe had nearly come untied again. Santa could see a hint of cleavage and her lacy nightie. She started toying with the rim of her coffee mug and glanced at the kidnapper's note, which was on the table. "I just don't feel like eating, Santa."

"I'll make you a bagel." He pulled one from the bread box, popped it into her rickety toaster oven, then placed the cream cheese on the table, suddenly wishing he could make her smile again, even if he wasn't Amanda's father. The events of the morning had been so swift that he'd barely been able to process that. Now he tried to tell himself it was for the best. What kind of father would he make, anyway?

"I'm toasting you a bagel," he finally said playfully. "Don't look so impressed by my culinary talents."

She smiled then, but only because it was expected. He continued gazing into her eyes, wishing she didn't look so vulnerable and beautiful. It was rare for Cyn to not be in complete control. Her softened features made him want to take her into his arms, to offer comfort rather than take his evenge. He served the bagel. "Should I change back into hat towel?"

"Oh, please, no," she said chuckling. "I think I've had :nough excitement for one morning."

At that, he grinned. He was pleased to see her lather an inhealthy amount of cream cheese onto her bagel, too. She ictually started nibbling, while he looked at the note. This one was on heavy white stock and the words were typewrit-en with a pica electric. It said, "I'll steal the closest thing o your heart."

"Could mean anything and it doesn't specifically men-ion Amanda," Santa finally said. "It's probably not the same person."

Cyn put down her bagel as if she'd suddenly lost her ap-petite again. "No, it's not."

His gaze shot to hers. "You know who sent this?"

Her jaw clamped shut and her green eyes turned as hard as glittering emeralds. He grabbed the chair nearest hers, scooted it beside her, then sat. He was so close that their knees touched. "Who?" he repeated.

"Jake Jackson." Her voice sounded low and lethal.

Santa's lips parted in defensive protest, but he quickly caught himself and remained silent. After a moment he de-cided he might have laughed, if she hadn't sounded so deadly. After all, Jake Jackson wasn't even in the running for the suspect list. He felt a gut-level twinge of guilt. His being here, without her knowing his identity, was begin-ning to feel like a bad joke gone way too far. Worse—not a half hour ago, she'd said she trusted him. And Amanda wasn't even his baby.

He realized Cyn was watching him carefully. "Jake was a past lover of mine," she finally said.

His first impulse was to demand to know just exactly how many lovers she'd had. To hear himself described so off-handedly as a past fling was unnerving. *I've got to leave. Right now. Today.* He forced himself to nod.

She exhaled shakily. "A few years back some college guys were romancing heiresses—" She paused and pursed her lips as if she'd just tasted something foul. "They called them-selves The Grinch Gang."

He shifted in his chair uncomfortably and fought to keep the irony from his voice. "I remember the story." Did she really think Jake Jackson would come back into her life, to hurt her or Amanda? Four years ago she'd lain in his arms, gloriously naked and so full of trust.... Or so he'd thought.

"Did you see me on TV? Or read the papers? Most of them printed the text of the trial." She grimaced, a slight flush staining her cheeks. "Heiresses being played for fools make good copy for the tabloids, I guess."

Santa didn't trust his voice. Lengthy segments of the trial had been replayed on newscasts. He'd seen her, all right. While he was on his back in a hospital bed, his calf and face undergoing reconstructive surgery, she'd positively blasted him. He felt himself getting furious all over again. He leaned forward casually and placed his elbows on the table. "I seem to remember seeing something about it," he finally drawled.

She reached over and squeezed his arm, as if thanking him for his support. Beneath his crisp white shirt, tingles skated along his skin. No matter how angry he felt, he still wanted her. It amazed him. He cleared his throat. "So you think it's this Jackson character?"

When she tilted her head, a lock of sleep-mussed hair fell over one of her eyes, making her look as mysterious as she did sexy. "During the trial, Jackson was hospitalized," she said slowly. "I had followed him to my parents' house. I saw him and two others robbing us, and called the police."

She slid a hand beneath her robe lapel absently. Apparently, her nightie strap had fallen. The simple, guileless gesture nearly took away Santa's breath. Didn't she have any idea what she was doing to him? "Why did you follow him?"

"Because I was an idiot," she said.

Unfortunately, that didn't really answer his question. At the trial, she'd said she'd trailed him because she hadn't trusted him all along. Santa didn't buy it. "Jackson," he continued casually. "He was the guy who got shot, right? A couple of rookie cops came in on the scene, and it turned out that one of the robbers had a gun."

"The man who got away with our jewelry," Cyn affirmed. "Some cash, too."

"So it wasn't Jackson who had the gun?" he prodded, feeling oddly triumphant.

"No," she conceded, sounding almost as if she wished it had been him. "But the jerk sure deserved everything he got, including getting shot," she added with uncharacteristic menace.

"Well, maybe he learned his lesson," Santa said. "Maybe he even reformed in jail. I mean, why would the man come back to haunt you?" Did Cyn secretly hope that Jackson still loved her? *Maybe he does.* Santa blinked, as if to make the thought vanish.

She shrugged. "Matthew Lewis—he was the only defendant present at the trial—got really mad at one point. He jumped up and screamed that they—all of them—would come back someday. He said—" Her voice suddenly broke. "That they'd steal the closest thing to my heart." Her eyes shot to his and misted with tears. "And that would be Amanda. Now, wouldn't it?"

"So it could be either Lewis or the man who got away," he said, trying to sound reasonable. "Why does it necessarily have to be—" He almost couldn't say it. "This other guy, Jackson?"

"It just is," she snapped.

"That doesn't make sense, Cyn," he returned softly. A thousand warring emotions were pulling him every which way but loose. He wanted to defend himself, he wanted to make her see reason. And yet, at moments—so drawn in by her lovely eyes—he nearly forgot he *was* Jake Jackson. Hell, hearing her vehemence, he was ready to kill Jake, himself. Worse, he wanted to take her into his arms and hold her tightly. "I'm going out of my mind," he muttered.

Her eyebrows shot upward. "Excuse me?"

"Nothing." He got up and crossed to the kitchen counter, as far away from her as he could get.

Unfortunately, her bare feet, complete with their dainty pink-painted toenails, pitter-pattered right behind him. She nearly leaned against him while she rinsed crumbs from her bagel plate. His hands itched to touch her soft thick hair and

the silk of her robe. His eyes flitted over her, yearning to se
every last inch of her skin. His mouth went dry with botl
desire and the urge to tell her the truth.

But the truth no longer mattered. He didn't love Cyn. Sh
hadn't trusted him. He didn't want a woman who bolted
when the going got tough, either. Besides which, he wasn'
even Amanda's father.

*She hates Jackson now, and when she finds out the truth,
she'll hate me.* The thought flashed through his mind, bu
he assured himself that wasn't the reason for his silence. He
wanted to rectify the past, perhaps, but he didn't want he
back.

He absently touched the scar on his jaw, thinking he had
so many motivations these days—some even running at
cross-purposes—that he couldn't keep track of them all.
And he didn't have to. He wasn't telling her. Period. And he
wasn't going to stick around until some telltale sign gave him
away.

She turned from the sink and reached past him, to grab a
dish towel. "I know Jackson's been here," she said as she
dried her hands. "The man's as slippery as an eel. When I
went out this morning and saw the door wide open, I just
knew it. I could sense it. I could *feel* him. In fact, I've felt
his presence for a few days." She stared intently at Santa. "I
never really believed in such things before, but do you think
it could be some sort of premonition?"

Santa's eyes roved over her face. If only her eyes were less
green and her lips were less full... "Well, maybe he was
here," he said gruffly.

Cyn placed her hand on his arm again and gazed at him
trustingly. "But he's gone now, isn't he?" she asked softly.

He could smell soap and the fragile scent of yesterday's
perfume. "Yeah." He swallowed hard. "I guess."

Without moving away from him, she said, "You know
something funny?"

That you're about one second away from being kissed?
His lips parted, and he licked them. "What?"

"Don't take this wrong." She came a step closer and their
thighs brushed.

The only wrong thing I'm going to take is you . . . in my arms. "I'll try not to," he managed to say.

She cocked her head and glanced upward, scrutinizing him with a quirky, flirtatious smile. "Heavens, Santa," she teased, poking his chest with her finger, "it's not a test."

He dipped his head and grinned, his mouth just inches from hers. "Well, if it is," he found himself drawling, "I sure hope I pass."

She leaned more of her weight against the counter. "You remind me of him a little."

His stomach balled in a knot. "Who?"

"Jake Jackson," she chided, playfully rolling her eyes.

He didn't even want to laugh this time. He cleared his throat. "Comforting, I remind you of a burglar."

She flashed him a quick smile. "Well, he was a cheat and liar, too."

When she shifted her weight again, the silk of her robe whispered against his fingertips. "Let's not forget that," he murmured.

"And a convict," she added.

He drew in a quick breath. "Thanks."

Although she was gazing into his eyes, she suddenly seemed to be staring right through him. For an instant, Santa almost felt as if he'd vanished.

"It's so very strange," she continued, sounding almost whimsical. "You don't look like him, or talk like him, even though you've got a bit of a drawl. You sure don't dress like him. And he was skinny, without a single muscle to speak of. He was a night owl, too." She frowned. "I just can't imagine him with a suntan. And he was so much shorter..."

Shorter? I'm the exact same damn height. "The man doesn't sound particularly appealing," he finally said.

"Try boy," she quipped. "And not nearly as appealing as you."

Boy? I can't believe I'm now being compared to myself. Did she really just admit she's attracted to me? "So do you always date unappealing men?" It was increasingly difficult to match her teasing tone.

She shrugged. "He was a jerk and I was young and stupid."

Actually, she hadn't been all that young. She'd been twenty-four. She was acting as if their whole affair were easily summed up in a sentence, too. *Boy, jerk, young, stupid.* "But now you're old and so very wise," he said roughly.

She didn't notice his tone. "There's just something about you. I can never quite put my finger on it. And—"

He glanced down, both wishing she'd move away from him, and that she wouldn't. "Hmm?"

Her cheeks colored slightly. The silk of her robe still whispered against his fingertips, as if calling him closer. Pressed against his muscular thigh, her hand felt soft and warm. "When you kissed me the other day—" She paused and swallowed. "You know, at the store..."

As if he could forget. Just a breath away, her lips seemed to beg for his. He swallowed around the lump in his throat. "Yeah," he repeated gruffly, "at the store."

"It just made me feel like...well, like..."

I've had all of this I can take. "Like this?" He grabbed her waist, feeling amazed at how small it was beneath the slippery robe. As he pulled her in front of him, he covered her lips with his own.

He'd taken her by surprise. He could feel it in how her thighs turned hard and unyielding against his, and in how her shoulders tensed against his chest. For a full minute her confused arms remained rigidly suspended in midair, while one of his circled her waist, keeping her close. His free hand raced up her back, under her soft hair, and cupped her neck.

Then her shoulder gave, curling into the crook of his. Her thighs went as soft as a pillow and nestled against his legs. Her arms crept around his neck. And the warm spear of her tongue began to tussle with his. He nearly moaned when he felt her long fingers knead the muscles of his shoulders.

In her bare feet, she was shorter than he, and as he plunged his tongue deep between her lips, he felt her strain upward on her toes. His hands automatically dropped down the length of her back, until he cupped her behind, almost lifting her. It had been so long since he'd felt her.... He almost leaned back, so he could see her face. Instead, he continued drinking her in, feeling as though he'd never stop.

His desire for her had been tightly wrapped inside him for oo long. Now it unfurled like a sail taking wind. He was eady to make love to her. Nothing mattered. Not the time or the place or the fact that she didn't know who he really vas.

She was kissing him so deeply that he could barely breathe now. And when she arched against his growing arousal, his hands began to rove over the soft rise of her backside. He ifted her quickly, and turned, so that her back, rather than his, was against the counter.

She drew away, with a shaky intake of breath. He let her slide down the length of him until her feet touched the floor again. Her green eyes looked as soft as water, and her lips were as swollen as ripe red berries. Her mussed hair looked ike hell. And sexy beyond any words Santa could think of.

"I want you," she finally whispered, sounding breathless.

He wasn't sure what he'd expected, but not that. Cyn had changed. She'd always been an unconscionable flirt, but never quite so bold. Now she was all grown-up, a woman conscious of her needs and desires. And he liked it. He glanced toward the doorway. The sound of Amanda's cartoons suddenly seemed to fill the kitchen.

She blew out a soft, satisfied sigh. "I don't mean now," she nearly whispered. "I think I just mean that I'm glad you're here. The holidays are always a little hard for me."

He was somewhat taken aback. "Glad to be obliging," he drawled, feeling a little breathless himself but determined not to show it.

She chuckled, and a teasing glint winked in her eyes. She poked his chest playfully with a finger, yet another new gesture he was getting to know intimately. "But the real question is whether or not you want me, now isn't it, Santa?" She gazed at him expectantly.

His mouth dropped open in mock astonishment. "Are you always so blunt?"

"One of the things I've found out in the past few years," she said, "is that life's too short."

"For old-fashioned courtship with the hired help?" he asked with a smile.

"You really don't have to answer me, Santa." She wriggled out from between him and the counter.

She was almost to the door when he said, "Cyn?"

She turned and raised an eyebrow.

"Just so your mind will be at ease..." he began softly.

She giggled like a schoolgirl. "Just so I can sleep nights?"

"Why, I'd hate to think of you tossing and turning," he said, drawing out the words, "and all because you couldn't quit wondering."

"Well, you better hurry up and tell me," she teased. "Because I've got to take a load of clothes out of the dryer."

His brows shot up in genuine surprise. "You mean, a woman like you does her own laundry?"

She rolled her eyes heavenward, then fixed her gaze on him. "Impressed?"

He smirked back. "No."

Her laughter filled the room. "Those clothes of mine are probably burning up by now," she singsonged.

"I don't know about the clothes," he said, his gaze never leaving hers. "But I sure am."

Her smile spread into the sexiest grin he'd ever seen. "Yeah?"

"Yeah. And I want you." He gazed deep into her eyes. "Something fierce."

She quickly held up her index finger, touched it to her tongue, then waved it in the air. "Pssst," she said. "Why the very air in here sizzles."

"But Cyn," he continued, feeling an odd mixture of anger and desire, "I don't have to have everything I want."

Her face fell just a little and, as much as it hurt him, he felt almost glad. "Don't tell me. Santa is above involving himself with his clients."

"That's right," he said softly. "I'm here to do a job."

She shot him a false smile, then whirled around and headed for the door again. "Pardon my saying so," she called over her shoulder. "But you don't look all that busy to me."

"A minute ago," he called at her retreating back, "I sure felt pretty busy. Didn't you?"

"LOOK, PAXTON—" Santa blew out a very loud, annoyed sigh. He had to get away from Cyn. He couldn't be in the same room with her without touching her. He had to get away from Amanda, too. The beautiful little girl wasn't his. And now she represented his most secret dreams . . . of the family he wanted but would probably never have. "I hired a temporary rent-a-cop to stay outside Cyn's door. And there are at least five other guys with my qualifications."

Paxton's hands shot to his hips. He was facing away from Santa, staring through his office window at the Rockefeller Center tree. "Name one."

"Strauss."

Paxton snorted. "Mr. Santa!" He turned around and stared into Santa's eyes. "Strauss is protecting the President of the United States! When we couldn't find you, we tried him."

When Santa leaned back in the office chair, something stabbed him in the back. He glanced behind himself; it was the handle of a "say and tell" toy. He sighed again, thinking that Carpenter was in South America, Gibson had slipped two disks playing tennis, and O'Conner never worked Christmas. "Hudson," Santa suddenly said. "Naomi Hudson."

Paxton's jaw clenched.

"She's a woman," Santa said. "But I assure you, she's good." With a woman, he wouldn't have to worry about Cyn. After all, Carpenter and Gibson both had legendary reputations with the ladies.

"I don't care that she's a woman," Paxton said defensively, "but she works full-time for a senator in Texas."

Santa frowned. "I haven't talked to her in a while," he admitted.

"With all the work I have to do this time of year, I can't worry about Cynthia and Amanda," Paxton said. "You have to stay. Especially since this morning's note looks like a real warning."

"I'm sorry," Santa said. "I can't."

Paxton's eyes narrowed. "Just what has Cynthia done to you?"

What hasn't she done? Santa couldn't help but take the opportunity. "In researching the background, hoping to get to the bottom of this, I've come up with certain..." He paused. "Discrepancies." Was it his imagination, or did Paxton look as guilty as sin?

"What kind of, er, discrepancies?"

"Harry Stevens isn't dead." Santa tilted his head and scrutinized Paxton. The man was hiding something. He could sense it. "When I work for people, I don't like being lied to about the facts. Turns out your daughter also had an affair with a convict."

"He wasn't a convict then! She didn't know!" Paxton plopped in his desk chair so quickly that it nearly swiveled in a complete circle. He righted himself, looking resigned. "Harry used to be a good friend of hers," he said, leaning his elbows on his cluttered desk. "He merely gave Amanda a name."

Santa wanted to rise to his feet but didn't. His chest felt as if it were being squeezed by a vise. "The kid," he said, fighting for control of his voice. "Amanda." He crossed his arms, as if the gesture might still his beating heart. "She's really Jake Jackson's daughter, isn't she?"

"You know about the case?"

Santa forced himself to nod. "Is she?"

Paxton's eyes widened. The man looked positively stricken. "I just don't know," he finally said. "Please, Mr. Santa, my daughter's been through the wringer. There was a lot of press at that trial." He waved a hand in the air. "Cynthia was devastated—just what you might expect when a young, vulnerable, sensitive girl has been betrayed like that."

At twenty-four, Cyn had been overprotected; still, she wasn't a girl.

Santa wasn't sure why, but he felt guilty. "So why did you declare Harry dead?"

Paxton shrugged. "It just seemed the cleanest way to end everything and explain Amanda."

Paxton was lying. Santa was sure of it. It would be easy enough to get Amanda down to a lab for a DNA test. And yet, somehow, Santa didn't want to do that. He wanted to hear the explanation from only one source. Cyn Sweet's lips. He simply couldn't believe how devious the members of the Sweet family were. "Whose child is it?" he finally asked.

"I really don't know," Paxton repeated, sounding almost sincere.

Santa thought about the way Cyn had been teasing and toying with him. Just how many men had she come on to in that way? He doubted she'd had an affair right after the trial, but it could be the truth.

"Will you stay?" Paxton's eyes were pleading him.

Sure. I'll seduce the information out of your daughter.

"I'll pay double what you're getting now."

"Fine," Santa said.

NINE DAYS TILL
CHRISTMAS...

Chapter Four

"Dad, I didn't *do* anything!" Cyn exclaimed, twirling the phone cord around her pinkie. She retied her robe, then glanced toward the TV, wishing Amanda was watching in the den, rather than the living room. Fortunately, her daughter was thoroughly engrossed in *Sesame Street*. "In fact—" Cyn lowered her voice "—I haven't even *seen* Santa since last night, when he left to—"

"To storm my office!" Paxton barked so loudly that Cyn leaned away from the earpiece and grimaced. "And quit his job! For what I'm paying, things must be pretty darn bad, if he wants to leave. I demand to know why things aren't working out."

Because he kissed me and I kissed him back so hard we could have made love. Her ego still stung from his rejection. How could he kiss her with Jake Jackson's verve and passion, then say he wouldn't act on it? And why had he tried to quit on her? Just where had he been all night? "I don't know why he wanted to leave. Santa can be a little—er—standoffish," she said in self-defense.

"I'd call it respectful, young lady," her father countered. She was sure Paxton was thinking of Jake Jackson, who hadn't respected her in the least.

"Daddy, when I'm sixty, are you still going to be calling me 'young lady'?" She hardly felt inclined to discuss what was going on in her own apartment. Or not going on, she thought, feeling frustrated.

"Don't change the subject," he said levelly. "If you ask me, you could do a lot worse than Anton Santa."

She gasped. "Worse than! For what?"

"You know exactly what I mean, Cynthia Anna."

Paxton never called her that unless he was truly mad. "All I need is for you to start playing matchmaker," she returned huffily, wondering what had gotten into her father. Usually she could do no wrong; now he was actually taking Santa's side. *I don't always have to have what I want,* she thought, mentally mocking Santa.

"Well, maybe you need a matchmaker." Her father's voice gentled. Knowing what was coming, she had to fight not to pitch the phone across the room. She grabbed it from an end table and cradled it against her stomach. "After all, you can't raise Amanda alone. You need someone. And you haven't—"

"Haven't done such a good job matching myself up?" she asked tartly. Her father was definitely making veiled references to Jake, and she was starting to feel like a pressure cooker that was about to blow.

"Santa's responsible," her father said. "He's protecting you and Amanda and you've got to appear appreciative, at the very least. He's just not the sort of man who'll put up with nonsense."

A quick image of Santa, clad only in his "Merry Christmas" towel flashed through her mind. She almost chuckled. "And he's good-looking and wears tailored suits, instead of leather jackets," she added, not bothering to hide her irony.

"He does dress nicely." Her father suddenly sounded agreeable.

Cyn's hand tightened around the receiver. "And so he must be the man of my dreams? Practically every man in New York wears suits, Dad!" Except Jake Jackson, she mentally amended.

"I don't see what you've got against him." Paxton's voice rose again.

"Why, not a thing." The words were delivered more sarcastically than she'd intended. "Maybe I should just marry him tomorrow."

"Maybe you should." This time it wasn't Paxton. It was Santa.

She whirled around. "Do you always eavesdrop?" Hot color seeped into her cheeks. Before she'd met Santa, she hadn't blushed in years. Only Jake had flustered her to that point. It was positively infuriating. So was his opening line. He meant to continue a flirtation, even though there'd be no follow-through. "How long have you been standing there?"

He smiled pleasantly, his eyes looking like dark round globes beneath his thick lashes. "Long enough."

"Well, you shouldn't creep around!" The receiver slid downward. She caught it between her jaw and her shoulder. "I didn't even hear you come in!"

His eyebrow arched in a way that was barely perceptible. "Should I take that to mean you were listening for me?"

The nerve of him. "All night," she returned drolly.

His powerful shoulders rolled slightly in their sockets, like a shimmying dancer's. "Twisting and turning and waiting and wondering..."

It was so true, she felt embarrassed. "Don't flatter yourself," she snapped.

He leaned forward idly, resting his elbows on the back of an armchair. "I'd much rather flatter you."

"Be nice to him!" Paxton warned over the phone.

"You could flatter me by vanishing," she said with a scowl.

"I said, be nice!" Paxton shrieked.

This time Santa clearly heard him. "I—I..." She didn't know who to address first, her father or Santa.

"Be nice to me," Santa mouthed, wagging a suntanned finger.

"I am being nice," she said into the mouthpiece.

"And let me know when you're off the phone," Santa said.

"Does Santa need to use the phone?" Paxton asked. "If he does, it's probably important. We'd better get off, Cyn."

Her lips parted in wonder. Santa's self-satisfied smile made him look like a cat who'd just lapped up the last of the cream. "Daddy, we need to go over the final plans for this evening's promotion!"

"Santa has an important call to make," her father returned.

Her eyes widened and she sighed. "Love you, Daddy."

"Love you, too," he said. "And be nice to Santa. I'll be watching you at the drawing for the tickets to *The Nutcracker*, to make sure you're behaving."

She hung up and glared at Santa. It was difficult. She could still feel his lips on hers. Her thighs suddenly tingled, as if he were pressed against her again. His sharply tailored, double-breasted chocolate suit made his eyes look darker. But, she had to remind herself, the first time he'd kissed her without mistletoe, he'd tried to quit his job. "When did you get so buddy-buddy with my father?"

Santa shrugged, looking genuinely puzzled. "He seems to like me."

She nodded as if he had just confessed to armed robbery. "Just what did you do to him?"

"The regular snow job." He flashed her an irresistible, glistening grin that made his eyes twinkle.

She sniffed. "And *he* fell for it," she said, as if to indicate that *she* hadn't.

Santa gazed at her steadily. The grin slowly tempered to an amused smile. "You're jealous."

As soon as he said it, she knew it was true. Her father had never taken someone else's side. "I thought you'd quit," she remarked lightly, wishing the man couldn't read her quite so easily.

"Changed my mind."

"Would you like to tell me why?" Had he really come back for her? she wondered. Maybe he'd worried all night about his ethics regarding clients, but couldn't get their kiss out of his mind, so he'd come back. Maybe she was being too hard on him. "Why?" she repeated softly.

He chuckled. "Every time I say no, your father pays me double. It's starting to add up."

That figured. "Good," she said with a lightness she didn't feel. "I was afraid you'd reconsidered your client-involvement policy." She eyed the armchair, wishing she could sit down. Her fool knees were buckling again.

"Oh," he drawled softly. "That, too."

"Ah—" She sucked in a quick breath, hating him for thinking she was that easy. "But in the gray light of another chilly New York morning, I'm sorry to inform you, I've cooled considerably."

They stared each other down for a solid minute. Everything in his eyes said he knew she was only saving face. "Didn't you say you had a call to make?" she asked innocently, holding out the phone.

He was still sizing her up with his eyes. "Sorry," he drawled. "*My* call's private."

She couldn't help but wonder whether he was phoning a woman. Given his looks, she imagined he found plenty to call. "Well," she said. "I hope you don't expect me to leave the room."

She wasn't sure but thought his shoulders were beginning to shake with laughter. He turned on his heel and headed for his room. "I guess I can play the gentleman. Once." He glanced over his shoulder and winked at her.

Now that Dad's on his side, I'm doomed, she thought.

She stared at his closed door, feeling more curious than ever about who he was calling. Was it a woman he'd been with the night before? As much as she hated herself for it, she found herself dragging the living room extension down the hallway and into the kitchen, away from the TV. She shut the door.

Don't do it. So far, your jealousy has gotten you nowhere but in a heap of trouble. She tried to keep reminding herself that the last supposed "other woman" she'd researched had led her to The Grinch Gang. Nevertheless, she very quietly picked up the receiver.

"Santa, I'm going to have to put you on hold for a minute," a woman said. The line went blank and Cyn held her breath. She felt like an idiot. What was she doing?

"Oh, Cynthia," Santa singsonged. "Who's eavesdropping now?"

Caught red-handed! She considered hanging up, but that would be even worse than an outright admission of guilt. "It *could* have been Amanda," she said coolly.

"But it wasn't," he returned. The last thing she heard before she hung up was Santa's resounding belly laugh.

"Ho, ho, ho," she muttered. Still, she knew it took an extremely powerful man to reduce her to such juvenile tactics. Mulling things over, she almost convinced herself that Santa hadn't come back for the money, but because of her. Hadn't he?

"SORRY, SANTA, just one more minute." Right before his friend put him on hold again, he heard her perkily answer the other line, saying, "Sally Steele, Riker's Island."

He'd spent the previous night rifling through desks at Too Sweet. He'd been determined to find stray bits of cut magazines, an X-Acto blade, or the typewriter on which the last note had been composed. He'd found zero. He'd paid for the rent-a-cop to watch Cyn's place out-of-pocket, too.

He removed his cuffs from where they were looped over his belt, tossed them onto the mattress, then leaned back on his pillows. Cradling the receiver against his shoulder, he decided that seducing information out of Cyn would be a piece of cake. She was angry, but only because he'd rejected her yesterday. Nevertheless, her supposed premonitions about sensing Jake Jackson's presence were making him nervous.

Why was it so important that he hear the information from between her lying lips? he wondered. As much as he fought it, he thought of her around the clock. He kept imagining the moment when he'd take her. It would happen quickly, without feeling, but sometimes now, the fantasy ended all wrong. She realized who he was, they forgave each other, and everything was hunky-dory. Why hadn't he simply pushed Paxton harder for the truth?

And how long could he wait? He was being jerked around like a lapdog. First he was Amanda's father. Then he wasn't. Then he was again. What was he going to do if he found out he was? Take Amanda from her mother to live with him? How could such a thing work? *Excuse me, would you mind watching my little girl...while I take a bullet for the Speaker of the House?*

The line clicked on. "Sally?"

"Hey there, Santa Claus! Haven't seen you out at Riker's Island lately. Guess you've been good this year."

If he wasn't careful, Amanda's nickname for him was going to stick. "Hey there," he said.

"What can I do for you?"

"Besides leave your husband?"

She giggled. Sally loved her husband more than life, and both of them knew it, but she always flirted with Santa. "It would be too cruel to leave him before Christmas," she chided. "But is there something else?"

"I'm checking on an inmate. He was arrested on a B and E four years ago. The name's Matthew Lewis."

"Guess you've been sunning yourself in the Caribbean again." Sally laughed. "Don't you watch the news?"

He sat up. "No, I've been reading the papers, though. Did he escape or something?"

"As far as I'm concerned, you're the escape artist," she said flirtatiously.

Santa chuckled. "Sally, honey, you're married."

"So true." Sally blew out a mock beleaguered sigh. "The guy you're looking for was released on a holiday pardon from our humble Riker's two weeks ago."

"He's been out for two weeks?" Santa repeated. That meant Lewis could have sent all the notes. Having worked with The Grinch Gang, Santa knew the man was skilled enough to get into Cyn's place, too. Prison might have hardened him and made him mean enough to steal Amanda. Maybe this time he wouldn't get caught.

"Should I call you back with an address for him?" Sally finally asked. "It's hard to find people this close to Christmas, but I'm sure I can track down his parole officer."

"That would be great," Santa said, giving her Cyn's number. "I owe you one."

Sally's ribald laughter cackled over the line. "Keep saying that," she said coyly, "and I just might try to collect."

"I'm sure you'd take it out in blood," he teased.

"I was thinking more in terms of flesh," she joked. "As in your hide. But perhaps your firstborn would do."

He thought of Amanda. "Oh, please, Sally," he said, "not that."

"Don't tell me there are little secret Santas out there," she said laughing. "Ones you've never told us about."

"Sally," he said before he hung up, "when I know, you'll know."

"I CAN'T STAND TO HAVE a man watch me cook," Cyn said, tightening a red-and-green apron around her waist. She shot him a taunting smile, then shoved a tray of cookie sprinkles in his direction. She'd changed into black wool slacks and a white silk blouse, through which he could see hints of a lacy camisole.

"Nothing worse than a feminist," he returned playfully, seating himself at the table. The aroma of freshly baked cookies filled the warm kitchen and made him think of home, hearth and family. Glancing between Cyn and Amanda, he wondered yet another time if this really *was* his family.

"What's a fem-nist?" Amanda lathered a cookie with icing, getting more of the green goo on her hands than on the cookie. She pushed it toward Santa, who was now on sprinkle detail, apparently.

"A mild annoyance," Santa teased. He chuckled, gazed into Amanda's adorable green eyes, then picked up her cookie. Instead of sprinkling it, he naughtily popped it into his mouth whole.

Amanda gasped, staring at him, slack jawed. Then her rosy cheeks dimpled and she giggled. "Mommy, Santa Claus don't help us bake right."

"It's *won't*, not *don't*, and men never do, honey," Cyn replied over her shoulder as she put another tray into the oven.

When she turned around again, Santa surveyed her with the most penetrating gaze he could muster. She leaned against the same counter where they'd kissed the day before. "But don't forget, there are some things *only* men can do in a kitchen," he said. Judging from the way she pursed her lips, she too was now thinking about kissing him.

"Yeah," Amanda said brightly. "Men can come and they fix the sink when the water goes everywhere."

"Right, Amanda," Cyn said, leaning against the counter and giving Santa the once-over, as if she couldn't have made the point better herself.

Still, he was pleased to hear that her voice sounded a bit faint. She was thinking of kisses, all right. The corners of his lips twitched. "Men can fix all kinds of broken-down things."

Completely forgetting Amanda, Cyn's eyes widened. "I sure hope you aren't implying that I'm somehow broken-down."

He shrugged. "No, but are you now implying I could fix you?"

"Put me in a fix is more like it," she said coyly, clearly unable to stop herself from rising to the bait.

"And then there's your father—" He grinned and leaned his elbows on the table, enjoying himself. "Who's trying to *fix* us up."

Cyn suddenly chuckled. She crossed her arms over her chest. "Well, I'm not *fixing* to let him."

Santa glanced at Amanda, who now looked thoroughly confused. "Granddaddy's a fem-nist," she piped in as she finished icing the last cookie.

Cyn's eyes narrowed to a squint. "How's that?" she asked as he leaned forward and sprinkled tiny pink stars over Amanda's cookie. The gesture won him endearing smiles from both Amanda and Cyn.

"Granddaddy calls and don't let me watch cartoons," Amanda groused, jumping up from the table.

Ever the patient mother, Cyn automatically repeated the won't-not-don't rule, then said, "How would that make him a feminist, Amanda?"

"He was 'noying me," Amanda said promptly.

Cyn's laughter seemed to make the kitchen even warmer. "No, what a feminist is—"

"I'm gonna get my dress to wear by myself," Amanda announced, interrupting her.

Cyn smiled. "You go pick out a dress. I'll call you when the next batch is ready for icing."

"If Santa Claus doesn't eat them all," Amanda said, shooting Santa a coy glance that she'd clearly copied from her mother. "I get in trouble. Mr. Santa should be in big trouble."

"As soon as you leave to pick out your dress," Cyn said gravely, "I mean to explain the rules to Santa."

"Rules?" As soon as Amanda had gone, he picked up another cookie and took a large bite.

"We don't eat without asking." Cyn tossed a dish towel over the lip of the sink and stared pointedly at his cookie.

There were some remarks even he wouldn't touch with a ten-foot pole. Still he couldn't help but imagine his mouth sliding over Cyn's smooth skin. When he said nothing, her face suddenly went from wintry pale to berry red in a second flat.

"You are so crude!" A faint, shocked smile curled the corners of her lips.

"*I* didn't say a word," he drawled.

"You don't have to. Is your mind always in the gutter?"

He downed the rest of the cookie and reached for another. "Perpetually, when I'm around you."

"You have a whole tray of sprinkles to finish," she said, suddenly sounding like a drill sergeant. "And I suggest you get to work. Otherwise, you'll disappoint Amanda."

Was Cyn really going to try to implement her own hands-off policy? Good luck, he thought. Given the energy between them, her resolve would never last. "Hmm," he finally hummed, picking up a container of sprinkles. "If I concentrate real hard on decorating, then maybe you won't be so likely to read my gutterlike mind."

"I sure hope I can't," she returned archly. "I'd probably collapse from the shock."

His gaze dropped from her face and lingered momentarily on her blouse. Looking at how the scalloped lace edges of her camisole formed heart shapes over her breasts, his smile almost faltered. "No probably about it," he said softly.

Her sharp breath seemed overly loud in the quiet kitchen. She grabbed the dish towel, dampened it, then strode to the table and began mopping in and around his elbows, as if he weren't even there.

"Missed a spot," he prodded as he put down the pink star sprinkles and reached for the tiny blue dots. When she glanced his way, he pointed at a glob of green icing.

"Thank you," she said a little huffily, swiping at the green smear with more force than was needed.

"Anytime." After a moment, he cleared his throat and watched her busy herself, cleaning up the kitchen. He'd debated for some hours about whether or not to tell her about Lewis. He didn't want to see fear in her eyes again. But he couldn't protect people who weren't aware of the danger they were in, either.

"Cyn," he said. "We need to talk."

She folded the dish towel, slapped it over the sink again, then rinsed dishes, as if she meant to ignore him. When they teased each other, there was always some truth in what was said. He wondered whether their words would heat up into a real argument or a kiss. This time he hoped they could simply talk.

She finally turned around. "Now, what do you want to discuss?"

"You might want to sit down for a minute."

"You mean, right next to you?" She chuckled. "Forget it, Santa. Our knees might touch or something. And even though you seem ready to forget it now, I am your client. Right?"

"If I happen to forget I'm sure you'll be the first to remind me."

Her smile broadened into a confident grin. "Why, Santa—" She was mocking his drawl now. "I'd just feel so downright wretched if I accidentally compromised your ethics."

His eyes never left hers. "Ms. Sweet as sugar," he returned, "it's not my *ethics* I'm worried about."

That stopped her cold.

Out of the corner of his eye, he saw a wisp of smoke. "And Cyn?"

She crossed her arms over her chest. "What?"

"I do believe your cookies are burning."

In the next instant, she went flying around the kitchen like a spooked bird. She looked so upset when she slammed the tray onto the counter that he said, "Sorry."

"It's not your fault," she quickly returned, as if not about to admit that he'd captured her complete attention. "Besides," she said as Santa rose and came up behind her, "Daddy likes them that way."

"Burned?"

"Crunchy," she corrected. A flicker of awareness sparked in her eyes. Santa was sure she was thinking what he was. That they'd been standing in this exact spot when they'd kissed the previous day. "So, what is it?" Her businesslike tone was as crisply brittle as her cookies.

He suddenly wished that he could protect her and Amanda, not just from Lewis, but from all the harm in the world. His mouth opened slightly and he licked his upper lip.

"Don't tell me," she teased. She was clearly aware of the emotion in his gaze but read it incorrectly. "You're going to propose to me now." She smiled wickedly. "It always happens after men have known me three or four days."

"I wish I were," he found himself saying softly.

Her eyes met his dead-on, and widened. "It's—it's something bad," she rambled. "I can tell, it's something bad. Dammit, Santa, what is it?"

Somehow, he wanted to be holding her when he told her. "Matthew Lewis is out of Riker's Island on a holiday pardon," he said.

She all but crumpled against the counter. The expression in her eyes had gone from viciously teasing, to fearfully surprised, to helplessly vulnerable—all in a heartbeat. "Jake Jackson," she demanded. "What about Jake?"

He should have expected that. And he didn't want to lie. He was digging himself in deeper with every single falsehood he uttered. But seeing the expression in her eyes, he knew he'd tell a million lies to erase it. "I think he's still in prison," he managed to say.

She gasped. "Think?" Those beautiful green eyes pleaded with his.

"Know," he corrected. He waited for her to say something more. She didn't.

"Come here," he nearly whispered. Before his arms were even around her shoulders, her face was pressed against his chest. Her body curled against his, feeling so right he was almost convinced they had never been apart.

He tried to remind himself that she hadn't been there for him. That she'd left him, lying on her parents' lawn with two gunshot wounds. She might have deprived him of his very own daughter, too. The woman who was asking for his strength now hadn't given him hers. Cyn was demanding his trust but hadn't trusted him.

Santa knew he was supposed to be seducing information out of her. Instead, he was almost sure he could fall in love with her all over again. But even if he could, he thought, he'd never forgive her.

"BUY NOW! Lotto tickets are distributed with every purchase!" Bob Bingley grandly barked commands over Too Sweet's loudspeaker. "At exactly seven o'clock—that's just five minutes from now, folks—we'll dispense the very last ticket and the drawing will begin. That ticket might be a winner! So make your final purchases now!"

As Cyn and Amanda headed for the makeshift stage on the ground floor of Too Sweet, Cyn wished that the elf hadn't called in sick. A flu bug seemed to have half of Manhattan under the weather. She leaned and adjusted her green leggings. The next thing she knew, she thought, she'd be dressed as Santa Claus.

She shot Amanda an encouraging smile as they took positions on either side of the air-driven lotto machine. Inside the transparent plastic, bright red and green balls printed with silver numbers whirled and tumbled.

How does Amanda stand this? Cyn wondered, plastering a smile on her face. Their matching elf outfits were bright green and consisted of pointy-toed, Aladdin-style slippers, thick leggings, and squarish, shorty dresses. What Amanda referred to as the Robin Hood hats had gargantuan red plumes. With Anton Santa staring at her protectively, Cyn felt more than a little idiotic.

She heaved a sigh of relief when the drumroll sounded. Over and over, Amanda pressed a button and the balls shot upward, landing in their ball-size pockets.

"Nine," Cyn called over the microphone. "Seven. Four..." There were to be twenty winners, each of whom would receive three free tickets to *The Nutcracker*, so that parents could accompany the child. Cyn wished all the kids present could win. "Six. Seven..."

As she called out the numbers, she glanced at Bob, who was recording them all. Then her gaze returned to Santa. No matter how hard she tried, she couldn't keep her eyes off him. He could be so sweet, when he wanted to be.

"Mommy," Amanda said in a stage whisper.

Cyn started. "Three," she called into the microphone, still watching Santa. "One..." She'd done her best to cold-shoulder him on their way out of the apartment, and now she was glad. In the few days she'd known him, he'd sent out more mixed messages than the post office. First he'd kept her at arm's length, which had made her want to flirt with him. When it had led to a kiss, he firmly rejected her, then tried to quit his job. Now he was seemingly ready to offer her comfort.

"Mommy!"

"Lucky number one again," Cyn said promptly. "Two. Nine..."

"That's us!" someone yelled.

Cyn's eyes darted over the crowd, settling on familiar faces—Eileen, Bob, Evan, Clayton. Somehow she half expected to see Matthew Lewis. Lewis made her think of Jake. *I've got to stay away from Santa,* she thought. "Three," she called. "Seven again! Five..." After all, Jake Jackson had taught her enough about mixed messages to last her a lifetime. She wouldn't have a man in her life who blew hot and cold.

"And now for the last lucky number!" she said brightly a few moments later as Amanda pushed the button. "Number nine!" She blew out a quick sigh, trying to forget that Santa's call this morning had been to a woman. She grinned at the crowd. "That wraps it up! Have fun at *The Nutcracker!*"

Amanda preceded her down the steps and right into Paxton's arms. "Good job, Amanda!" he said.

Meaning to avoid Santa, Cyn hurried toward the employees' door. Glancing over her shoulder, she realized the man in question was right behind her. Paxton was following, too, with Amanda on his hip.

She needed to take a roll of wrapping paper home, so she ducked into a walk-in closet that served as a supply room. The place was a mess, cluttered with tumbled stacks of boxes and scattered bows. Cyn smiled. A disaster area meant that today's sales were good. Just as she glanced over the pickings—gold foil, red foil, and red-and-green wreath print—she heard steps. Then the door behind her shut.

"What exactly did I do wrong?" Santa leaned casually against the door. Even though they were at opposite ends of the storage closet, he was a mere four feet away.

"Not a thing." She ignored him and bent over. Her hands fumbled over the various papers, even though she'd already decided on red. Suddenly she stood up straight. Just how short was her skirt? She forced herself not to grab at the hemline nearest her backside, and glanced at Santa. *Pretty short, judging by his expression.*

A loud series of raps sounded on the door. *Saved,* she thought, watching Santa cross his arms over his broad chest as if he didn't intend to budge.

"Are you in there, Cyn?"

She smiled at Santa as if to say that he wasn't going to get away with trapping her. "Yes, Daddy!" she called brightly.

"Santa?" Paxton called.

"Right here."

Then the worst imaginable thing happened. The lock turned over. Her father had locked the door from the outside! What in thunder did he think he was doing?

Santa had the nerve to chuckle. "Your Daddy's sure got a juvenile streak," he remarked.

She sighed. "Why else would a man start a toy company?"

He shrugged. "The real question's why my favorite elf ducked in here to hide."

Favorite elf? His eyes gave her the once-over. She wished she was clad in anything other than a felt dress, and that the supply room was larger. "I'm not hiding," she said pointedly.

"Does Cyn not want to join in our reindeer games?" he drawled.

She grabbed a roll of paper, feeling so flustered that she accidentally picked up the green rather than the red. She wanted the man, there was no doubt about it. But she was just as sure it would be a mistake. She stalked toward the door. "I'm an elf, not a reindeer. Remember?" She pounded on the door. Hard. "Dad?"

"Sorry," Santa said softly. "But I think we're at his mercy."

Her gaze met his. "Let's wait it out, like adults, shall we?"

He threw both hands in the air. "Is it something I said?"

She arched her brow as if she had no idea what he was talking about. Still, she'd made such a point of avoiding him that he couldn't have missed it.

He shot her a knowing smirk. "You know what I mean."

"All right," she said levelly, leaning her shoulder against the door. "I'll tell you."

He turned so he was facing her. "Please do."

"Number one, you're toying with me," she said, leaning even closer. "Number two, you blow hot and cold, and I don't like that in a man. And number three," she said, her voice rising, "I don't play silly games." She flashed him a quick smile. "Reindeer or otherwise."

The fact that he was still smiling truly annoyed her. "I'm sorry I blow hot and cold," he said. "But you know something?"

"What?" She just couldn't help but ask.

"Right now, I'm blowing hot."

Before she could even respond, the fool man was kissing her again. She dropped the wrapping paper, and her arms flew up in protest. As his lips claimed hers, one of her hands somehow wound up on his shoulder. The other, fortunately, remained rational. With it, she began pounding on the door, as if to save her life.

It flew open in the next heartbeat.

Thank heavens, she thought, just before she realized they'd been leaning on it. She and Santa tumbled outward, sprawling toward the floor. Having no choice, she clutched him for support, but he was airborne.

His lips never left hers, but he somehow managed to twist his muscular body so that he hit the hard tiles first. Her hat lurched off her head and then, because of the plume, floated slowly downward. Santa kept rolling, until he was right on top of her.

Cyn wrenched away, only to find that she was trapped by Santa's weight. "Daddy!" she nearly shrieked. She looked up, into Paxton's eyes. He seemed to be towering over her.

"Something wrong, dear?" Paxton stared down at her calmly. In his arms, Amanda clapped excitedly.

"Look at what this man just did to me!" Cyn burst out, her eyes shooting Santa daggers. She unpinned one of her arms and tried to pull down the hemline of her ridiculous elf outfit. It was bunched nearly to her waist and she now realized that one of her slippers had come off in the melee. "Just look!"

"What?" Paxton was all innocence. "Oh, I suppose I should thank Mr. Santa. After all, he just broke your fall with an astounding display of professionalism and expertise. Excellent job, Santa," he continued as he began ambling away. "Excellent." He glanced over his shoulder, suddenly chuckling. "Oh, and Santa?"

The man was staring deeply into her eyes, and the full length of his body still covered hers. Cyn was sure he could feel her heart pounding against his chest. He finally glanced at Paxton. "Yes, sir?"

"Do keep up the good work."

I'M DEFINITELY getting out of shape. Across the river, in New Jersey, a man grunted and leaned against a wall, debating if he should contact Club Med or buy a StairMaster. Then he lugged the heavy typewriter up the rest of the stairs. "What a workout," he muttered when he reached his bedroom. He dropped the typewriter onto the mattress. It was so heavy that it bounced.

He fished through the odds and ends in his bedside drawer. When he found the key to his walk-in closet, he hoisted the typewriter into his arms again, carried it inside the closet, then shoved it behind a row of shoes. Then he locked the closet.

Things were getting serious, all right. Anton Santa had scrutinized the contents inside every drawer in the Too Sweet corporate offices. Santa had also looked at every typewriter. Worse, the last letter that had been sent hadn't even been mentioned in this morning's meeting. It hadn't made the papers, either.

He wanted that toy company! If it were run as something other than a family business, it could become a franchise. He'd make a fortune. Contrary to what the other execs thought, bad press always lost Too Sweet money. But the notes hadn't generated publicity.

He sighed. Maybe it was time he truly took matters into his own hands.

*EIGHT DAYS TILL
CHRISTMAS...*

Chapter Five

Santa glanced at his clock. He'd finished the papers and his police procedural by six-thirty this morning, and was halfway through a thick forensics book now. He finally dogeared the page and stood and stretched, hoping he'd given Cyn enough time to dress. It was ten, but he still hadn't heard the shower. One more look at her in a bathrobe, he thought, and he'd attack her.

How anyone could sleep past five or five-thirty was simply beyond him. The cartoons hadn't even come on until eight. "Ready or not, here I come," he chanted.

He flung open his door and found himself staring at the empty living room. He ambled in the direction of the blaring cartoons, only to find the den vacant, too. He tilted his head, listening. *Nothing.*

Both Cyn and Amanda knew better than to leave without him, he thought. Had someone forced them to? He crept down the hall. No one was in Amanda's room. Her bed had been made and the toys she'd played with the previous night had been put away.

He checked all the rooms, then warily pushed open Cyn's door. The room was a mess. Struggle or mere slobbishness? It was hard to tell. He circled her bed cautiously, half hoping the twisted sheets indicated a struggle, since he was neat to a fault. *How could I ever live with this woman?* He squelched that thought and squinted at her covers. Mere slobbishness, he finally decided. He didn't know if he felt relief because Amanda was probably safe, or because the mess meant his and Cyn's personal habits were so different.

In spite of the circumstances, he leaned and ran a hand over the sheets. They were of pink satin and so tangled that he could easily imagine they'd spent the night together. The whole room smelled like a woman who'd bathed and perfumed just for him, and the vanity was strewn with feminine trappings—powder-tinged makeup brushes, tiny crystal vials, delicate colored bottles, and crystal sprayers with pumps. Her blouse of the previous day had been sheer enough that he recognized the lace camisole on the floor. He had to fight not to pick it up.

He strode into her private bath and crouched down. The tub was dry, which meant she definitely hadn't showered. Suddenly his eyes widened, and he snagged a bottle from the lip of the tub. He scrutinized it so carefully that it might have been evidence at the scene of a murder.

"I'll be damned," he whispered, shaking his head. Cyn Sweet dyed her hair. The label really said Blonde. And all this time, he'd thought of her as a natural.

When he stood again, one of the soft silk stockings that hung over the shower rod fluttered against his face, then trailed over his shoulder. "She still wears garters, too," he murmured. *And I've got to get out of here.* He turned abruptly, reentered her room proper and checked the closet opposite her bed. He found nothing but rods hung with clothes that smelled of Cyn. "Cyn?" he called, heading toward the kitchen. "Amanda?"

Her folded note was hidden under an angel-shaped refrigerator magnet. It said, "Don't worry, we weren't kidnapped or anything."

He rubbed the scar on his jaw while he stared at the note. He was angry at himself for becoming so engrossed in his book, and furious at her. In fact, what he was feeling was out of proportion with the situation. He felt as if he'd just raced back in time. It was four years ago, and he was running through her parents' front door. She took one look at his face, then turned and fled toward a cop cruiser. He felt abandoned.

He sighed. The kidnapper had a line on Cyn's daily activities, judging from how the last note had been delivered. He or she could have forced Cyn to write the note.

"More likely you just took off." He grimaced in the direction of a window, as if he might actually see Matthew Lewis, trailing Cyn and Amanda down the crowded avenue below. How could Cyn have left when they knew the man was out there somewhere?

"Why did you do this?" But he knew why. Last night, after the promotion, Paxton had insisted they all have dinner, and her father's matchmaking tactics had clearly infuriated Cyn.

She was sweet as sugar during their meal at The Russian Tea Room, of course. But as soon as Paxton was out of sight, her smile had vanished and she'd closed up like a clam. Santa wondered, as he had the previous night, what exactly had caused the rift between Paxton and his wife. *Who knows?* he thought now. *Women are impossible.*

He headed back down the hall to get his coats. As he shrugged into a gray suit jacket, he suddenly chuckled. "Some things never change," he said. He knew exactly where she was.

"WHAT DO YOU THINK, honey?"

Amanda was perched on a raised platform in her cotton undershirt and underpants. She shrugged. "Is she gonna come with my stuff?"

Cyn turned one way, then another, sucking in her stomach. "The lady from children's will bring your things in just a minute," she murmured, deciding that the emerald dress clung like a second skin. Too obvious. "Maybe I should try the red again."

A woman rapped on the door to the spacious dressing room, then nudged inside, her arms piled high with clothes. "Sorry for the delay, but we've brought up everything you liked from downstairs." She laid the clothes on a chair, while Cyn stripped back down to her slip.

"Did you like the red one better?"

Amanda pawed through her own pile. "I like black."

"It was better?" Cyn asked thoughtfully. She'd awakened this morning, deciding that she wanted to look smashing for *The Nutcracker*. After all, Amanda was going, which meant Santa was going. As she preened, Cyn told herself she just didn't want him upstaging her in one of his dashing suits.

"The black is for Mr. Santa," Amanda said, as if reading her mind. She marched up to her mother and craned her neck upward.

"Who said it was for Santa?" Cyn asked wryly, staring down. She realized Amanda had put on a sweatshirt backward and chuckled. "Here, honey, raise your arms." She turned it around, thinking the top was positively adorable. It was green, with Rudolph appliquéd on the back. A puffy Santa Claus adorned the front. When the string that hung from his cap was pulled, his eyes blinked.

Amanda stared in the mirror for less than a second. "Goody," she said. "We'll buy it." She tossed it onto her pile and found the matching leggings.

"We can?" Cyn laughed. "The next thing I know, you'll be asking for a gold card." She flashed Amanda a grin. "Please do me a favor though, and don't ask before you're at least five."

Amanda plopped down on the platform and wriggled into the pants, with a concentrated expression. "You're so very definitely my daughter," Cyn said wryly. She could swear that Amanda had been dressing herself before she could even walk. Suddenly she felt a twinge of loss. If anything ever happened to Amanda, she couldn't bear it. A lump formed in her throat and she swallowed. She forced herself to tug on the red dress again.

Staring at it, she realized she should have listened to Amanda. The black dress was the one, hands down. She stepped out of the red, reaching for it. The sleeveless velvet sheath could be worn with opera-length gloves. It would have Santa's eyes popping out of his head.

"Mommy?"

Cyn glanced down and had to fight not to laugh. Amanda had donned a black velvet dress, too. The scoop neck came down to her navel. It seemed to point out that her baby was years away from having breasts. Cyn felt relieved, somehow.

"I gotta get a dress for Santa," she nearly wailed.

"Well, we're going to concentrate strictly on you now, honey," Cyn said soothingly. "Shopping takes practice."

"We practice lots," Amanda said glumly. "I wanna be a knockout."

A knockout? Did they use terms like that on *Sesame Street?* "Sure, honey," Cyn managed to say.

HE FOLLOWED their trail from Barney's to Macy's to Bloomingdale's, back to Barney's, and then to Bergdorf Goodman. He found them in Saks. By that time, he was so steamed, he didn't let the sales personnel stop him. He rapped once on the door, then flung it open, thinking, *Hell, Cyn, I've seen you stark naked before.*

Amanda screamed.

Santa gulped. Cyn was fully clothed, and Amanda was scared to death. She scurried toward a corner, clutching a green wad of velvet against her undershirt.

She whirled around. "You gotta say who it is!" Amanda's mouth gaped and her green eyes were wide.

What he'd taken for modesty, apparently wasn't. A furious Amanda flung down the dress and put her hands on her hips. He guessed it was all right to be in her underclothes in front of a man, just so long as she was acquainted with him.

"Sorry, Amanda," he managed to say. He glanced at Cyn, who was clearly enjoying his discomfort.

"Try the blue one, honey," she said to Amanda.

"He can't see it," she whined in protest.

Santa felt like an idiot. "I'll wait outside."

"I don't care!" Amanda stomped her foot. "It's ugly."

"Sweetheart, anything'd turn pretty if you put it on," he said soothingly. That helped. She smiled just enough that her dimples started to show.

"Santa, why don't you wait outside," Cyn said, sounding tired. "We need to get this over with."

Her tone put him on edge. "I have been charging all over Manhattan," he said softly. "Do you know how many women's clothing stores there are in this town?'' He shot her one long, penetrating look, then glanced pointedly over the shopping bags in the dressing room. ''But of course you do.''

''Well, why didn't you just stay home?'' she returned saucily.

He didn't want to argue with her in front of Amanda, but he wasn't going to let her get away with a stunt like this, either. She couldn't play silly games, not when she might be endangering Amanda. ''Whatever's between us is between us.'' His voice was soft yet carried a warning. ''But you don't jeopardize the safety of yourself—'' he glanced quickly at Amanda ''—or others because of that.'' She looked so guilty he almost wanted to retract the words.

''We were just shopping,'' she said defensively.

''Shopping,'' he echoed, trying not to sound as disgusted as he felt.

She folded her hands primly in her lap. ''Well, we had to finish Christmas shopping.''

His eyes trailed from one shopping bag to another. He fixed his gaze on hers again. ''Everything you've bought is for yourself,'' he chided.

Her blush told him it was the truth. Suddenly her lovely green eyes narrowed. ''How did you know where to find us, anyway?''

The same way I know you take cream in your coffee. I know you inside out, lady. ''Just a lucky guess,'' he drawled, his eyes never leaving hers.

''Mommy's sorry, Mr. Santa Claus,'' Amanda said tearfully.

When he looked down, the little girl—so very probably his little girl—looked like her whole world was about to collapse.

''Mommy was bad and she won't do it again,'' she vowed. She looked as if she were making a life-and-death oath.

Cyn looked at Amanda for a long time, then at him again. ''I really am sorry,'' she said, sounding genuinely contrite.

He nodded. ''I'll be outside.''

''Santa Claus?''

He turned at the door. "Yes, Amanda," he said, more sternly than he'd intended.

"We got somethin' not for us, 'cause Mommy let me. You got a present you can't have till Christmas. Okay?" Her eyes begged him to say that everything was all right between them.

His heart skipped a beat. This kid was bringing him to his knees. "Thank you, Amanda," he said softly.

Outside, he took a seat in an armchair facing the dressing room. The man next to him was asleep and snoring. *My sentiments, exactly.* That women could shop for an entire day would never cease to amaze him.

It was a good thing he was patient, he thought. After all, waiting was his job. It was good that he could hide his feelings, too. Otherwise, he would have given Cyn a tongue-lashing that neither she nor Amanda would be likely to forget. But he could wait—through all the hours of shopping, and until he heard the truth about Amanda from Cyn's own lips.

Another full minute passed before he realized his heart was pounding. He blew out a long, relieved sigh. *They're safe,* he finally thought. *My girls are safe.* This time he didn't even consider that neither might belong to him.

MORE WAITING. Santa glanced at his watch, then stared at the football game again. His team was winning. Was he really missing the play-offs because of a ballet? Between shopping and *The Nutcracker*, he was sure he'd fall asleep like that poor fellow in Saks. Not that he'd ever been to a ballet before, of course.

"Ta-da," Cyn called out.

When Santa turned around, he forgot footballs even existed. Cyn's thick blond hair was pulled into a French twist. Springy silken tendrils framed her face and wound around the dangling clusters of her pearl earrings. Her wide, full lips were glossed a kissable, glistening pink.

But it was the dress that caused an almost uncomfortable tightening in his groin. The black strapless velvet sheath was long enough to look classically elegant, but short enough that no man—least of all, him—could ignore those sexy,

perfectly shaped legs. Black gloves stretched all the way up
her arms, and a single strand of gleaming pearls looped all
the way down, past her waist.

It was almost impossible to imagine that this was the same
woman who'd left him for dead just four years ago. But he
remembered, all right. She moved behind an armchair and
rested her palms on the back of it. Even though he wanted
to tell her she looked lovely, he found himself gruffly saying, "Aren't you going to freeze?"

Her face fell, but she recovered quickly enough to shoot
him a false smile. "Since when is my body temperature any
of your concern?"

As of right now. "As a bodyguard," he said, rising lithely
from the sofa, "bodies always concern me." He strode
across the room and stood in front of the chair.

"Ah—" She tossed her head, showing off the long,
smooth touchable column of her throat. "But temperatures are another matter."

"Perhaps, but whatever perfume you're wearing is sure
making mine rise." He decided that it had been easier to remember the past and why he should avoid Cyn when he was
on the other side of the room. Why had he moved?

When she leaned her elbows on the chair back, he was
half-sure she was intentionally accentuating her cleavage for
his benefit. "It should," she said. She reached out coyly and
grasped his tie between her gloved thumb and fingers. "It's
called Flame."

What had come over the woman? She was driving him
crazy. His every muscle and sinew tensed with need. He
wanted her. Getting close would be the easiest way to find
out about Amanda, too. And yet he knew it was a mistake.
If they made love, she'd realize who he was. Unfortunately,
he *liked* to play with fire. Besides which, it was she, not he,
who was going to get burned. If she really thought he cared
about his client ethics in this particular case, she had another thing coming.

Ever since he'd arrived, they'd circled each other as warily
as caged tigers. Judging from her behavior of the moment,
she'd decided to pursue him again. He was fairly sure she
was no match for him when it came to boldness. His gaze

dropped to her breasts. After a moment he blinked and looked into her eyes.

"Since I'm going to be so chilly—" Her voice was lazy, and she lightly tugged his tie. "I'd ask you to keep me warm..." She rolled her head around her shoulders, as if she were desperately in need of a massage. "But..."

He leaned forward, placed his hands on either armrest and brought his lips within inches of hers. She dropped his tie as if it had just caught fire, and he nearly smiled. "But?" he prodded softly.

"But—" She wriggled her elbows on the back of the chair, as if getting comfortable. "I have a coat."

"I doubt it's as warm as I could be," he said, wishing his own voice wasn't starting to sound so husky.

"But it's fur," she countered.

"Not very politically correct," he remarked dryly, even though an image of Cyn in nothing but fur flashed through his mind.

"I've had it nearly ten years," she returned guiltily. "And it *is* warm."

"Like I said—" He leaned an inch closer. "So am I."

She leaned away from him in a barely perceptible movement. The wafting scent of her perfume was so overwhelmingly feminine that he didn't exhale for an instant. It made him think of how mysterious women really were—of top drawers crammed with lace and hidden compartments that contained love letters and cloth diaries full of secrets.

He had no idea how long they merely gazed at each other. "I dare you to come around this chair," he finally said.

She blinked. "What in the world for?" she trilled. She'd been going for casually flirtatious. She sounded breathless.

"You know what for."

Faint pinkish color stained her wintry pale cheeks. "Can't you just escort Amanda and myself like a normal person?" she asked.

He chuckled and raised an eyebrow. "I take it a normal person is a man who isn't attracted to you?"

She smiled, obviously feeling as attracted to him as he was to her. "Well, yes."

He was about to say that normalcy was highly overrated, when he heard steps bounding down the hallway. He glanced toward the door.

Cyn leaned over the chair and whispered, "Tell Amanda she looks like a knockout."

"A knockout?" he managed to ask. Cyn's minty-smelling breath lingered by his ears.

"Yes," she hissed, just as Amanda appeared.

She stood uncertainly in the doorway. She was wearing a blue velvet dress, with a full skirt and wide sash. A tiny matching pocketbook hung from her white-gloved hands, which were clasped nervously in front of her. Two small blue bows held her wavy curls back on either side. It was on the tip of Santa's tongue to tell her she looked cute as hell. Instead, he crossed the room and knelt in front of her. "Wow," he said, "you're—er—a knockout, Amanda."

He didn't know what he'd expected, but it wasn't to have her glare at him suspiciously. "Mommy told you to say it."

He mustered his best dumfounded expression. "Well, she didn't. Was she supposed to?"

"I'm a knockout," Amanda said proudly, not bothering to answer him.

Once their coats were on and they were headed out the door, Santa caught Cyn's hand and guided her arm through his. "And so are you," he whispered.

She smiled up at him. "I knew you'd come around."

"CAN YOU HOLD the pocketbook, Mr. Santa Claus?" Amanda asked as the houselights dimmed. She snuggled down in the seat between her mother and Santa.

"Sure, honey," he said gruffly.

Cyn fought back a chuckle as she watched Amanda's teeny blue bag vanish beneath one of Santa's hands. He set it so gingerly on his knee that it could have been a kitten. Clearly, he wasn't quite sure what to do with it. Cyn nestled back in her own seat, ready to watch the show. *If I can keep my eyes off Santa.*

Even when she wasn't looking, she was conscious of every inch of him. It was almost as if she'd known him before. And tonight, entering the theater on his arm, she'd felt more like a woman than she had in a long time. He was so controlled and strong and handsome in his charcoal suit, starched shirt and silver silk tie that she'd felt smaller and infinitely more delicate.

She trained her gaze on the stage longer than she'd thought she could. After all, she was still waiting for her own nutcracker, wasn't she? With a sigh, Cyn imagined she was Clara. She received the nutcracker from her uncle and was astounded when he became a handsome prince. Cyn's heart thudded with fear as the rats, with their long noses and tails and colorful costumes, leaped across the stage.

And yet, as the first act became the second and third, she found she wasn't thinking of herself, but of Amanda. As she watched Clara's transformation, from a naive girl to a young woman, Cyn hoped that her daughter's initiation would be more gentle than her own. *Damn Jake Jackson.*

She glanced at Santa, and her lips parted. The man seemed as engrossed in the ballet as he had been in the playoffs. Were his thoughts anything like her own? Did he feel faint twinges of sadness as he watched Clara's first glimpse of love? Did he wish he could be that young, just one more time? In some sweet, soft part of Santa, did he wonder if he could ever become her prince?

Cyn's eyes narrowed. For the first time, she wondered if he'd ever been married. Had he ever been madly in love? What had his life been like before they'd met, just a few short days ago?

Santa turned and looked at Cyn, as if he'd felt her gaze. She glanced down at the top of Amanda's head quickly. Less than a second passed before she raised her eyes again. He was staring back steadily.

After a long moment, she smiled and turned her attention to the stage.

But she could still feel those eyes.

Their caress was so strong and bold and real, it was as if his hands were actually touching her.

"IN YOU GO, SWEETHEART," Santa said.

Cyn removed her gloves, shoved her hands deep into her coat pockets and leaned in the doorway. She watched as

Santa attempted to slide Amanda between the sheets. Her
daughter had slept while she and Santa slipped her into her
nightclothes, but now Amanda seemed unwilling to relinquish him.

Her small pudgy arms were flung around his neck and her
legs remained wrapped around the waist of his camel coat.
Santa pried her loose ever so gently, clearly trying not to
awaken her. Then he seated himself beside her on the canopied bed and tucked her in. He remained there, simply
watching her, as if he'd forgotten Cyn entirely.

*Why is it that every time I see him with Amanda, I think
I could fall in love with him?* Cyn wondered. She tried to tell
herself that it was only because the dainty, feminine room
made him look so much more masculine. His hands seemed
larger and darker against the tiny pink throws, his back
seemed broader beneath the frilly canopy, and his feet—clad
in shiny dress shoes—looked adultly male next to Amanda's girlish pocketbook, which had fallen to the floor.

A tug of sadness pulled at Cyn's heart. She'd barely dated
in the past four years. It had seemed best to focus on
Amanda, to try to give her everything in the world. But she
hadn't given Amanda the thing she most wanted. A daddy.
Right now, seeing such a strong man watch over her little
baby, the absence of a father almost hurt. *Jake Jackson isn't
coming within a mile of Amanda, no matter how much she
needs a dad.* Cyn sighed. She was a daddy's girl, herself. She
was approaching thirty, but she simply couldn't imagine a
life without Paxton, or her mother.

Amanda had accepted Santa so easily. What would happen when the threats were gone and he left? Even now, Cyn
feared the effect on Amanda. *And on myself.* In a few short
days Cyn had come to want him. Maybe that was fine, she
decided. If she made love to him, he would leave. He would
be a man who briefly touched their lives—without leaving
heartbreak in his wake.

She sucked in a sharp breath. As if remembering that she
was watching, Santa gently smoothed the hair on Amanda's forehead. He leaned, retrieved Amanda's pocketbook
from the floor and placed it on her bedside table carefully.
Then he reached for her lamp. Its shade was scalloped and

its base was a pink porcelain ballerina. The tutu seemed to shrink beneath his hand as he turned out the light.

"Sleep well, Amanda," Cyn heard him whisper in the darkness. "And dream of a nutcracker prince." The whole room grew quiet and seemingly smaller and Cyn felt oddly self-conscious.

"It was a big night for her," Cyn whispered as she and Santa tiptoed into the hall.

"For me, too," he said softly as he opened the coat closet. He looked sleepy, and the dim light transformed his eyes so that they softened to a gleaming gold. He stepped behind her. When he removed her coat, his fingertips grazed her bare shoulders and glided gracefully over her skin.

"So, did you have an all right time?" she murmured, facing him in the hallway's dim light. Was it her imagination or were his hands really luxuriating in the sensual feel of the fur?

He nodded as he hung her coat for her, then shrugged out of his own. "It made me think of lost childhoods," he said in a dreamy-sounding drawl.

"And lost first loves?" she asked, before she'd really thought it through.

He hung up his coat, then leaned against the door frame. "Those, too."

There wasn't much light, but it caught in his slicked-back hair and streaked it with a gold that matched his eyes. She smiled. "Just how many lost first loves can one have?"

His eyes suddenly seemed so all-knowing that she nearly flinched. His lips parted slightly, then closed, as if he'd been about to say something but then changed his mind. "Only one," he finally said.

She tilted her head, wondering what he'd decided not to say. "Who was yours?" Her voice lowered huskily.

He merely stared at her, as if he could do so forever. A look she could swear she'd seen a thousand times in his eyes now touched them. It was of sadness, longing and desire—all combined. "Who was yours?" he countered softly.

Jake Jackson, she thought, wishing there was just one other name . . . one other man. One other time when she'd been touched to the depth of her very being. "Bad topic?"

she suggested. She tried to tell herself that the raspiness of her voice was caused by sleepiness, not Santa. And yet, she knew she wanted him.

"Afraid so," he murmured. He leaned lithely and touched her pearl necklace. His fingertips lingered against her collarbone, then he lifted the strand just inches into the air. He thoughtfully turned it one way and another, as if watching how the pearls caught the light.

The thought flashed through her mind that she'd thrown her pearls before swine, with Jake Jackson, and yet when Santa carefully replaced her necklace all she could think of were those tanned fingers that remained on her skin.

Say something, she thought illogically.

"Good night, Cynthia."

He said it, but he didn't move away. Instead, his fingers traced across her upper chest, then slid up the column of her neck. Just when she remembered to breathe and sucked inward, his hand turned and cupped her chin.

Her lips parted. Slow heat curled in her stomach like trailing smoke, and fire seemed to lick its tongue into the corners of her body. Her mouth went as dry as cinders. *He's going to kiss me,* she thought. *Oh, how this man's going to kiss me.*

He leaned and pressed his lips against hers with an astonishing gentleness. She'd expected feverish fury and fiery intensity. She'd expected to feel his whole body crush against hers. Heavens, she'd expected the kiss they'd shared in the kitchen. But the almost chaste, steady pressure of his lips was even more intimate. She realized she was holding her breath.

He leaned back. "Sweet dreams," he murmured softly.

Her heart was hammering, her knees were wobbly, and she still hadn't breathed. Santa's golden eyes flickered as if lit by inner fires, and his broad shoulders looked strong enough to carry the weight of the world. Cyn exhaled shakily. "Ah, Santa," she managed to whisper, "who needs to dream?"

*SEVEN DAYS TILL
CHRISTMAS...*

Chapter Six

"A fine dinner, as usual, Cynthia," Paxton said. He took a last quick bite of cheesecake, then leaned back and sipped his espresso. He tilted his head toward the CD player, as if listening to the soft classical music. "You'll make a man a fine wife, someday." He glanced mischievously in Santa's direction. "Won't she, Santa?"

"Perhaps sooner than she thinks," Santa drawled from the head of the table, where Paxton had insisted he sit. She'd dimmed the lights, and Santa's eyes danced in the candlelight. For a second his penetrating stare made her feel particularly transparent. She could swear he knew her innermost secrets.

"Amanda needs a father figure," Paxton continued.

"Now, Daddy," Cyn protested weakly. Her gaze drifted to where his shirt cuffs peeked from beneath his suit sleeves. As usual, her father was missing a cuff link. She wished he'd concentrate more on dressing himself and less on marrying her off. She simply couldn't believe how Paxton had warmed to Santa.

"Well, they always say that second marriages are the best," Santa said to Paxton, picking up the thread.

Is it my imagination or does Santa know something about Jake and Harry? "So glad you could come, Daddy," Cyn piped in, for what had to be the umpteenth time. Why wouldn't her father take the hint? Not that she wanted to be alone with Santa. All her five senses longed for him, but her sixth sense kept screaming, "mistake." She'd avoided him today, since he hadn't attended church with them. Instead, he'd rifled through drawers at Too Sweet again.

Paxton sighed, placing his napkin beside his plate. "I'd glance in on Amanda, but I don't want to wake her."

"You won't," Cyn said quickly. "You know how soundly she sleeps."

Paxton ignored her and turned to Santa. "Real cute, isn't she?" he prodded.

Santa's eyes, which had seemed so nondescript just days ago now steadily met Cyn's, making her whole body tingle. "Cyn or Amanda?" he finally asked, his gaze never leaving hers.

Paxton chuckled. "Amanda."

Santa nodded. "She sure is." Everything in his expression made Cyn sure he was thinking of her. And not in terms of cute, exactly. She appreciated the easy way in which he humored her father. Still, she was starting to feel testy.

"Next time Mother can't make dinner, I'll call," Cyn said, more pointedly than she'd intended. Her parents traded Sunday night dinners, and this one belonged to Analise. Cyn wished her mother hadn't worked tonight, too. She half expected her father to come right out and beg Santa to marry her.

"Yes, Amanda *is* cute, isn't she?"

"I think you said that, Daddy," Cyn reminded.

"As a button," Santa said. From the opposite end of the table, he shot Cyn a grin, as if to say he was as aware of Paxton's machinations as she was.

"Heavens!" Cyn cleared her throat loudly and looked at a clock. "How time flies!"

Paxton scrutinized her, then Santa. "Oh!" he exclaimed guiltily. "I guess you two want to be alone."

Cyn's cheeks warmed. "That's not what I meant! I mean—er— I just need to start cleaning up...."

"I'm no fool," Paxton said, sounding pleased. Feeling flustered, Cyn slammed her demitasse cup onto its saucer.

Santa smirked, seemingly enjoying her discomfort. "I'll walk you to the door, Paxton."

Cyn busied herself by gathering up the dessert plates. She was nearly to the kitchen when she heard Paxton say, "You'd be a good man for my daughter, Santa."

Santa's laughter rang in her ears. "You just don't quit, do you, Paxton?"

In the kitchen, Cyn put her hands on her hips and sighed. As much as she loved to cook, she'd also managed to dirty every dish in the house. She headed toward the dining room again and collided with Santa. He caught her in his arms, and once more she felt sure he was going to kiss her.

Instead, he said, "You rinse. I'll carry." With that, he playfully marched her back toward the sink.

"Sorry about my father," she said.

"You sure rushed him out." Santa's breath whispered by her ear.

"I'd had about all the male bonding I could take," she managed to say. Feeling Santa's broad chest press against her back, she half wished he'd responded differently to her father's last words. He could have said he was Mr. Right, for instance. Instead, he'd laughed.

"The Super Bowl is male bonding," he said, depositing her in front of the dishwasher. "What your father engages in is old-fashioned matchmaking."

Watching him amble back down the hallway, Cyn almost wished it had worked. He was obviously attracted to her, and she was fairly sure he wasn't bothered by the ethical question of their involvement. Ever since he'd tried to quit, his eyes had flickered with invitation. On the one hand, a casual affair, which was all a traveling man like Santa could offer, seemed perfect. And yet, Cyn wasn't sure she was capable of it. She'd end up wanting more. She sighed and started cleaning with a vengeance.

"Why doesn't a woman like you have a cook?" Santa asked moments later. He grabbed a towel and began hand-drying the sterling silverware.

She shrugged. "I like to cook." When she glanced at him, she realized he'd removed his jacket. His suspenders were off his shoulders and hung in loops by his thighs. "Besides, I love turkey dinners." She smiled. "I even make them in the summer."

He leaned casually against the counter, while he polished a serving spoon to perfection. "At least someone to clean up..."

She placed the last pot in the drain board. "Why?" she asked saucily. "When I have you?"

"Ah—" he drawled. "But do you have me?"

She decided not to pursue that one. "Honestly, I don't really like having people around all the time. My mother always did."

He chuckled. "Is that a not-so-subtle hint?" He slapped the towel over his shoulder and crossed his arms over his chest. "Just what am I getting in the way of?"

"Oh," she managed to say lightly, "of my many dates." *What am I saying? What dates?*

He grinned wickedly. In the next instant, the towel snapped off his shoulder and he playfully swatted her behind. "Meet me in the living room." He shoved away from the counter with his hip.

He'd nearly reached the hall before she asked, "What for?"

"You know." He turned in the doorway. "I'll take you out, squire you around town. We'll have dinner. Take in the show..."

"A show in my living room?" she asked archly.

He turned and strode down the hall with such lean-looking long strides that her heart started to race. "Always," he called over his shoulder. "If you're there, sweetheart."

"I guess we could watch TV," she yelled.

Another throaty chuckle floated to her ears. "I was thinking more in terms of fireworks."

"So, is this where you bring all the girls?"

For a moment, Santa kept staring through the living room window at the snow flurries. Would it ever really snow? And did he dare seduce her? Wouldn't she realize who he was? He forced himself to turn around.

He watched her smooth her crepe cream dress beneath her behind as she sat daintily on the sofa. She sat right in the middle, too, which meant she intended for them to get cozy.

Her thick hair was drawn into a soft, seductive knot. He almost wished he'd extinguished the candles and turned on all the lights. "It might be more to the point," he finally drawled, "to ask if this is where you bring all the boys."

"Ah—" She flashed him a quick smile, then glanced at the two glasses of wine he'd poured and left on a coffee table. "Many a man has lost his virtue here," she said. The tremor in her voice almost convinced him it wasn't true.

"Not to mention his heart, I'm sure." Santa's own skipped a beat, and he wondered just how much truth there was in what she'd said. He was a little jealous by nature, and he couldn't help it.

"A man's heart," Cyn returned lightly, "is the very last thing I need." She picked up a glass and took a quick sip of wine.

He crossed the room and sat next to her on the sofa. She looked as lovely to him as she had the previous night. Through the transparent sleeves of her dress, her skin glowed. "So, it must be a man's hand you're looking for...." he said in a teasing whisper.

She smiled. "Oh please. Not that."

He burst out laughing. "Just what part of a man do you *want*, Ms. Sweet?"

Her smile broadened. "Do you really want to know?"

He managed to straighten his face. "Actually—" He casually laid his arm along the back of the sofa, above her shoulders. "I'm afraid to ask."

She took another sip of wine and replaced her glass on the coffee table. Then she turned and looked at him boldly. In the dim candlelight, her eyes seemed as darkly green as a forest at midnight. Just looking, he felt himself getting pleasantly lost. "You should be," she said, holding his gaze.

Many times, he'd noticed that Cyn had grown up. But this was too much. How many men had she talked to this way? He knew he hadn't been her first lover. And yet, she said there'd only been one other man, one time. All along, he'd assumed it was Harry Stevens. Maybe it wasn't.

When he said nothing, she leaned forward again. When she lifted her wineglass, her stocking-clad knee brushed his slacks, begging the question again: Could he possibly make love to her without her recognizing him? She took a sip that left her mouth wet and glistening. The classical CD fell silent between movements of a symphony, and in the sudden, hushed quiet, her glass tinkled against a coaster.

Without even thinking, he leaned forward as she leaned back, and his arm left the sofa and curled around her shoulders instead. In a second, her cheek was pressed against his chest. "I've lost my fear," he said huskily. "Just what part of a man do you want?"

The hemline of her dress had risen and how her long, perfect legs twined at the ankles suddenly captured his whole attention. He wasn't sure, but he thought he felt her smile press against his shirtfront.

"What part of a woman do you want, Santa?" She poked his chest lightly with one of her long, polished nails.

He chuckled softly. Everything about her—her playfulness, her nearness, and her scent—was arousing him. The pressure of her hip against his was warm. "Depends on the woman."

She snuggled closer, nuzzling her cheek into his shoulder. "What about me?"

"You?" He dipped his head and breathed in the clean, fresh scent of her hair. As he brushed his lips across her thick bun, he thought about removing her hairpins. Heat coiled in his abdomen and his whole body felt heavier. His slacks began to tug perceptibly. *My face is different. My hair's another color. I'm more muscular. But my inner self, the way I am when I lose control, when I make love . . .*

"Who else but me, silly?" she finally murmured.

When he inhaled, his mouth went dry. He licked his lower lip, knowing he couldn't take much more of this. Not the constant teasing. Not the soft, almost accidental touches when they brushed past each other. Not the way her legs could twine around his waist if he only pulled her on top of him. He wasn't wondering about Amanda at the moment. He had to know if he was her father, but right now, all he knew was that he wanted Cyn.

Finally he said, "You're not the kind of woman that I could break down into parts." He dropped his arm from around her shoulder and slid his fingertips down the length of her arm.

She giggled throatily. "So the whole of me is greater than the sum of my parts? Isn't that some law of chemistry?"

"Philosophy, I think," he murmured. He tightened his arm around her, thinking that he was nearly ready to make love, even though he hadn't even kissed her yet. "But chemistry will certainly do."

"Is that a compliment, Santa?"

"No, sweetheart," he said, kicking off his shoes. "It's an invitation."

"Am I supposed to RSVP?" Her voice lowered so that it was barely audible. She kicked off her high heels.

"Immediately."

When she sat up, he wished he was still wearing his suit jacket. As it was, there was nothing to hide his aroused state. Her gaze flitted toward his lap, and rose immediately to his eyes. The sheer vulnerability he saw in her face made him sure he was making a dangerous mistake. Her confidence was gone. So was the jaunty smile that preceded her saucier come-on lines.

"I don't want—"

She was speaking so quietly that he had to lean forward to hear. He glanced toward the hallway. "Are you worried about Amanda?"

She shook her head. "She's a sound sleeper and my door locks."

"Condoms?" he asked softly.

"I have some."

Bad sign, he thought. Who was she keeping them for? After a long moment, she licked her lower lip and swallowed. "I just don't want any serious involvements," she whispered in a quick rush. "I really don't."

He tried to tell himself that he just wanted to know whether or not he was Amanda's father. But right now he didn't care. He tried to remember that moment, four years ago, when she'd deserted him, but couldn't. He was ready to take her on any terms she offered. Shadows wavered across her skin, just as her resolve seemed to waver. "But you want me?" he said.

She nodded. "For just—just one night."

Why doesn't she want something more? Is it because I'm Amanda's bodyguard? Because I'm living in the apartment with her? Because I remind her of Jake Jackson? His warring emotions were tugging him apart. He reached out and touched her cheek. "No strings attached," he assured softly, wondering if he meant it.

Even in the dim light, he could see the flush that was beginning to stain her cheeks. She had the embarrassed look of a woman who wished that things would quickly be decided, one way or the other.

"Yeah—" She smiled quickly, clearly trying to banter but failing. "No tomorrows and all that."

His chest closed around his heart like a vise. "And no yesterdays," he said gruffly. Beneath his fingers, the skin of her cheek felt as soft as silk. His gaze never leaving hers, he dropped his fingertips lightly to her chest, just inches above her breasts.

"Heaven knows," she whispered, her voice catching. "There are a few yesterdays I'd like to forget."

He caught her hand and rose lithely from the sofa, pulling her with him. "Maybe this will help," he said, claiming her lips.

SANTA LOCKED THE DOOR and turned around. Hints of lamplight shone through her window into the intimate darkness. Cyn was standing by the window. One of her long arms hung rigidly at her side; the other lifted a corner of the curtain. *Ah, Cyn,* he thought, wanting to tell her that he liked her just the way she was. *This new you is just a disguise. I can see that you're as soft and sweet as you ever were.*

She'd warmed to his kisses in the living room, but now, in her bedroom, she seemed tense. He crossed the room and approached her from behind. His arms circled her waist and his hands rubbed slow circles on her abdomen. When he hugged her tightly, and she felt how aroused he was, her back stiffened and then slowly relaxed. Together, they stared through the window. He could hear her swallow. "It's cold out there," she finally said.

Her hand was trembling and the curtain fluttered. "That's why I'm in here tonight," he said. "With you."

She turned in his arms, letting the curtain fall. "To keep me warm?" She gazed into his eyes, her voice tremulous.

He drew her closer, pressing her against the length of his body, and kissed her, slowly probing her lips. "Ah, Cyn," he chided softly as he leaned back, "don't tell me you're scared."

He smiled, feeling glad it was dark, knowing there was less chance he'd be discovered this way. "Brassy Cyn," he murmured, nuzzling his cheek against hers. He began to let down her hair. His other hand roved over her back. When her hair cascaded around her shoulders, he raked his fingers through it, caught it in fistfuls then let it fall again.

"It's been a long time," she said breathlessly.

For an instant, his hand froze on her back. "How long?" *Four years?*

"Too long." Her hands cupped his chin. "How'd you get that scar?" she asked huskily.

He was surprised to find that the question didn't even anger him. He smiled. "Knife fight."

Her chuckle caught in her throat. "Somehow I doubt it," she whispered as her hands dropped to his chest. As she began to unknot his tie, his lips settled on hers again.

He tried to remind himself that he was supposed to make love to her quickly and without foreplay. But as he kissed her, his hands dropped gently from her hips, to her thighs. He lifted the hemline of her dress with nothing more than his fingertips, until skin met skin and he was touching the bare silken inches that lay above her stockings. As he loosened her garters one by one, she drew in a quick breath against his mouth.

He was more adept than she was. Slower, too. Within moments she was rising on her tiptoes and arching against the most intimate part of him. And yet, in her fury to undress him, while he kissed her, she suddenly seemed to forget her own pleasure. She fumbled with his buttons, tugged at his shirt without managing to remove it, and nearly ripped the cuff links from his wrists. Santa let her. Until she reached for his zipper.

"Cyn," he said softly, "we have all night."

"Sorry." She leaned back in his arms.

"Don't ever be sorry," he whispered, "but you're coming at me like this is something you want to get over and done with."

"I'll admit that ever since I first saw you, that's pretty much how I've felt." The sheer frustration in her soft voice made him smile. She slid open the ends of his shirt, ran her nails through the curling hairs on his chest, then pressed her face against him. She smiled against his skin. "You're the most controlled person I ever met," she murmured.

His eyes had adjusted and he could just make out her features. He wondered if making love to her might get her out of his system for good. She was so incredibly beautiful that he somehow doubted it. Still, he did mean for this time to last him the rest of his life. *That's what I want, isn't it?* That, he thought, and to push any other men she may have had from her mind forever.

Will she know who I am?

"Santa?" she whispered throatily, sounding a little bereft.

"I'm right here." A soft sigh escaped her, just as his mouth captured hers again. He lifted her and carried her to the bed.

"I want you," she whispered against his cheek, as his hands deftly removed her remaining clothes, then his own. When her hands glided over his back, he swallowed a moan and drove his tongue deep between her lips.

He shut his eyes, and while his tongue dueled with the wet, warm spear of hers, he fought for control over the depth of passion this woman could arouse in him. As his hands rose and fell over the contours of her flesh, he told himself he wouldn't relinquish his whole self. Some part would remain distanced and detached. Untouchable.

But then her thighs parted. In the darkness, they looked like silver, glistening fish in deep, mysterious waters. As his palms roved slowly over them, toward the most feminine, intimate part of her, he felt as if he were drowning. She moaned when he began to touch her, and he felt his control slipping away.

But she'll know ... she'll know.

"Santa..." she murmured. Her silken thighs relaxed, parting more for him. All he could think was that she was so open and that he was touching her. Her sighs suddenly caught on the air. She whimpered. "Anton..." And then she cried it out. "Oh, Anton."

His heart nearly broke. He'd never heard her say his real name. And to hear it spoken with such need ... "Say my name again," he whispered.

She grasped his shoulders, arching to both meet his touch and to kiss him. "Anton..."

"Oh, Cyn." His own voice was nothing more than a ragged sigh. She captured it with her lips as she rocked against him. He found a condom, then rolled fully on top of her. For a long moment, he merely hovered above her.

How can you not know who I am?

As he slowly sank into her, he almost wished that she would discover him. If she didn't, he might tell her. What if—driven by desire—he confessed the truth?

"Anton..." This time, his name came in a short, quick gasp, as she caught his rhythm.

He drove into her steadily, repeatedly, kissing her neck, her cheeks, her breasts ... until her skin turned damp and warm and until he felt her losing his rhythm and straining with all her might for her own. Against his mouth, her breath came in fits and starts. She held it, then let it go in shudders that urged him deeper inside her.

Damn you, Cyn. Tell me you know who I am.

Her legs wrapped around his back like a vise. He was a controlled man, but now, caught in the tangle of her arms and legs, crazy images started flashing through his mind. He could no longer damn her, but only kiss her, over and over again.

For an instant, he was almost sure they were lying in a warm field of dew-damp grass and yellow spring flowers. A thousand white butterflies took flight. They hovered just above the flowers, like angels. When the tiny palpitations of Cyn's body closed around him, her flesh fluttered as gently and as urgently as those wings.

When she rocked against him, uttering one long soft whimper, the last vestiges of his control gave away. He was with the one woman on earth who could make everything vanish—past, present and future. The one woman who could take all the parts of him—heart, body and soul. And with one final kiss that seemed to go on forever, Santa completely lost control.

"WHERE'D YOU GET the scar on your leg? Another knife fight?" Cyn murmured.

"Yeah," Santa said softly.

She glanced dreamily at her digital clock through heavily lidded eyes. "It's after two in the morning," she whispered huskily, stretching her long legs against the length of his, and nuzzling her face against him.

"Hmm."

She smiled, hearing that hum rumble deep within his chest. When he nodded, she didn't see but only sensed it. She rolled to her back, luxuriating in how she felt. Her limbs were limp and languid, her whole body warm. Hours had passed, but time seemed to stand still. No man had ever loved her the way this one had. Certainly not Harry, her one love before Jake Jackson. And not even Jake Jackson himself.

Thinking that, she realized she wanted no secrets to come between her and Santa. "Santa?"

"Hmm?"

"You know when I told you about Jake Jackson? I mean, about going out with him?"

This time Santa didn't hum. Had he fallen asleep? Heaven knew, she was about to. She reached across a scant space between them, then grazed her fingertips from his thigh to his chest. Tiny muscles leapt to life beneath her touch, assuring her that he was still awake. She folded her hands beneath her breasts, then blew out a long, satisfied sigh.

"You were saying?" he finally murmured.

"I didn't tell you the whole story."

He rolled toward her slowly, scooting so that they barely touched. She could feel his breath on her shoulder. "What

PLAY
HARLEQUIN'S

LUCKY HEARTS
GAME

AND YOU GET

- ★ **FREE BOOKS**
- ★ **A FREE GIFT**
- ★ **AND MUCH MORE**

TURN THE PAGE AND DEAL YOURSELF IN

PLAY "LUCKY HEARTS" AND YOU GET...

★ Exciting Harlequin American Romance® novels — FRE

★ Plus a Lovely Pearl Drop Necklace — FREE

THEN CONTINUE YOUR LUCKY STREAK WITH A SWEETHEART OF A DEAL

1. Play Lucky Hearts as instructed on the opposite page.

2. Send back this card and you'll receive brand-new Harlequin American Romance® novels. These books have a cover price of $3.50 each, but they are yours to keep absolutely free.

3. There's no catch. You're under no obligation to buy anything. We charge nothing — ZERO — for your first shipment. And you don't have to make any minimum number of purchases — not even one!

4. The fact is thousands of readers enjoy receiving books by mail from the Harlequin Reader Service. They like the convenience of home delivery...they like getting the best new novels months before they're available in stores ...and they love our discount prices!

5. We hope that after receiving your free books you'll want to remain a subscriber. But the choice is yours—to continue or cancel, anytime at all! So why not take us up on our invitation, with no risk of any kind. You'll be glad you did!

NOT ACTUAL SIZE

This lovely necklace will add glamour to your most elegant outfit! Its cobra-link chain is a generous 18" long, and its lustrous simulated cultured pearl is mounted in an attractive pendant! Best of all, it's absolutely free, just for accepting our no-risk offer!

HARLEQUIN'S

With a coin — scratch off the silver card and check below to see what we have for you.

154 CIH AQZD (U-H-AR-12/94)

YES! I have scratched off the silver card. Please send me the free books and gift for which I qualify. I understand that I am under no obligation to purchase any books, as explained on the back and on the opposite page.

NAME

ADDRESS   APT.

CITY   STATE   ZIP

Twenty-one gets you 4 free books, and a free pearl drop necklace

Twenty gets you 4 free books

Nineteen gets you 3 free books

Eighteen gets you 2 free books

THE HARLEQUIN READER SERVICE®: HERE'S HOW IT WORKS

Accepting free books places you under no obligation to buy anything. You may keep the books and gift and return the shipping statement marked "cancel". If you do not cancel, about a month later we'll send you 4 additional novels, and bill you just $2.89 each plus 25¢ delivery and applicable sales tax, if any.* That's the complete price—and compared to cover prices of $3.50 each—quite a bargain! You may cancel at any time, but if you choose to continue, every month we'll send you 4 more books, which you may either purchase at the discount price... or return at our expense and cancel your subscription.

*Terms and prices subject to change without notice. Sales tax applicable in N.Y.

happened?'' he asked, now sounding almost fully conscious.

"I—'' She started to admit that she'd loved Jackson, but then decided that wasn't exactly wise, given the circumstances. "He's Amanda's father.''

"Really?'' Santa's voice lowered. "I thought Harry Stevens was her father.''

She sighed. "Harry was just an old friend. And, after all the publicity of the trial, we thought it would be better if another father was somehow named.'' She took a deep breath, then exhaled.

"We?''

"Daddy, mostly. Mom thought it was horrible to lie, and it was. It is. But I didn't want Amanda to know her father was a criminal. I thought it would really hurt her. And Dad didn't want my name raked any further through the mud. Amanda knows anyway,'' she said unhappily. "She has ears.''

"Amanda knows Jake Jackson is her father?''

Was it her imagination, or did Santa sound mad? She hoped he wasn't. Even if he was, she meant to say her piece. She was determined to ensure that this relationship begin in a completely honest way. And it was the beginning of something Cyn now knew she wanted to last. He raised slightly on his elbow. She nodded. "Amanda threatens to tell people all the time,'' she finally said softly. "When she doesn't get her way.''

When Santa didn't respond, she continued. "After Harry Stevens agreed to give Amanda a name, he wanted to marry me—for real. I mean, we did marry, but he wanted for us to live as a couple. I didn't love him, though. It could never have worked. For Amanda's sake, I wish it could have. Harry's change in attitude caused a rift between us, so my father declared him dead. That way, people would think I was a widow and there wouldn't be questions.'' Cyn sighed in relief. "Jake was really bad news,'' she admitted. "I should have known it all along. He told small lies. He'd be late to meet me and arrive with explanations I shouldn't have believed.''

Cyn glanced at Santa. In the darkness it was hard to make out his expression. "I'm glad that part of my life is over," she continued. Looking at Santa, she knew it was. Jake Jackson was the furthest thing from her mind.

Santa rose stealthily from the bed. "The switch is on the right wall," she said sleepily, thinking he was headed for her bathroom.

He wasn't. She heard him rummaging around on the floor, gathering his clothes. By the time she realized he was actually dressing and flicked on her bedside lamp, he'd already pulled on his slacks and shirt. She squinted against the light. "Where are you going?"

His expression was unreadable. "To sleep."

"You can sleep here for a while," she murmured, wishing a pleading tone hadn't crept into her voice.

His fingers slid deftly from shirt button to shirt button. In a fluid movement he tucked in his shirttails and zipped his trousers. He folded his suit jacket almost mechanically. Then, instead of resting it over his arm, he dangled it from the hook of his finger and swung it over his shoulder, making her wonder why he'd folded it in the first place.

She gulped and sat up. "Did I say something wrong?" He merely stared at her, and her heart began to thud. When her hand flew to her chest to cover her heart, she realized she was sitting there, stark naked. Moments ago it wouldn't have mattered. Now she knew it did. She grabbed the sheet and pulled it up, clutching it against her breasts.

"You knew I had had a past lover when you slept with me," she said, trying to keep her voice level. *Is that what's wrong? Why did I bring up Jake?* "You think I'm dishonest," she tried, starting to feel angry. "But you don't know what it was like. I was an overprotected kid, and I was pregnant by a man I simply couldn't have in my life. A criminal…" *I'm losing him. I'm going to lose Santa.* "Can't you understand that?" she asked, trying with all her might not to wail.

Why is he staring at me like that?

Was this really the same man who'd loved her body so completely? She'd been so amazed she could almost believe their lovemaking hadn't happened. The self-consciousness she'd felt in the past—the tiny worries about how she looked and sounded, about her scent and the dampness of her skin—had all been forgotten. He'd touched her thoroughly, matter-of-factly, with complete, loving acceptance.

But now, there was nothing more than cold judgment in his eyes. Or was she imagining that? "You just don't understand..." she repeated.

He pivoted gracefully on his heel and strolled toward her door. His soft drawl floated over his shoulder. "Maybe I understand more than you think I do."

SIX DAYS TILL
CHRISTMAS...

Chapter Seven

Monday, December 19, 1994

Cyn was waiting for him in the predawn hour, which was when the fool man got up. Outside it was still pitch-dark, and the light in the kitchen had taken on a yellowish cast. She'd barely slept and her eyes felt itchy. Not his, apparently. At precisely 5:30 a.m., Santa breezed into the kitchen. He looked so relaxed, she felt sure she'd conjured their night together in her dreams.

But I didn't. He made my knees weak and my head spin and my heart beat out of control. He touched me in the way only Jake could...so much like Jake that I just can't believe it. Except Santa's in a whole other league. I've been with him and now I'll never stop wanting him.

He nodded, headed straight for the cabinets and fixed himself a bowl of cereal. He was showered, shaved and wearing a fresh deep amber wool suit. His sparkling white shirt looked so crisp Cyn was sure she could snap it like a cracker. He turned, watching her as he munched. "Unusual to see you up at this hour," he finally remarked, between bites.

She'd spent the past few hours stewing, mentally rehearsing sweet apologies and speeches that were downright mean. Now she was so unnerved by his control that she couldn't remember them. "You're a pretty up-front guy, right?" she asked, keeping her voice level. She drew her chilly bare feet beneath her in the kitchen chair, and wrapped her robe more tightly around herself. "I mean, you always call things pretty much as you see them?"

He crunched his cereal and nodded. She realized his gaze wasn't anywhere near as ambivalent as she'd previously thought. Those eyes of his smoldered beneath his heavy eyelids. "Are you really going to pretend that last night didn't happen?" she finally snapped, wishing that each movement of his hands and hips and lips didn't remind her of it.

He leaned and placed his bowl in the sink behind him, without breaking their gaze. "You don't want serious involvements," he said softly. "Remember?"

She exhaled huffily. "Maybe I changed my mind." She sounded haughtier than she'd intended, as if determining the course of their relationship was entirely up to her.

"You should have thought of that before you laid down your ground rules," he returned gruffly.

Play it cool, Cyn. Don't let him get the best of you. Once he does, you're a goner. As angry as she was, her gaze roved over the broad shoulders she'd clung to during the night, then dropped to the chest she'd nuzzled against. "You're not mad about all the family secrets I told you, are you? I mean, a man in your line of work has undoubtedly heard worse."

He shoved his hands deep into the pockets of his trousers. Her eyes followed the movement inadvertently, and alighted on the space where the fabric tightened across his hips. He shrugged. "Yeah—" He caught her gaze when she raised it. "I've heard it all."

"Well then, hear this," she said calmly. "In the past couple of hours I decided—" *I want to marry you. Oh, don't say that!* Something in his expression—a warning, perhaps— stopped her.

He looked alert, but his brown eyes seemed sexily lazy. She decided he was intentionally trying to look bored.

"Don't tell me you couldn't sleep?" he asked.

She uncurled her feet beneath her. They slapped the tile floor when they hit it. "I think you're afraid."

He merely surveyed her with that trademark Santa look, where his lips parted but he didn't speak, and his eyes looked heavy but he didn't roll them heavenward. Everything in his gaze said there was nothing he feared.

She tossed her head so that her loose hair fell behind her shoulders. "You travel a lot, and you're used to being on your own," she said. "Having things your own way..."

"So, I'm afraid?"

"Maybe." As if to undercut her own seriousness, she managed to shoot him an unconcerned smile.

"Of what?"

"Loving me."

He chuckled softly. "Don't kid yourself."

She shrugged, as if it didn't matter to her one way or the other. "Well, I know why I wouldn't fall in love with you." She wished the smile she'd plastered on her face wasn't making her cheeks tingle.

He sighed. "Do tell."

"Oh, well—" She busied herself by picking up crumbs—some real, some imaginary—from the tabletop. "You're a globe-trotter, and you're involved in a dangerous business. I mean—" She clapped her hands together above a saucer, dusting off the imaginary crumbs. "You could get shot at any moment."

"My, my, don't you sound bloodthirsty."

He sounded annoyed now. She suddenly hoped she could make him every bit as irritated as she felt. "Not at all," she returned lightly. "But I think it's sweet that you don't want to involve yourself with a woman on account of that."

"Cyn" he said flatly, the veneer of banter vanishing. "That has nothing to do with—"

"Well then, what does?"

He didn't look particularly happy about being caught in her verbal trap. "You said you wanted to sleep with me, for just one night. So, I did. That's all."

"That's all!"

"That's—" He paused and swallowed. When he spoke again, his voice was unnervingly calm. "That's right."

"Right after you kissed me, when the note concerning Amanda came, you tried to quit." Her voice leapt upward and she couldn't rein it in. "When I needed you most, you walked out. Do you *always* leave when people need you?"

"That's enough," he said levelly.

"Apparently, *I'm* not," she returned in a steely tone.

He was clearly trying not to react, but his expression softened. "You're my client," he nearly whispered.

She rolled her eyes. "Amanda's your client."

"I'm an up-front guy," he countered. "And I'm calling it like it is."

It was clear he'd taken his position and didn't intend t_ budge. But she didn't, either. In those long, cold, wee hours of the night, Cyn was just too sure she'd finally found a mar she wanted to be with. He was amazingly strong, but he could be so caring and gentle....

They were still staring each other down when the phone rang. "Who could be calling at this otherworldly hour?" she muttered, reaching it first.

"May I please speak to Anton Santa?"

She held out the phone. "It's a woman," she said, not bothering to hide her pique.

When he reached for the receiver, his fingertips grazed the back of her hand. She wanted to hang up the phone and feel the strength of his arms around her again. She wanted to be held. He turned his back to her. "Yeah? This is Santa."

Cyn crossed her arms over her chest and listened to his hmms and sighs. After a moment, she decided that something was wrong. "Thanks for calling as soon as you got the information, Sally," he finally said. "I owe you one."

"What is it?" she asked as he hung up and turned around. His eyes were even more disturbing than the call. She was almost sure that he was considering offering her comfort again. *It's bad. I can feel it.* A shiver of both fear and longing raced down her spine.

"I got an address on Matthew Lewis." Santa's voice gentled for the first time that morning. "He's nearby. At a house in Jersey."

"I'M COMING WITH YOU!"

"You're staying with Amanda and the rent-a-cop," Santa called over his shoulder, listening to Cyn's flat boots thud after him, through the parking garage. He turned the key in the driver's side of his rented sedan. Just as he opened the oor, Cyn elbowed him with such force it nearly took away is breath. Before he could grab her, she'd scooted in and lid across the seat.

He glanced over the items she'd brought with her: overize pocketbook, picnic basket and thermos. He removed his andcuffs from where they were looped over his belt and ossed them onto the seat, next to the car phone. Then he ot in and slammed the door. Hard.

He felt half-inclined to tell her he was Jake Jackson, if for o other reason than that she'd hightail it back to the partment. But he meant to tell her in his own good time. Like when he figured out what he wanted to do about Amanda, for instance. If he'd ever felt he was exacting reenge by keeping his identity hidden, it was doubly true 1ow. When he told her—and he'd have to, since Amanda vas his daughter—Cyn would never recover from the blow. Not after he'd made love to her. He tried to tell himself that 1e didn't care. She was a liar and two-timer and he didn't vant her back.

"I know what Matthew Lewis looks like," Cyn finally nnounced breathlessly as she rummaged in her pocket-100k, pulled out a plastic band and drew her hair into a 100se ponytail. She pulled on a little black knit hat, then tuffed her stray hairs beneath it. "And you don't."

"Fine," he said, wishing she didn't look so cute in her riliculous undercover getup, and thinking he knew damn well vhat Lewis looked like. If Cyn came with him, Lewis might ee the two of them together, and identify Santa. After all, 1e man had seen him clean shaven and in a suit. As soon as Santa had left the hospital, he'd questioned him. Well, Santa thought as he turned the key in the ignition, he'd just nake Cyn stay in the car. When the sedan roared to life, he elt half-inclined to squeal out of the garage. Instead, he omehow managed to calmly back out of his space.

"I bet this'll be kind of fun," she said as he pulled onto Eighty-eighth Street. "I mean, a stakeout and everything. I nade some turkey sandwiches, either with or without mayo, ind a whole thermos full of coffee, with the cream sepaate, of course, since I know you like yours black."

He hit the brake at a light and slowly turned his head
staring at her pointedly. His gaze dropped slowly over he
outfit and, suddenly, he had to fight not to smile. She wa
wearing all black—tights, hooded sweatshirt, suede coat an
hat. She looked like an adorable thief in a TV movie. Sinc
it was daytime, she looked pretty obvious, too.

"Maybe you like peace and quiet when you drive," sh
said, after a moment. She made a show of primly foldin
her hands in her lap, then glanced away from him and stare
through the windshield.

He took the FDR, doubled back into midtown, then too
the Lincoln Tunnel. He didn't know which was worse, he
silence or her chatter. He didn't know why he was so furi
ous, either. After all, hadn't he suspected Amanda was hi
daughter, all along?

But hearing Cyn say the words had changed everything
He was a father. She was a liar. And he didn't have th
slightest idea what to do about any of it. Oh, he'd clain
Amanda. He had no intention of letting her go through lif
believing her father's name was Jake Jackson. Still, once h
claimed her, what in the world was he going to do with her'

He drove in silence for some time, trying to tell himself h
hated Cyn, even if having her had only made him want he
all the more. Being trapped in the cramped, closed confine
of the car made things infinitely worse. Not a second passe
without him feeling conscious of her nearness. He could pul
her silly hat from her head, release her hair band, and al
that disheveled, luxurious hair would cascade around he
shoulders. Beneath the scents of bath powder and per
fume, Cyn's own scent filled the car. Resting one hand
lightly on the wheel, Santa cracked his window with th
other. The chilly rush of air smelled like burning leaves, bu
it didn't help.

Because he was thinking about Cyn, he made a wrong
turn and landed on an expressway. He braked at a toll
booth harder than was necessary, rolled down his window
and handed over the money, thinking that maybe he could
start a securities business in the city. Images of picking
Amanda up and dropping her off at Cyn's flashed throug!
his mind. *What a mess.*

Cyn. Was that really what he was mad about? Threads of their conversation kept replaying in his thoughts. Had she really had the nerve to accuse him of walking out when she'd needed him? That was rich. She'd left him lying in her parents' yard with two gunshot wounds. As badly hurt as he'd been, he'd chased after her. He'd saved her life, too. Now he pulled off the expressway and tried to get his bearings.

"Such cute decorations," Cyn remarked pleasantly. As Santa wound down the circular streets, he couldn't help but follow her gaze. "Oh, look! Look at that!"

She pointed excitedly at a house with candles in the windows. A German shepherd, wearing a green bow for a collar, thumped his tail on the front porch and pawed the door. In another yard, a huge plastic Santa sat on a sleigh, driving a team of reindeer. In front of a quaint two-story stone place, tall brass lanterns tied with red bows marked either side of a brick walkway. Dark smoke plumed from chimneys, then trailed through the whitish winter sky. Wreaths hung from nearly every door.

He hazarded another glance at Cyn, thinking that she'd deprived him of this. Of some homey little neighborhood somewhere with her and Amanda. Of holidays with a family he could call his own. Maybe he and Cyn would even have had other children by now. Four years had passed, three Christmases where Amanda had squirmed on Santa's lap and torn crinkling shiny paper from her presents. *Damn.*

"I just love the decorations," Cyn crooned softly. "Don't you?"

He didn't know whether it was her proximity to him in the seat or the fact that he was breathing in her perfume with every breath, but he found himself nodding. "Yeah."

She whirled around, laughing. "Was that a yes, Santa?"

"Can't a man like decorations?" he asked gruffly.

"Absolutely." Her eyes were twinkling but he was fairly sure her attitude correction was a ploy. She was still furious. Cyn didn't take no for an answer when she wanted something. And she wanted him. *Too bad,* he thought. He battled another sudden urge to reveal himself. The information would go down like a bad medicine, but it would definitely cure Cyn of her desire for him.

He pulled to a curb. "See the brick place down there? Th
one with the lit-up dogwood tree?"

Cyn nodded.

"That's Lewis's mother's."

She scooted up and peered through the windshield
"Can't we get any closer?"

He shook his head, then leaned and stretched his arm ove
her knees. When he did, she nearly jumped out of her skin
He wished he didn't want to smile at the proof that he
newfound perkiness was nothing more than show. He slowl
opened the glove compartment and took out his field
glasses.

"Oh," she murmured. "You were just getting your bin
oculars."

"Don't worry," he said as he raised them to his eyes. "
won't attack you."

"WHERE DO YOU FIND the patience for this stakeout stuff?'
Cyn asked hours later. She raised her arms above her head
and yawned lazily, looking at Santa.

"I'm a patient man," he returned. He polished off the
last bite of his second turkey sandwich and washed it down
with a gulp of coffee.

You sure are, she thought. Images from their night to
gether touched her mind, but that wasn't the only reason she
had to know him better. Paxton liked him. Amanda felt a
strongly about him as she did, herself. Santa had seemed less
perturbed by her presence as the day had worn on, too
"Don't you start feeling like you just have to *do* some
thing?"

"No." He glanced at her. "Like what?"

"We could make out," she teased. "After all, we *ar*
parking. It's cold in here, too. We haven't turned on the ca
or the heater forever."

He shook his head in mock censure. "You're a woman
with only one thing on her mind."

She curled her legs in the seat and turned to get a bette
look at him. She felt all rumpled and he looked as dapper a
he had at the crack of dawn. "Are you trying to tell me
you're less focused?" she asked, as if she felt sorry for him.

He relaxed in the seat and tilted his head, his eyes roving over her face. "Maybe I have only one thing on my mind, too."

She arched her brows and stared back at him innocently. "What?"

"Making sure Amanda's safe," he said levelly.

Cyn gulped, wishing they were here for some other reason. "I know you will," she said, meaning it. Santa was so patiently diligent about his work that Amanda could have been his own daughter. Could he ever truly accept Amanda as his own? And, after having Amanda to herself for so long, how did Cyn really feel about sharing her? With Santa, she thought, perhaps she could.

Her eyes drifted over him as they had a thousand times that day, and she thought, as she had each time, that he seemed like the strongest man in the world. While she was looking at him, his whole body suddenly tensed.

"There he is," Santa whispered.

She whirled back toward the windshield and gasped. "How did you know it was him?" Her blood boiled as she watched Lewis cross the yard and get into a compact car. Was it her imagination or did he look nervous?

"Is it him?" Santa asked.

"Yeah," she said, staring the man down. An almost murderous hatred pumped through her veins. The sensation couldn't have been more intense if she had seen Jake Jackson himself. After all, Lewis was one of the men who'd nearly destroyed her life four years ago. And now he might be coming after Amanda.

Santa started the car, then pulled out, keeping a good distance away from the compact. Cyn fell silent and glanced between Santa and the other car. He was good at tailing people. Half the time she was sure they'd lose the man, but they never did. The longer they drove the more anxious she became. Suddenly all the lovely Christmas decorations seemed a little menacing.

"Damn," Santa muttered under his breath.

Something in his voice made Jake Jackson's face pop into her mind. *It's only because we're tailing Lewis.* "What's wrong?" she asked, her heart pounding.

"Er—nothing." He sounded surprised, as if he hadn'
meant to curse out loud. He sighed. "If I'd known we'd be
following him, I wouldn't have let you come."

"I'm not going to get hurt," she said defensively. Why
did he think she couldn't handle herself? She felt touched
He was worried about her, which was a good sign. Up
ahead, Lewis pulled to a curb. Santa backed into a drive
way.

After a moment his wry chuckle filled the car. "Just don'
make me take another bullet for you," he said. "Okay?"

She leaned across the seat and playfully poked him in the
ribs. "*Another* bullet?" she teased. "Have you been having fantasies about protecting me or something? I mean, I
don't remember that first one."

He flashed her a quick grin. It seemed to light up the
dreary winter afternoon, but it didn't completely hide the
sadness in his eyes. What was it in this man's past that
haunted him?

"Maybe you just didn't see it coming," he finally said.

"Stay put," Santa said roughly, feeling desperate to ensure that Lewis and Cyn didn't get within view of each other.
"And I mean it this time."

"But, Santa—"

He shot her a long, penetrating glare to communicate his
seriousness. He had a hunch about what was happening. It
had come from a thousand subtle impressions: the way
Lewis squared his shoulders, fidgeted with his hands, tensed
his thighs, paused before he rang a doorbell. Santa felt he
was standing at the most precarious impasse he'd ever en-
countered. Should he keep Cyn away from Lewis ... but at
the risk of not capturing the man who might be threatening
Amanda?

"I mean it," he repeated, grabbing his cuffs.

"Whatever you say." Cyn sounded resigned. She wasn't
happy about it, but everything in her expression said she
meant to stay in the car.

Santa quietly shut his door, then casually ambled toward
the house Matthew Lewis had entered. It was a shingled two-
story, surrounded by boxwoods. A rough-hewn wooden

deck had been added onto the back, and at either end were stairs that led into the backyard. It faced a privacy wall that presumably hid an alley.

As Santa neared the house, Lewis stepped onto the deck with another man. Looking at them, Santa could bet his bottom dollar that the second man—a man Santa had only seen in a mask—was the one who'd escaped from the Sweets'. He was also the man who'd pulled a gun on the cops. He was wearing only jeans and a flannel shirt, and his hands were shoved deep into his pockets for warmth. When he spoke, his breath fogged the air.

As soon as the men turned their backs, Santa bolted through the yard at a silent crouching run, then stealthily crept beneath the deck. He squatted down, glanced up through the spaces between the boards and listened.

"What are you doing here?" It was definitely the man who'd gotten away. Santa recognized the voice. The man bounced up and down as if he were cold, making the boards above Santa creak. "This is my mother's house. We could have met somewhere." ·

Oh no. Santa drew in a breath and glanced over his shoulder. He could hear Cyn's boots crunching over the frozen grass from a mile away. Fortunately, the men above him were too engrossed in each other to notice. Santa tried not to think about the last time Cyn had taken it upon herself to follow him into a dangerous situation.

"I kept trying to get a number for you, but couldn't. I tried every John Christopher in the tri-state," Lewis groused. So that's the man's name, Santa thought just as Cyn crept up beside him. When he realized she'd brought her pocketbook, he nearly rolled his eyes. "So, I just started coming by here every day," Lewis continued.

"Guess you want your part of the last haul," Christopher said. "That's why you came, right? You knew I was going to keep it here."

Santa shot Cyn his steeliest stare, then pressed his finger to his lips. Small puffs of her breath clouded the air, and her cheeks, which looked even paler than usual against the black of her hat, had turned red in the cold. For the briefest instant, he shut his eyes. Why couldn't the woman have just stayed in the car?

"No, you don't understand!" Lewis's voice rose. "We've got to give it all back!"

"Keep your voice down," Christopher growled. "My mother's in the kitchen, making a ham, and she'll hear you." He stamped his feet on the deck as if that might warm them. "The stuff was way too hot after the trial to pawn," he continued. "So, I've still got it." His voice lowered, persuasively. "Did you really think I'd try to rip off a partner?"

Santa watched Cyn's eyes widen in disbelief. She was clearly starting to get the picture. The two men were talking about the Sweet jewelry. Santa glanced upward. Through the cracks in the planks of the deck, he could see the soles of the men's shoes. Christopher started pacing. "Wait here," he finally said. "I'll get them. You can take your share."

Above, steps sounded. A screen door snapped shut. A storm door slammed. The boards creaked as Lewis walked to the edge of the deck, leaned his elbows on the railing and stared out over the yard. He now had the same view as Santa and Cyn. The yard sloped toward the privacy wall. Brown dirt patches peeked through the frozen whitish grass. A concrete birdbath had been disconnected from its base and overturned.

Honor among thieves, Santa thought, shaking his head. Lewis hadn't choked up Christopher's name or revealed that Christopher had kept the jewels at his mother's.

"He's not listening to me," Lewis said to nothing but the thin air.

"You're not just going to sit here, like this, are you?" Cyn finally whispered, looking furious.

He had half a mind to clamp his hand over her mouth and drag her back to the car, since he was beginning to suspect that this had nothing to do with Amanda. It was about the Sweet robbery, and nothing more.

"We have to do some—"

"Shut up," he mouthed, just as Christopher returned.

"But we—"

This time Santa did silence her. He deftly reached around her shoulders, drew her against him and pressed his palm over her lips. She tried to wrench away, but in her effort to stay quiet, the move was completely ineffective. Santa felt her lips purse against his skin. *Good. She's not going to talk. I'll hear everything I need, get her out of here, then come back.*

He gazed down at her eyes, which were riveted on the deck above them. He glanced up again. Christopher was holding out a bag. Gazing through the cracks, it was hard to tell, but it looked like a regular brown bag. The large sandwich kind.

"Well, take it," he said angrily.

"You're not listening!" Lewis burst out. "We never should have stolen these things. We've got to return them. We could just mail the bag back anonymously. You won't get caught."

"Get caught?" Santa imagined that Christopher's mouth was gaping open in astonishment. The brown paper bag swung down with his arm and dangled at his side. "Did you get reformed in jail or something?"

"As a matter of fact," Lewis said stiffly, "I did."

Christopher's low chuckle sounded menacing. "And here you are," he taunted. "Out on a holiday pardon, and just dying to play secret Santa to the Sweet family. Why, Matt, where's your little red suit?"

"Leave me alone," Lewis said just as Cyn tensed in Santa's arms. "If nothing else, I'll return my half."

"I don't think so," Christopher countered. "The Sweet family has undoubtedly collected and spent the insurance. They're never going to see this stuff again."

Cyn wrenched quickly in Santa's arms. "Oh, yes, they are!" she shrieked, scrambling toward the stairs.

"Oh, Cynthia," Santa muttered. He bolted after her.

"Don't move a muscle!" She charged up the stairs, digging in her pocketbook. "Don't even think about it."

"Who the devil are—" Christopher began, instinctively dropping the paper bag. He began backing away stealthily.

"It's Cynthia Sweet!" Lewis exclaimed, sounding as pleased as he was dumfounded.

"And she's got a gun," Christopher said flatly.

Sure enough, she'd gotten his gun out of the glove compartment. Fortunately, since Cyn had a gun, the two men were more interested in her than in him. Santa watched her train the weapon inexpertly on them, while she slung her pocketbook over her shoulder. The safety was on, and he was positive she'd have no clue about how to release it. At least he hoped not.

She bent with graceful agility, scooped up the paper bag, then glanced inside. "My class ring! The little diamond studs Daddy gave me for my sweet sixteen! And Mom's necklace!" she exclaimed, glancing over her shoulder at Santa. She looked at him a second too long.

Christopher barreled across the deck, lunging for the gun. Christopher knew how to use it, too, Santa thought as he raced forward. Cyn's arm flew upward. Santa caught both her hands, then the gun and, completing the arc, tossed the weapon far behind him, in a stand of trees.

"What's going on out here?" The screen door swung open and a fiftyish woman peered out, wiping her hands on her apron.

"Get back inside," Christopher said, his gaze still riveted on the bag in Cyn's hand.

"I will," the woman said. "But this time, I'm calling the police."

The second the door slammed shut, Christopher charged at Cyn again. She swung her pocketbook at his head, and when Santa leapt between the two, the bag caught him square across the jaw. Christopher took the opportunity to sucker-punch his ribs. He wrestled Christopher to the ground, anyway, then hauled him across the deck. Reaching for his back, he grabbed the cuffs and hooked Christopher to the railing.

When Santa turned around, Cyn was staring at Lewis with her hands on her hips and murder in her eyes. And Matthew Lewis was beaming at her.

"You all stayed together," he said, shaking his head.

"What?" she demanded in a tone that was nearly as menacing as Christopher's.

Santa found himself wishing the earth would open, and swallow him up. "There's something I think I should tell you, Cyn," he said quickly.

"We can talk in the car," Cyn said. "Right now, I want to know what this cretin has to say in his defense."

"You and Jake stayed together," he repeated, nodding at Santa.

Her eyes narrowed. "Jake?"

Lewis chuckled. "Or should I say Anton Santa?"

Cyn gasped. She pivoted around slowly and stared at him. Long moments passed. She tilted her head. Her eyes widened, then she squinted.

"It's true," Santa began, keeping his voice calm. "I can explain every—"

"I almost didn't recognize you, because of the weight you've gained," Lewis interrupted, in a booming voice. "How are you, Anton?"

"This is the craziest thing I ever heard," Cyn murmured, sounding more puzzled than angry. Santa blew out a long sigh and waited for whatever was about to come. He'd let her get it out of her system, then he'd explain. She was still looking at him oddly, as if unable to make out any resemblance between him and Jake Jackson.

"Look, Cyn," he said. "It's not what you think."

"Oh, it isn't?" she finally bit out. "Well, Jake..."

"It's Anton," he managed to say. "Anton Santa. That's my real name."

"Well, Jake or Anton or whoever you are," she snapped. "I just wanted to inform you that your partner in crime or suspect or whoever *he* is—" Cyn raised her finger and pointed "—is getting away."

Santa whirled around. Sure enough, the cuffs were dangling from the rail and Christopher was halfway over the privacy wall. Santa glanced at Cyn again, just in time to see her pivot on her heel and storm down the stairs.

"Cyn, wait," he called, just as a siren sounded in the distance. Who was he going to lose—Cyn or Christopher? His gaze shot from one to the other. Then he leapt over the deck railing and sprinted across the grass.

FIVE DAYS TILL
CHRISTMAS...

Chapter Eight

Tuesday, December 20, 1994

'Twas five days before Christmas and all through the house, not a creature was stirring, not even a mouse. Santa was reclining on Cyn's sofa, with his hands folded on his belly and his feet propped on her coffee table. He stared at the lighted-up Christmas tree, then at the door, then at the tree again, wishing Cyn would come home. As he listened to the early morning silence, he told himself he had no right to be furious. He'd spent more than a week pulling the wool over *her* eyes.

But what was a mere week, compared to the three long years he could have been Amanda's father? By the time he'd recaptured Christopher, Cyn had vanished with the car. Then he'd had to wait for the warrant to search the Christopher place, in order to get a ride back to the city in a cop cruiser. He'd grilled Lewis and Christopher, of course. Still, by the time he'd reached Cyn's apartment, Cyn, Amanda and the rent-a-cop were gone.

It wasn't until midnight that he'd found Analise, with Amanda and the cop at the Plaza Hotel. Not that he'd gone there. Cyn had gone elsewhere, but Analise hadn't known where. As long as Amanda was with the rent-a-cop, she'd be fine. Besides, he meant to give Cyn time—not much more, but some—so she could mull over their unusual situation. And boy, he thought wryly, was it unusual. Maybe they were even now.

I should have chased Cyn, not Christopher. "No," he muttered. "I had to do my job." And he'd wanted the Sweets' belongings returned, so that the past was laid to rest and he could get on with his life—as Amanda's father.

He just wished Cyn's place didn't feel so empty without her and Amanda. He couldn't help but miss their early morning sounds: the whoosh of the water jets in Cyn's shower, the patter of Cyn's bare feet on the kitchen tiles, and the cartoons blaring when Amanda turned on the TV.

The cheery holiday decorations made their absence more intense, too. Every red and green knickknack reminded him of it. The apartment felt as empty as the hotel in Washington where he'd spent the previous Christmas. And the one in Singapore, the Christmas before that. And the one in North Dakota...

I've been traveling a long time. That's what he'd said the night he'd arrived. Now he found himself waiting for Cyn to walk right through that door, without anger or malice, and accept him back into her life...their lives. Not that she would. But he'd been traveling too long. And Anton Santa wanted to come home.

Another hour passed, during which Santa decided he was tired of waiting. He'd waited in countless hotel lobbies, on platforms and stages, beside closed doors during corporate meetings, and in parked cars outside the gates of mansions. He'd waited in crowded airports from Amsterdam to New York to San Francisco. All over the world, he'd waited.

Now, never moving, watching Cyn's door, Santa decided that he'd never been waiting for the people he'd been hired to protect. Never for a high-ranking Swedish official, or a low-level French dignitary, or to take a bullet. No, all that time, in all those places, he'd really been waiting for Cyn Sweet. And what he'd been waiting for was her love.

Just as he realized that, the key turned in the lock.

REMEMBER THAT HE'S AS *slippery as an eel. He'll try to persuade and cajole, but don't listen, and stay as calm and cool as he is,* Cyn thought. She'd left Analise and Amanda with the rent-a-cop, then she'd gotten her own room at The Carlyle. She'd wanted to be alone, and she'd wanted to think.

Now she felt as if she were about to confront the devil himself. Her hands were shaking so badly that she could barely manage the electronic keypad. "No doubt he was trying to keep me out of my own apartment," she muttered just as her keys rattled against the door. One by one, the dead bolts clanked, turning over. She took a last, deep breath, then flung open the door.

He was there all right, just as she'd known he would be. She stormed inside, slammed the door behind herself and leaned against it. He was seated on her sofa, in a soft-looking cream wool suit, as casually as you please. She realized, with a quick shock, that even under the circumstances she couldn't help but react to the way he looked. *How can I be attracted to someone so horrible? What's wrong with me?*

For long moments she merely stared at him. How could it be that this man was also Jake Jackson? They looked nothing alike. Their voices were different. And yet his kisses had told her the truth. Oh, how they'd told the truth, if she had only listened. All night she'd wondered why Jake Jackson would carry handcuffs and seemingly arrest John Christopher. Now she didn't care how Jake had come to be here. She just wanted him away from her daughter.

"About time you showed up," he finally said. "Where's Amanda?"

His voice, which was every bit as soft as it was gruff, more than hinted at the South now. It had become pure Mississippi Delta. His more clipped, nearly Northern, accent had been nothing but a calculated ruse. Her lower lip began to tremble.

"Where is she?" he repeated. The words rose and fell in an almost lilting cadence.

She shook her head. She was looking at Anton Santa but hearing Jake Jackson's voice. "In a safe place," she finally returned. Everything in her voice indicated that Amanda wasn't safe with him. *Stay cool, Cyn.*

He crossed his long legs. The perfectly tailored lines of his elegant suit made him look somehow draped across her sofa. His hands remained calmly folded in his lap. He could

have been on an ad page in *GQ*. "With a kidnapper run
ning around," he said, "I'm not sure The Plaza's so safe."

Her lips parted in astonishment. Clearly he meant t
evade the issue of his presence in her life. "You got you
kidnappers," she snapped. She reached for the doorkno
just to steady herself. "And if you knew where we were, wh
did you ask?"

He lifted one of his shoulders in a graceful shrug. "Lewi
and Christopher aren't involved." His voice was unnerv
ingly gentle. "As for The Plaza—" His lips stretched int
what might have been a smile but wasn't. "I wanted to se
if you'd tell the truth."

I wouldn't tell the truth! She pushed herself off the door
then fought the impulse to fly across the room and punc
him. She had to keep her distance. Even now there was
chance she'd wind up in his arms. The only comfort was tha
he didn't know she'd stayed at The Carlyle. That meant sh
could escape his clutches if she wanted to. "Whether *I'd* te
the truth," she finally repeated, assuring herself it was an
ger, not desire, that made her voice turn raspy.

He nodded. "In four years—" he began tersely. Sh
watched him clench his jaw, then swallow. When he spok
again, his tone was as even as her hemlines, and as silky a
the fabric of her dresses. "In four years," he continued
"you never bothered to mention that Amanda was m
daughter."

She tossed her hair over her shoulder with a quick jerk o
her head. "Sorry—" She wasn't about to let him think sh
was shocked to find he had another identity, or that sh
wondered why he was now carrying handcuffs. "But Rik
er's Island isn't exactly one of my haunts."

He rose so lithely from the sofa that she gulped audibly
Fortunately he didn't head for her but strolled idly to th
window, making her wonder how she'd ever thought hir
ordinary. He lounged against the bars he'd installed, hi
whole body looking dangerously lean and sensuously lan
guid. He carried his weight in his hips, not his shoulders
and now they swayed outward, barely perceptibly. H
looked as restless and calmly predatory as a caged cat.

"So...Santa, Jake, Anton...where all have you been?" he asked with mock politeness. "Or should I say, 'where have you *all* been?'"

"You mean, where did I go after I took the bullet that could have killed you?"

It was the last thing she expected. Her wry chuckle filled the room. "You seduce me, rob my family, then try to tell me you saved my life!" It was so ludicrous that she relaxed against the door, crossed her arms over her chest and stared at him, openmouthed. "I can't wait to hear this one."

"Good," he said levelly, without bothering to look at her. "Because you're about to."

"Well, get on with it," she quickly returned. "Because your time's running out."

Now he did glance her way. His muscular shoulder rolled against the bars and he barely turned his head. His profile nearly took away her breath. The nose was straight, the jaw firm, the forehead high below his slicked-back hair. When his eyes, which looked nearly black today, shifted from her face to the stocking-hung mantel, they looked mysteriously deep. How could a liar and a thief manage to look so arrogant?

"I used to be a cop," he began slowly. "Undercover."

He looked directly into her eyes, but she was too shocked to respond. During the night, the possibility had occurred to her, of course, but she'd rejected it. The man was too dishonest. If he'd been an undercover cop, he would have called her during the trial, to explain. He turned back to the window.

"I was pulled out of the academy before I'd even graduated. They set me up in an apartment in the Village." A faint smile touched his lips. "But then, I guess you remember that."

Her mouth went dry, as she thought of the apartment where she'd made love to Jake...to Anton. He sounded totally serious. Could he be telling the truth? *No way.* Watching him lounge against the window bars, it was easy enough to imagine him in a cell. The detective in charge said her testimony had put him away, too. After Jake left the hospital, he'd gone straight to jail. *Don't listen to him!*

"...and I was enrolled in a class in every school in the city Columbia, NYU, the midtown CUNY. They were alread pretty sure that the people burglarizing the outlying area were students. Which they were—" He glanced at her "Lewis and Christopher were enrolled at NYU."

"I had classes with them." She shot him a steely stare hoping to communicate that she didn't believe a word h said.

He turned fully away from the window, leaned his hea against the bars and shoved his hands deep into his trouse pockets. His gaze was as unflinching as hers, but his voic remained calmer. "You have no reason not to believe me."

"Oh, no!" she exclaimed. "And why is that?"

"Because nothing else makes sense."

She sighed, then tried her best to sound bored. "So, yo grew your hair long...."

"It was long already."

"But you dyed it, and grew a mustache and beard and los a lot of weight...."

"Gained," he corrected. "Since then."

"I can't believe I'm hearing this," she said flatly.

His gaze still met hers dead-on. His low, throaty, almos bitter chuckle filled the air. "Oh, but sweetheart," he con tinued. "It gets even better."

No matter how much she wanted to, she couldn't tear he eyes from his. He was so self-possessed. All her sense heightened when she took in his casual attitude and under stated elegance. Only his eyes alerted her to the emotion that seethed beneath his surface. "I'll just bet it does," sh said coolly.

"Sometimes truth's stranger than fiction."

"Especially when we get to the part where you save m life." She blew out a piqued sigh.

"You followed me...." His voice lowered a notch. "Be cause of you, two rookie cops who didn't have a clue wha was going on stormed into your parents' house."

A lump lodged in her throat and she swallowed, knowin that much was true. She arched a brow in his direction *Whatever he's going to say is a lie.* "Go on."

He shook his head. "Why *did* you follow me?"

"I was wrong to call the police?" she snapped. Her eyes widened. "I was just supposed to sit there while you carted off all of our worldly possessions?"

"The only thing that got carted off was me," he said flatly. "On a stretcher." He suddenly shrugged, as if the rightness or wrongness of her actions didn't concern him. "The two cops burst in, Christopher pulled a gun, and one of the rookies fired a shot, hitting me instead of Christopher. The bullet grazed my jaw."

He absently rubbed a thumb across the scar now, as if to prove it. Had she really nearly gotten him killed? "So you took a bullet for Christopher." She spoke in an overly innocent tone, realizing she'd just caught him in one of his infernal lies. "That's not exactly saving my life, now is it Jake . . . Anton?"

He looked as if he wanted to kill her. "Well, after that shot was fired, you suddenly hopped out of the front seat of a cruiser and ran toward the house. Why did you do that, Cyn?" It wasn't a question, it was a demand for an answer.

Because I was afraid you were going to be killed. And I was going to save your life. But then you flew through the door, with blood on your face, and I got scared. More scared than I'd ever been. She sighed shakily but didn't answer him.

"And Christopher, either because he wanted revenge because you'd turned us in, or because he needed to fire some cover shots, so he could get away, aimed right at you."

That's why you ran into the yard? All she remembered was seeing his face, feeling scared, hearing a shot and seeing him leap into the air. She'd turned and fled. Now she realized that it explained the scar on his calf. "You're lying," she said weakly.

"Feel guilty yet?"

If I believe this, every word of it, I have no excuse to keep him from Amanda. Her heart suddenly thudded in her chest. Her worst nightmare had just come true. Jake Jackson had come back to claim their daughter. And for a second time he'd stolen into her life under completely false pretenses.

"You're lying," she said with resolve, her voice as cold a
the winter day.

"You just can't face it, can you?"

"You can tell ten million lies—" She strained to keep he
voice level. "But you'll never get within sight of Amanda
again."

He crossed the room silently, looking every inch the
predator. The sheer energy radiating from the man had he
backing herself up against the door. He stopped right in
front of her. Then he sprawled an arm alongside the door
his elbow claimed the space next to her head. He leaned so
close his hips grazed hers. "You want to repeat that?"

"You're not getting anywhere near my daughter!" He
voice sounded high-pitched and thin. Her mouth went dry
and her breasts suddenly felt full and heavy. With his lips so
near and his breath warming her skin, there was just no way
she could fight her body's traitorous response.

"Need I remind you," he drawled, "she's my daughter
too."

He *had* come for Amanda. And she had to be strong
"You steal into my life," she returned coldly, "and each
time, you pretend to be someone other than who you really
are. Now, like four years ago, what you intend to do is rob
me. Cop or no cop, you're a thief."

"And you're a liar," he countered, leaning just an inch
closer. "What about your marriage that never was? O
poor, dead Harry? Or how you live as a grieving widow? O
about how you mean to deny me rights to what's mine?"
His eyes now looked as dark as a starless night. "Sounds to
me like you're the thief, Cyn."

Whose heart did she hear beating, she wondered, sud
denly feeling dizzy. Her own or his? "You've used me one
too many times," she managed to say huskily. "This time
to get to Amanda. Last time—" His eyes held her spell
bound. She forced herself to blink. "I—I don't know why."

"It was my job," he nearly whispered.

"And you did it so very well." The words caught in the air
as if each one had a barbed hook buried deep inside it. "I
bet you enjoyed it—seducing a rich, extremely overpro
tected college kid until you made her..."

"I did enjoy it." His hand dropped to the sleeve of her luxurious coat. "But what was it that I *made* you do?"

Everything in his dangerously dark gaze reminded her that she'd always gone willingly into his arms. Her mouth had become so dry that her throat ached. "Nothing," she croaked.

"Did I make you love me, Cyn Sweet?"

The truth made her feel a little faint. She clenched her jaw. "Did you use me, Jake Jackson?"

"Anton Santa," he corrected. His eyes narrowed. "I had no family, no money and nowhere to go," he continued persuasively. "I'll admit, I liked the excitement of my job, and that I was hungry...." The last word hung in the air as his gaze roved over her face. "To make good," he finished abruptly.

"You did use me," she said in shock.

His jaw hardened and his eyes seemed to judge her. "What did *you* love? The man you see now? The man I am? Or some scruffy bad boy from down South? Some guy with a motorcycle and a leather jacket, of whom your parents would never approve."

She licked her lips against their dryness. "Touché," she whispered.

"That's why you didn't recognize me," he continued with that hypnotic voice.

"What are you talking about?"

"You didn't recognize me because you were in love with a myth. And then, when you felt betrayed, my looks got all scrambled up in your mind. Maybe you couldn't even remember what I looked like at all."

Cyn's mind raced while she listened to him. "You're sending the notes!" she burst out. "You sent them so that you could get this job, so that you could see Amanda—"

He gasped. "What?"

She stared at him, not knowing what was truth and what were lies, and only knowing that perhaps none of it mattered because she still craved his lips.

His eyes widened, as if all his questions had suddenly been answered. "Why did you follow me?" he demanded again.

She decided to tell him. Maybe the truth would hurt him. Maybe he'd realize what he'd lost by betraying her. "I thought you were with another woman," she said.

"And where were you last night?"

Did he think she'd been with another man? "At The Carlyle." As much as she wanted to let him wonder, she wasn't about to appear dishonest. "Alone."

"Oh, Cyn," he whispered, his expression softening.

"Don't 'Oh, Cyn' me. You've no excuse for not calling me during the trial. You could have explained."

"I was in the hospital, doped up, with my whole head bandaged. My boss wanted my cover kept a secret, so that I could go after Christopher when I got out."

His every word was making her furious again. "You could have made someone tell me the truth."

"I was about to—" His voice was raspy, tinged with longing. "When you announced your engagement."

She sucked in a quick breath. Maybe he'd really loved her. But if she believed it, she'd have to forget the past, and he'd take Amanda. "You sent those notes!" she accused again.

His hand savagely cupped her chin and he leaned so close that the tips of their noses nearly touched. "There are bad guys," he said softly. "And they're out there and they're real. But I'm not one of them, Cyn."

His mouth settled on hers with a quick vengeance, as if a kiss could convince her. She wanted to wrench away but couldn't, not when his lips probed hers farther apart and his hand dropped into her hair in the softest caress she'd ever felt. She found herself weakening against the door, softening against his strength, and kissing him back.

It wasn't fair that no other man had ever felt so right or fit so snugly against her. It wasn't fair that only he could kiss her with such dangerous, almost primal need. Her knees nearly buckled beneath her as he drew back then pressed his lips to hers again. Completely against her will, she felt herself arch toward him as his tongue plunged between her lips. Her breasts tingled with awareness, the aching tips straining against the lace of her underwear.

I can't do this! She violently jerked away. His hand cupped the back of her head swiftly, before it connected with the door. They merely gazed at each other, their breaths coming in gasps.

"Would it really be so terrible," he finally said, "to have me in your life . . . to have a father for Amanda?"

"We have a life." A pleading tone stole into her voice. "A good, stable life. And you used me. I can't forget it."

His gaze dropped from her eyes to her lips, then to her chest. He sighed. "C'mon, Cyn," he said calmly. "Get away from the door."

She stepped away before she'd thought it through, then watched him get his coat. *He's leaving. Good.* As he opened the door, her relief was replaced by heartfelt terror. She assured herself it wasn't because she was losing him, but because she needed him to protect Amanda. "Where are you going?" she asked uncertainly.

"Where do you think?" he returned. "To get my daughter."

"STOP! STOP RIGHT THERE! At least wait! You can't just . . ."

For the second time in two days, Cyn was chasing him through the parking garage. This time, her high heels clicked and clattered against the concrete. She was running. Hard.

He'd already learned that she didn't take no for an answer, so he unlocked the passenger door first, then held it open for her. She whooshed past him breathlessly, in a rush of that sweet-smelling perfume. Once she was inside, he slammed the door.

"Do you mind telling me what you—er—what you—" She gasped as he slid into the driver's seat and started the car. Too winded to continue, she threw her head back against the headrest and gulped down long, deep breaths while he pulled out of his space and onto Eighty-eighth Street.

"I mean—" She whirled around to face him. "Once you *get* Amanda, just what exactly do you intend to *do* with her?"

"You know," he said, glancing at her. "I was kind of hoping you'd help me figure that one out."

Her expression softened a little. "Oh," she murmured in surprise.

His hands tightened on the wheel. "If it hadn't been for some very strange coinci—"

"If it *was* a coincidence."

"I didn't send the notes." He sighed. He didn't believe they'd met again, by coincidence, either. The first notes had been juvenile, and Paxton had a childish streak. Was it possible he'd known that Jackson and Santa were the same man? Had Paxton sent the notes, in hope of reuniting his daughter with the father of her child? If so, why hadn't he admitted it when he'd been asked directly about the identity of Amanda's father?

"As far as I knew," Santa finally said, "you were still married to Harry Stevens. I would never have come here. But now that I have... now that I've seen Amanda, I can't just walk away."

"You mean, you're not going to tell her when we get to The Plaza?" Cyn asked.

The sheer hope in her voice made him mad all over again. What right did she have to deny him his daughter? "When I saw Amanda," he managed to point out reasonably, "I thought she might be mine. I've known that she is for over twenty-four hours, and I haven't told her." He braked at a light. "Eventually, I mean for Amanda to know she has a father. An honest one who cares about her." The light changed and he pressed the gas. When he glanced at Cyn, she looked a little flushed.

"All right," she finally said. "I can never forgive you for using me... but all right."

He was so surprised, he nearly missed the circular entrance to The Plaza. He concentrated on driving for a moment, until he'd braked again. He stared ahead at the long line of limos and cabs that were also waiting for the parking valet. "You'll let me tell her?" he finally asked.

For long moments, she didn't say anything. He glanced through his side window. Various ice sculpture angels were displayed in front of the hotel. As beautiful as they were, they were nothing next to the flesh-and-blood woman beside him. When he glanced at her, she tilted her head and gazed at him.

"Amanda was told that Harry Stevens was her father," she said softly. "Then she overheard the truth." She shot him a sad smile. "Mom certainly never approved of the way Daddy handled things. I mean, having me marry Harry was sort of his idea. And Harry—because he wanted to marry me, for real—agreed. It was Daddy who later sort of declared him dead. And then one thing led to another," she finished in a rush.

Santa nodded. He'd heard all this before. "So?"

"Well, Amanda heard Mom and Dad arguing about it, and then she found out about…Jake. Amanda thinks Jake, who is in jail, is her father."

For the first time, how things might look from Amanda's point of view really sank in. "How could you let her think a criminal's her—"

"Santa, that's what *I* thought!"

At least she was calling him Santa now, he thought. Maybe Cyn could forgive him, too, in time. "Well, she can't go through life thinking that."

Suddenly her eyes shimmered and looked misty. He almost hoped she'd break down and cry, so he could pull her close, under the guise of comfort. She gulped audibly and blinked. "I just need to think it through," she said softly.

Was it the truth? Or was she buying time, while she figured out how to get him out of their lives? He shook his head, as if to clear it of confusion. If nothing else, she was the mother of his child, and he was going to trust her. He had to.

"Amanda's so young," she continued. "I don't want her to be any more confused than she already is. Maybe we should even bring in a counselor. I want to decide when to tell her." Cyn scooted across the seat and one of her long slender fingers reached up and traced the scar on his jaw. "Can you understand that?"

He nodded. The last thing he wanted to do was to confuse his little girl. "Why didn't you stop Paxton from telling all those lies?" he asked. "Why did you let him make such a mess of things?"

"I'd been through the ordeal of the trial. You were gone. I was twenty-four, unmarried and pregnant," she said, a hint of bitterness touching her voice.

Everything in her tone said he'd broken her heart. He expected her to say it outright. Instead, she scooted back across the seat. "You'll have to leave my apartment as soon as possible." The farther away from him she got, the more her voice seemed to harden with resolve. "There can be nothing between us. First, because I'll never want a man who lies to me. And second, because this is going to be confusing enough for Amanda as it is."

"I'll leave as soon as Amanda's safe," he said gruffly. He tried to tell himself that he'd gotten what he'd wanted— Amanda. To hell with Cyn.

He realized horns were blaring all around him and glanced through the windshield. Sure enough, all the cars in front of them were gone. One glance into Cyn's eyes, he thought, and the whole world ceased to exist. *Forget it. Just concentrate on getting Amanda.*

"MOMMY! I ATE THREE candy bars and watched lots of TV!" Amanda flew into Cyn's arms. She was getting heavy, but Cyn managed to swing her around in countless, dizzying circles. Then they collapsed on the bed in The Plaza's suite.

"Tickle fest!" Cyn exclaimed, wiggling her fingers against Amanda's ribs.

"Grandmama and Granddaddy are gonna take me to the Christmas trees from around the world!" Amanda broke into a fit of giggles. "I won't go if Mr. Santa can't." Amanda rolled away from Cyn and shot a guilty glance at the rent-a-cop. "And Mr. Thomas is gonna come."

Cyn glanced up. She'd left Amanda with Mr. Thomas and her mother, but both her parents were in the suite. Together. In the same room. For a moment the only sound came from the TV. *It's a Wonderful Life* was on. Cyn blinked, then looked at Santa. He seemed surprised, too.

"Santa Claus!" Amanda lunged off the bed and shot toward Santa. He caught her in his arms and settled her on his hip.

Cyn's heart dropped to her feet. *He lied. He's going to tell her now. Why did I listen?* The seconds ticked on, feeling like eternity.

"Why, hey there, you knockout you," Santa drawled.

"Now that we've spent the night here, do you mind telling me what in the world we're doing at a hotel?" her mother asked, gazing between Santa and Cyn. Cyn watched her mother smooth the skirt of her suit, then recline in an armchair. She could feel Santa's gaze on her back; it nearly raised the hairs at her nape.

Her father wiggled his brows. "Now, Analise, it's not nice to pry," he chided.

"I just want an explanation." Her mother smiled wickedly.

"It's so long and involved you wouldn't want to hear it," Cyn said in an embarrassed rush. Did her parents really think she'd gotten Amanda out of the house so that she could sleep with Santa? A guilty flush warmed her cheeks. Little did they know. She inadvertently glanced at Santa. The way she caught him looking at her, they might have come from making love. When she looked away, it was straight into her mother's merry grin.

Cyn had a few questions, too. She wanted to ask her parents what they were doing together, but then she decided she might hex the situation by asking if they were a couple again.

"Well, wherever you've been," her father began, "we waited until you arrived to do the honors."

"Honors?" Analise asked.

Paxton grinned. "The police called yesterday evening and asked me to identify a few things."

As if sensing what was to come but not daring to believe, Analise leaned forward. "My necklace?" she murmured.

"Not just a necklace," Paxton returned softly. "A chain of time...the Christmas and anniversary gift that marked off each of our many wonderful years together."

Analise gasped. "They really found it?"

Paxton circled around her chair, pulling the necklace from his pocket. He leaned slowly, looped it around her neck, then clasped it.

"Oh, Paxton," she whispered.

He place his hands gingerly on her shoulders and leaned close. They looked so romantic and wonderful together that Cyn pressed a hand to her heart. The whole last year of their estrangement seemed to slip away.

"I knew you'd want to see it again," her father murmured. "The other items were all recovered and they're in the safe." With every word, he seemed to be asking Analise to come home.

"I hope there were some cuff links in the bottom of that bag," Cyn whispered softly, looking at her father's open shirtsleeves.

Paxton patted Analise's shoulder. "Matthew Lewis was released on a pardon, and he went to John Christopher's house. Santa followed him and found Christopher. He was the man who got away."

"I helped catch him," Cyn pointed out.

Analise's throaty laughter filled the room. "Well done, you two. Now, if only Jake Jackson stays in jail. Somehow, I doubt that man will ever reform, no matter how much time he serves."

Cyn was about to hazard a glance at Santa when Paxton chuckled. "Oh, he just might, Analise. I mean, you never know."

The twinkle in her father's eyes nearly convinced Cyn he knew the truth. But that was impossible, she assured herself. The way Jake—Anton Santa, she amended—had stormed back into her life was just making her paranoid. The fact that he'd betrayed her twice wasn't helping, either.

She felt a warm hand rest on her shoulder and nearly jumped out of her skin. It was Santa. When she glanced up, Amanda—who was still in his arms—waved at her. Her chest constricted, but she managed to smile. *I'm going to lose my baby to this man.*

Her mother's voice brought her back to reality. "I've got to go."

"So soon?" Paxton cleared his throat. "I thought you and I were taking Amanda to the museum."

"You all run along," Analise said, her voice catching.

"I thought that necklace was supposed to be lucky," Paxton returned softly.

Analise's gaze alighted on Cyn's eyes, then fluttered upward to take in Santa and Amanda. "Oh, who knows?" She flashed Paxton a sudden smile. "Maybe it will turn out to be a lucky year, after all."

FOUR DAYS TILL
CHRISTMAS...

Chapter Nine

Wednesday, December 21, 1994

The phone's shrill ring pulled Cyn from a deep, disturbed sleep. Maybe all of this—Jake's return, his transformation into Anton Santa, the fact that she'd actually slept with the man, and the threats against Amanda—had been nothing more than a nightmare, she thought groggily.

"No such luck," she muttered, her fingers fumbling over her sweat-damp, tangled sheets. She accidently knocked the receiver to the floor, scooted and leaned to retrieve it, then barked, "What do you want?"

She quickly recovered. "I'm sorry. It's just that it's—" She glanced at the clock. "Twelve o'clock." Midnight? She squinted at her curtains and could see light peeping through. Noon!

She bolted upright just as her father said, "Your mother and I taught you manners, young lady. Would your highness mind telling me what's wrong?"

She shut her eyes, feeling thoroughly disoriented. "Please, Daddy," she whispered hoarsely. "I'll call you back in five minutes. I promise." She opened her eyes long enough to hang up the phone.

Then she stumbled into the bathroom and rinsed her face. It barely helped. All night she'd either wanted to creep into Santa's room and make love—or storm in and kill him.

What a strange few days it had been, she thought, squinting at her reflection. Jake Jackson had waltzed right back into her life as Anton Santa, and now he wanted to play Daddy to Amanda. "No play about it," she muttered, trying to force herself to face the facts. "He *is* Amanda's father."

Yesterday she'd accompanied Paxton, Santa and Amanda to the exhibit of Christmas trees from around the world. She'd wanted to avoid Santa, but she couldn't bear to leave him alone with Amanda. The worst thing was that he was the perfect daddy. He'd piggybacked Amanda through the museum, held her hand and let her buy postcards at the gift shop. Because of his world travels, he was able to tell funny stories about the kids he'd seen in every country for which there was a tree. Her little girl adored him.

But what about his lies? Cyn wondered as she brushed her teeth. Wouldn't he betray Amanda eventually, just as he'd betrayed her?

She rinsed her mouth, gulped down a healthy amount of cold water, then glared in the mirror. She looked downright horrible, but with a life like hers, who could concentrate on beauty sleep?

How come I didn't recognize him? She headed for the phone again, thinking of the reasons Santa had enumerated. Her image of Jackson had definitely colored him in memory—and not favorably. *Did I not recognize him simply because I didn't want to?* Now she couldn't see anyone *but* Jake when she looked at Santa.

Suddenly she cocked her head. No cartoons! "Amanda?" she yelled. She ran across the room and flung open her door. "Santa? Amanda?" *He's taken her. He's gone and he's taken her with him,* she thought. *But he wouldn't do that. Not Santa.* She ran to the phone again.

"Paxton's at your mother's office," Eileen said, when Cyn got her father's assistant on the line.

"Is Santa with Dad? Is Amanda there?"

"I don't know." Eileen sounded harried.

"Thanks, Eileen." Cyn hung up and tried her mother.

Her father answered on the first ring. "Paxton Sweet here."

"Daddy?" Cyn perched on the edge of her bed and coiled the phone wire around her hand nervously.

Her father sniffed. "I certainly hope you're calling to apologize," he said, a little huffily.

"Is Jake there? Does Jake—oh, heavens, I mean Santa," she corrected in a rush. "Is Santa there? Does he have Amanda?"

"Jake!" her father burst out. He lowered his voice, as if there might be other people in her mother's office. "For once in your life, you've got a respectable man after you, Cynthia Anna Sweet. You may choose to ignore it, but I've seen how Santa looks at you. He has a profession, character, he adores Amanda..."

Cyn was waking up fast. As her father ticked off Santa's attributes, it was right on the tip of her tongue to tell her father that his oh-so-respectable golden boy *was* Jake Jackson. She bit her lip as if to keep herself from talking. If anyone heard that piece of news today, it was going to be Amanda.

"When are you going to straighten up and fly right?" her father finally finished.

"Is Santa there with Amanda or not?" she asked, trying to stay calm.

"He most certainly is," her father returned. "Humph. I take it you're still in bed?"

Her father sure was in an uncharacteristic bad mood. "I couldn't sleep very well," she said in a conciliatory tone.

"Well, the early bird gets the worm. While you've been sleeping, Santa has been doing his job. He's found the kidnapper."

Her mind was suddenly reeling. As soon as she'd agreed to let Santa tell Amanda that he was her father, he'd found the kidnapper! Was he that anxious to leave her apartment? Had he known who it was all along? Had he merely waited until he'd gotten what he'd wanted—namely, Amanda—before he exposed the person who'd sent the threatening notes? Didn't Santa care about her at all?

"I'll be right there!" Cyn exclaimed.

Only after she'd hung up did she realize that she'd forgotten to ask the identity of the culprit.

"CLAYTON?" CYN GASPED. She scrutinized the elderly man in front of her as if she'd never seen him before in her life. *Clayton, who'd always bought her ice creams when she was a kid? Clayton, who was so involved with the store that he was almost a member of the family?*

Sure enough, Clayton Woods was seated behind her mother's desk, with the notes in front of him and Amanda on his lap. Analise was all but petting Clayton's hand, in order to soothe him. Paxton kept a firm hand on his head buyer's shoulder.

"It was—it was me. Me, Cynthia," Clayton said brokenly. "I'm so—so sorry. I—"

"There, there," Analise crooned softly, patting him with one hand and twining the fingers of her other through the links of her Christmas necklace. "Take a few deep breaths, dear. Paxton, why don't you run and get Clayton something to drink?"

"What about some nice hot tea, Clayton?" Paxton asked, scurrying toward the door. "I should have brought Eileen with me. We need to make some tea!"

"Heaven's, Paxton—" Analise sounded suddenly angry at the mention of Eileen. "Why don't you get it yourself? It amazes me that you can't even make a drink without your assistant."

Something in her mother's tone gave Cyn pause. So did Clayton's guilt. Still, even that couldn't erase Santa from her thoughts. He was leaning casually in the windowsill, with his arms crossed over his chest and a self-satisfied smile on his face. He was looking right at her.

Clayton seemed barely aware of the people present. Not even of Amanda, who flung her arms around his neck and gave him a sloppy kiss on the cheek. "It's okay," she murmured. "You can kidnap me, Uncle Clayton, and you don't have to write any letter."

The older man shook his head, as if confused. "I just had to heal the company." He glanced at Cyn.

"The company?" she managed.

"There're rumors of a takeover attempt," he said more firmly. "When we were joking in the board meeting, I just thought . . ."

Out of the corner of her eye, Cyn could see Santa. She could feel his gaze rove over her. In spite of the circumstances, she hoped she didn't look as underslept as she felt. She tried to focus her attention on Clayton. "Thought what?"

She tried to tell herself she should be angry, but she knew Clayton nearly as well as she knew her own father. Clayton had gotten a little absentminded and addled in the past few years, but he was still like family. Besides, all she really felt was relief. And Santa's eyes.

Clayton ran a hand over his bald scalp. The tufts of gray hair on either side looked springy and uncombed. He blew out a shaky sigh. "I thought maybe—" He hazarded a glance at Analise, then at Paxton, who breezed in with Clayton's tea. "Well, I thought maybe you all would have to interact. If you just got back together, even enough to have a good working relationship, the company might pull through. The talk on Wall Street is that someone's desperately angling to get inside...." Clayton's eyes seemed to plead for mercy from those who loved him.

Paxton squinted. "You've actually heard that down on Wall Street? Not secondhand?"

Clayton nodded sheepishly. "I go down there every once in a while," he said, his breath becoming more even. "Bob's there all the time, too. He loves to hit the Seaport and schmooze the ladies after work. Anyway, a few days after our meeting, I ran into an assistant from Holmes and Furrows and she said someone was actively pursuing us, but she didn't know who."

"Get Evan on it," Paxton said to Analise. "He knows practically everybody downtown by name."

Analise sighed. "According to Evan, someone's been buying up the employees' stocks."

Paxton gasped. "And you didn't tell me!"

"We weren't exactly speaking," Analise returned defensively.

"Well, we are now," Paxton said. "And we're going to pull together on this one. You, me, Clayton and Cyn have the lion's share of the stocks in the store."

"I haven't sold a one," Clayton quickly said.

"Of course you haven't," Analise said matter-of-factly.

"Me, neither," Cyn said.

"I wouldn't sell my store," said Amanda, making Clayton crack the first hint of a smile.

There was a long silence. Then Clayton said, "Can you ever forgive me, Cyn?"

"You really scared me," she said, speaking honestly. "I can't deny that. But I'm relieved to know the truth."

"When Mr. Santa arrived, I knew you'd feel safe, and then when you two got along so well, kissing at the store, under the mistletoe and all..."

Cyn's face was getting hotter by the minute. Santa seemed to be enjoying her blush immensely. "Mr. Santa has been of great help," she admitted in a businesslike tone.

"I only wanted your parents to start talking again," Clayton repeated.

Paxton clapped his back. "Well, Clayton—" He smiled at Analise. "Maybe your scheme worked." Paxton turned and winked at Cyn. "And just think, Clayton," he continued, with a quick glance in Santa's direction. "If you'd never sent those notes, my future son-in-law wouldn't even be here."

"Daddy!" Cyn nearly shrieked.

Santa's low belly laugh suddenly filled the room. "Why Cyn, didn't your Daddy tell you about the marriage he's arranged for us?"

SANTA CAUGHT CYN'S WRIST as she rounded a corner in the hallway near her mother's office. She'd been walking so fast that she swung toward him, still moving on sheer momentum, and nearly crashed into a water fountain. "Aren't you going to congratulate me?"

"What do you want, Santa?" she asked drolly. "A medal?" The woman was clearly in no mood for pleasantries. Her eyes were flashing and her lips were stretched into a thin line. "Or perhaps I should simply be pleased, since you've caught a man I consider to be my uncle." She raised her brows archly. "But then, maybe it's you who should congratulate me. After all, you and my father have arranged my marriage." Now Cyn smiled sweetly.

He was fairly sure her pique was due to the fact that she still wanted him and wished she didn't. "Can't you take a joke?" He playfully tightened his grip on her wrist. Beneath his fingertips, he could feel her pounding pulse beat.

"I'm merely worried about my father," she returned lightly, withdrawing her hand from his and placing it on her hip. "He seems to think you're so wonderful—" She lowered her voice. "And he's going to be upset when he finds out the truth."

Somehow Santa doubted it. "He's not going to dislike me for having been a cop."

She shook her head. "When he finds out you and Jake Jackson are one and the same, he'll be crushed."

He tried to assure himself that he only wanted the go-ahead to tell Amanda the truth. Then he was leaving. "Do you think he'll be crushed," Santa said softly, "because you were?" *Why do I keep hoping she'll admit she cares for me?*

"I was not!" She heaved a quick sigh. "I just don't like the way you're snowing my father. I'd appreciate it if you'd quit acting so buddy-buddy."

Eileen rounded the corner. Apparently, feeling as if he couldn't do without her, Paxton had called and told Eileen to rush over. "Hello, you two," she said pleasantly.

The way she said it, they might have just been caught kissing. Both he and Cyn smiled dutifully at Paxton's assistant until she'd passed. Then he said, "There's no reason for you to be jealous, Cyn. I get along with your father and I think it's a good thing. It'll be good for Amanda."

"Jealous?" she burst out, as if it were the craziest thing she'd ever heard.

"You don't want to share your dad," he said calmly. "And you sure don't want to share Amanda." In spite of her anger, he couldn't help but notice her kissably pursed lips. He almost wished he'd just arrived in New York. He would be playing it cool; she would be flirting mercilessly.

"I don't mind sharing," she finally said with a toss of her head. "It's all a matter of who I'm sharing with."

He reached for her hand again, lifted it quickly, then pressed it against his chest. "Sometimes—" He gazed deeply into her eyes, wishing she'd be more reasonable. "We've shared pretty well."

"Oh, please," she whispered miserably. "Don't remind me."

"Can you really forget?" He drew her a fraction closer.

"Believe me—" The huskiness of her voice seemed to belie her true emotions. "It's as if I've been stricken by a case of total amnesia."

He chuckled softly. "A serious medical condition." He realized she was almost in his arms. "Maybe I should jog your memory."

"The only jogging I'd like to see you do is in sweatpants. And of course—" She shot him an innocent smile. "You'd be running far away from me."

"Still convinced I'm a bad guy?"

"More than ever."

"If I'm already condemned, then I've got nothing to lose." He swiftly pulled her against him and delivered a fast, wet kiss. Then he tilted his head and looked into her eyes again. "How was that for bad?"

Her glistening lips almost curled into a smile. "Pretty bad," she conceded softly.

She's giving in as surely as if she'd cried uncle. He chuckled. "I can get worse."

"I'm well aware of that," she said throatily, a deep flush now spreading over her features.

"Not as aware as you could be."

Her jaw clenched and her eyes turned cold. She all but leapt back a pace. "I don't want you taking off with my daughter again."

"She's my daughter, too."

"Not yet."

Santa leaned against the water fountain. "She always has been my daughter, and she always will be my daughter," he said, wishing he didn't think of taking Cyn to bed every time he looked at her. "She doesn't become my daughter simply because you say so."

But when would it all come true? Would there really be a day when Amanda would fly into his arms, calling him Daddy? He could easily open a business in the city and find an apartment. He'd decorate a room for Amanda that would be every bit as enticingly little girlish as her room at Cyn's.

Finally Cyn sighed. "Now that your case is solved, I assume you'll be moving out of my apartment."

Didn't Cyn—in some small part of herself—want him to stay? Wasn't she having occasional fantasies about the two of them getting together and parenting Amanda? He guessed not.

"Well, are you?"

"You seem to have forgotten something." He drew an envelope from the inner pocket of his suit jacket and held it up for her to see.

"I—I thought," she stammered. Was it his imagination or did her gaze really flit to his as if she wanted his support again? "I thought Clayton was the one who—"

"Clayton didn't leave the typewritten note," Santa said.

Her eyes darted down the hallway as if seeking the culprit. "Who left it?"

"I don't know." He leaned closer to her. "But you can count on one thing."

"What's that?"

"That I'll be staying at your apartment until I find out."

CYN MANAGED TO AVOID Santa through the afternoon promotion and dinner. When they'd finally gotten home, she'd gone to the one place where Santa wouldn't follow—at least not in the early evening—her bedroom. Now she felt trapped.

Why should I be stuck here while he and Amanda watch movies? she fumed, momentarily forgetting that she was in self-exile. It was nearly Amanda's bedtime, which meant she'd been cooped up for hours. The longer she'd sat on the edge of her bed, the more she thought of things she needed to do.

If it weren't for Santa, she would be cleaning, baking, wrapping presents and planning a menu for Christmas morning brunch. She could read her magazines, which were on an end table in the den. She, not Santa, would be cuddling with Amanda on the sofa, watching videotapes.

"I can't live like this," she muttered. She got up, opened her door, then headed down the hall. *I'm not going to vanish simply because he insists on being here. I'll just sit down, pretty as you please, and watch television with my daughter!* Unfortunately, when she reached the den, a tape was rewinding.

"*Beauty and the Beast* is over, Mommy," Amanda said.

Cyn's gaze drifted from her daughter to Santa. "Oh," she said wryly, "I wouldn't be too sure about that."

Cyn did a double take, just as Santa drawled, "I take it I'm the beast and Amanda's the beauty?"

"Boy, aren't you quick." She had to fight to keep her voice light, since she couldn't take her eyes from him. He was wearing a white hooded sweatshirt and jeans. She'd never seen him in casual clothes, at least not since he'd been Jake Jackson. Throughout the day, she'd tried to remind herself that Santa had rights with regards to Amanda, but she could barely force herself to be civil, no matter how good he looked.

"*Beauty and the Beast* is over, Mommy," Amanda piped in, sounding confused.

"Yes, it is, honey," Cyn said, just as the tape stopped whirring. She crossed the room and returned it to its box, glad for the excuse to turn away from Santa. He looked as elegant as he did masculine in his suits, but his jeans left less to her imagination.

"I *was* a beast—" Santa's soft voice filled the room and seemed to take the very air from it. For a second, Cyn couldn't breathe. "But then Amanda kissed me and turned me into a prince."

Amanda giggled. "We gotta do *Aladdin* now."

"It's nearly bedtime," Cyn said quickly, wishing she didn't get so nervous and anxious when she was in the same room with Santa.

"Bedtime's not for another hour," Santa said. He seemed well aware that she'd been hiding to avoid him. Sure she couldn't take another second of this pins-and-needles feeling, she strode to the window and drew the curtain cords. The floor-to-ceiling curtains rattled on their rods and swept open.

"Snow!" Amanda shrieked. "It's snow, Mommy! Snow!"

In an instant, Amanda was at her side and hugging her leg. It was coming down hard and had been for some time. At least three inches had accumulated on the ground below. Just looking at it, and touching her daughter's shoulder, Cyn's anxiety vanished. She felt nearly as excited as Amanda. The first real snow! "C'mon—" She lifted Amanda into her arms. "Let's bundle up and make a snowman."

"On our roof?" Amanda asked breathlessly. "Can we?"

"Yep." Cyn breezed past Santa, with Amanda on her hip.

"I'll get a carrot for the nose," Santa called softly behind them.

Sure enough, he was waiting for them at the door. He'd put on soft-looking gloves and pulled a leather jacket over his sweatshirt. A carrot peeked from one coat pocket, and a hat and scarf from the other.

They headed to the roof and he flung open the door. The three of them stopped on the threshold and huddled together against the sudden rush of wind, as if some silent communication had passed between them.

"You just don't wanna mess it up," Amanda nearly whispered.

Cyn double-checked the high safety fence that enclosed the perimeter of the roof, then her gaze followed her daughter's over the blanket of glistening, untouched snow. There were no footprints or dirt smears or slushy tracks. The old tar roof had been transformed into a winter wonderland.

"I always love the first snow," Cyn found herself saying.

"Snow's a magic trick," Amanda said.

"It's like you've just discovered a whole new world," Santa said.

To hear such sweet words spoken so gruffly almost made Cyn smile. She was sure Santa was thinking of *their* new world. The one that was glimmering and beckoning at the edges of her consciousness . . . calling to her to give him another chance, and to let him be a father.

"You first, Amanda." Cyn gave her daughter a tap on the behind.

Amanda bolted from the threshold and zigzagged through the snow with her arms outstretched, leaving a trail of pint-size footprints. When she'd nearly reached the fence, she whirled around, collapsed in the snow and waved. Cyn chuckled. Amanda looked so adorable—sitting in the snow in her ski pants and parka, with her knit hat pulled nearly all the way down to her eyes.

She glanced at Santa. He was leaning against the door frame and gazing into her face as if he'd been doing so for some time. He pushed himself off with his shoulder, stepped onto the roof, then turned and extended his hand with a flourish. "Ready?"

She smiled at his mock courtly gesture. Why couldn't the man always be this charming? she wondered as she placed her mittened hand in his gloved one. Even though he'd come to take her little girl, it was difficult to stay angry. "Lead the way," she said grandly.

He moved back a pace and she stepped over the threshold.

For a moment he merely grinned. "Bet you can't catch me," he whispered, leaning close.

He suddenly dropped her hand. Then he—like Amanda— flew across the roof, leaving Cyn to contemplate how his large footprints left a winding path right next to her daughter's.

"You better watch out!" Santa yelled just as the season's first snowball left his glove. It smashed against the door frame next to Cyn's head.

"You better not shout!" Amanda called. She started singing the well-known Christmas carol.

Cyn wondered whether or not Santa Claus *had* come to town. "Well, Mr. Santa sure has," Cyn murmured. She sucked in a breath of the harsh wintry air, wondering how things would work out.

When the next snowball broke against the door frame, Cyn took off, too. She bolted toward Santa and her daughter, flying alongside the trail of footprints they'd left in the

now, her own heels kicking up great sprays of powdery
ust.

What was it about running through a first snow that made
er feel so free and happy and alive? She only knew that it
id. Because as she ran toward Amanda and Santa, all kinds
f images flashed through her head. She thought of Es-
imo kisses, and the hot chocolates they might share when
ley were good and cold, and of wrapping paper crinkling
n Christmas morning. She thought of something else, too.
f the warmth that existed nowhere on earth—except in
nton Santa's embrace.

THREE DAYS TILL
CHRISTMAS...

Chapter Ten

Thursday, December 22, 1994

The typewriter could be anywhere.

Santa's breath fogged the air as he took in the Rockefeller Center tree, the ice rink, then the life-size, decorative old angels that were grouped around Rockefeller Plaza. He crossed Fifth Avenue, where adults—who were parents, just like he was now—waited in long lines in front of the windows at Saks. Their bundled-up kids clung to the red velvet queue ropes with little gloved fists; they looked inside with such wide-eyed wonder that Santa imagined their eyes might be attached by springs.

In the windows, elves busily hammered toys, a little red choo-choo train chugged along its track, and Santa Claus squeezed down a chimney. The other Santa decided to take a walk, since he had plenty of time before Too Sweet's evening promotion, which was a caroling trip to a home for children. He ambled on down Fifth, as if he might actually find the missing typewriter on the sidewalk or on display inside the Godiva chocolate shop.

Where was it?

And who would send such a note? Santa could only hope the culprit didn't intend to kidnap Amanda on Christmas. He'd spent all morning rifling through the employees' drawers at Too Sweet again, analyzing the personnel files and rechecking the typewriters. The perp had to be someone who worked for the company, someone who was inti-

mately acquainted with both the promotion schedule an
Cyn and Amanda's habits. But who?

And what am I going to get Cyn for Christmas? H
paused in front of the Warner Brothers Studio Store. As
crowded, glassed-in elevator rose, he realized that a large
than-life Superman was pushing it upward. He smiled an
kept walking. Choosing an appropriate gift for Cyn wa
plaguing him nearly as much as finding that fool type
writer. Somewhere—in this city that had everything, ir
cluding Superman to push the elevators—the appropriat
gift had to exist.

It couldn't be something too big. After all, he didn't know
whether she'd gotten him anything or not. Besides which, h
hadn't even kissed her for what felt like eternity, at least no
so that she was kissing him back, which was the only kin
of kiss that counted. Although they'd played in the sno
like schoolkids the previous night, they sure weren't lovers

And yet the gift couldn't be too small, either. Perfume
and scarves and gloves didn't seem right. Neither did choc
olates. A new blouse might be nice, but Cyn had closetsfu
Her toaster oven was embarrassingly ancient, but he simpl
couldn't bring himself to buy the mother of his child an ap
pliance.

If he only knew where he and Cyn stood, then he'd au
tomatically know what to buy. All he knew was that he ha
to touch her again, to kiss her and to make love to her. H
could still hear her cries of pleasure as surely as if she wer
standing next to him on Fifth Avenue.

But could he really love her again? It was hard to tell. H
feelings about her were getting all mixed up with his fanta
sies about having Christmas with a family. Maybe thos
sappy commercials they showed on television this time c
year were getting to him. Every program he watched wa
interrupted countless times by moms, dads and kids wh
called relatives, opened packages and hung stockings.

It made him feel as if everyone but him was having th
picture-postcard family Christmas that he'd always wante
He'd been so far from attaining it for so long that he'd nev
even admitted he wanted it—until Amanda. Still, could Cy

be the right woman? He hardly believed that a child could keep an adult relationship together.

He was so lost in thought that he nearly stopped in the street, while a crush of shoppers bustled around him. When a bag swung against him, he sidled closer to the storefronts.

Great. I would come to a dead halt right in front of Tiffany's. He stared in the window. A tiny gold pen for her appointment book? he suddenly wondered. He could have it engraved, which would make it more personal. But with what message? *To Cyn. Christmas 1994.* Hardly.

The door swung open. "Coming in, sir?" the doorman asked.

Santa nodded. A great whoosh of wind from the avenue propelled him inside. Pressed on by the crowd, he ambled past the gleaming glass countertops. Every dazzling jewel imaginable stared back at him, making him think briefly of The Grinch Gang. Then one particular ring captured his attention.

It was perfect. Santa didn't know much about diamonds, but it was rectangular, set in a no-nonsense thick gold band. It looked bold. Classic. It was so simple that it made all the other rings seem overly flashy.

If Santa *was* going to ask Cyn to marry him someday, it was the ring he'd buy. After a moment a hand appeared beneath the glass and withdrew it. Santa felt a little piqued, as if someone had just snatched away his own personal prize.

"I do believe this is what caught your eye, sir?"

Santa glanced up.

A clerk smiled back. "She must be a very special lady, if you're considering this one," the man said, holding out the ring.

Santa didn't know what to do, so he pinched the band between his thumb and finger and smiled down critically, as if "diamond buyer" were his middle name.

"Lovely suit," the clerk continued conversationally. "Christian Dior?"

I've come a long way from my past and childhood, Santa suddenly thought, looking into the clerk's eyes, which held an unmasked appreciation for the well-dressed, cosmopol-

itan man and potential client in front of him. Santa glanced
at the ring again.

"It's part of our Imperial collection," the man continued. "It's known as the Giancarlo gem because it was cut
last year in Amsterdam by Giancarlo, of whom I'm sure
you've heard."

Santa nodded as if Giancarlo from Amsterdam were his
best friend.

"It's an absolutely flawless diamond...."

"What it would be is presumptuous of me," Santa said
flatly. But then he thoughtfully turned it one way and another, and slowly raised it to the light.

"DOES EVERYONE HAVE their music?" Analise asked as she
hurried down the hall of the Harrison House, clutching a
stack of song booklets.

"I've got mine," Cyn called. "We'll do 'Holly Jolly
Christmas' first."

"Mr. Santa Claus and me gotta share," Amanda piped
in.

"Paxton?" Analise's voice rose. "We've got to find Paxton because he has the sack of gifts."

A man leaned in a recessed window at the home for children, watching and listening. Santa, who was carrying
Amanda, looped an arm casually around Cyn's shoulder
and headed toward him. *What a happy little family they'd
make,* the man thought, feeling annoyed. But not for long
he assured himself. One thing had led to another, and now
he had no choice but to kidnap Amanda. After all, the notes
hadn't garnered any negative press.

Still, kidnapping Amanda tonight would be impossible.
There was a time when taking her would have been as simple as stealing candy from a baby. In fact, whenever the
child was bored at Too Sweet, she'd often come to his office to round up stray toys. Now Anton Santa and Cynthia
were sticking to her like glue.

There was definitely no way he'd get to her tonight. The
many volunteers from the marketing and promotion departments filed past him. Unwittingly, most of them had
sold their Too Sweet stocks to him. And who could blame

them for wanting to sell? he wondered. The company wasn't worth nearly what it had been the previous year. He'd make it a fortune, though, once it was his.

His jaw suddenly clenched when he saw Paxton kiss Analise's cheek. The two were more intimate than usual, which was striking sheer terror into him. If they had a good heart-to-heart, his cover would blow sky-high.

Yes, time was running out, but all he needed was to strike one final blow at the company. With any luck the bad news of Amanda's disappearance would give the papers every reason to republish the particulars of Cyn's past, too.

Someone tugged his sleeve, and he turned.

"Hiding?" Cyn lowered her voice conspiratorially. "Playing the Grinch and trying to escape your caroling duties?"

"Me?" he joked. "Never."

"Well, c'mon," she said, pulling him forward. "Amanda's waiting for you."

"Oh, is she?" he returned, fighting to keep the irony from his voice. He only wished it were true.

"YOU CAN SING, SANTA," Cyn said. It was almost as amazing as the fact that she'd accidentally spied him in Tiffany's that morning. She just wished she'd been close enough to see what he'd bought. Paxton and Analise were ahead of them, heading down a long hallway and toward the stairwell. Amanda was snugly tucked between her grandparents, clutching their hands.

Santa's fingers tightened on Cyn's shoulder. "I mean, really sing," Cyn continued. As "Holly Jolly Christmas" had given way to "Frosty the Snowman" and "It's Beginning to Look a Lot Like Christmas," his smooth baritone had almost shocked her into silence.

"So, you like my fa-la-las," he teased.

How did that terse macho drawl manage to produce such clear liquid notes on other occasions? "Don't tell me," she said drolly. "You have yet another secret life."

He tensed beside her, breaking their stride, then relaxed again. "Other secret life."

"Oh, you know—" She smiled at him. "You accompany the New York Philharmonic in your spare time." His face became so serious that she was sure he was still hiding things from her. She desperately hoped he wasn't. No matter how much she wanted Amanda to herself, she also found herself wanting to give Santa a second chance.

"Close," he finally said.

Cold fear knotted in her stomach, making her realize how much she wanted to trust him—both with her and Amanda. "Close?"

"Backup for Pavarotti," he said gruffly.

Cyn giggled in relief. "A backup singer? I thought that was for people like Diana Ross, when she was with the Supremes."

"Ah, Cyn—" He grinned. "You're showing your age."

The way he said it made her feel that she was getting older by the minute—without a man. Without him. "I'm all of twenty-eight," she protested.

His face became stern. "And you're right."

"About what?"

"I used to sing with the Supremes," he said gravely as he swung open a fire door. Above them, the rest of the carolers passed through the upstairs doorway. As it slammed shut, Santa looked deeply into her eyes. "Can you still respect me?"

Her lips quivered with laughter. He put his arm around her shoulders again and began slowly taking the stairs. "Well," she said, her voice growing husky. "I guess I can live with your wretched past, as long as you never dressed up in one of those spangle gowns."

Santa turned and leaned his back against the stair rail, pulling her with him. His hands crept beneath her red blazer and settled on either side of her waist. She could feel their warm pressure through her blouse. "You think you could?"

She rested her fingertips against his chest. "What?"

"Live with it?" he asked softly.

One look in his eyes told her that he was no longer referring to his supposed past as a pop singer. She was pretty sure he didn't mean *live with it,* either, but *live with him.* "We've gotten ourselves into a pretty complex situation." She wanted to do whatever was right for Amanda, which meant not involving herself with Santa. Nevertheless, her fingers crept farther upward, over his pin-striped shirt.

Gazing into his eyes, she wondered what he'd been doing at Tiffany's. She'd gone there to pick up a gift for him. It still wasn't engraved, and she didn't even know if she'd really give it to him. After all, she'd also bought him a tie.

"Yeah," he finally said. "Things are complex, all right."

"We'll just have to see how things go," she murmured. *Between us.*

He cocked his head and smiled. "Well, there are certain things I've come to feel I can't live without."

"Like what?"

His hands slid around her back in a tight, intimate circle, and he nipped her lower lip lightly with his teeth before covering her mouth with his own. Cyn shut her eyes, feeling languid in his arms, and teased him with the flickering of her tongue. After a moment, she forced herself to lean away. "They're probably at 'Silent Night' by now."

He chuckled. "Maybe we could kiss till 'White Christmas.'"

"Surely, you don't mean for the next two whole days," she said raspily.

"That's exactly what I mean," he murmured, as if carols were the last thing on his mind. His palms roved upward on her back, pressing every last vertebra, then traveled down again, over her backside. Somewhere in the proximity of her thighs, he found her hand and his fingers twined with hers. "C'mon," he nearly whispered. "You haven't heard anything until you've heard me do 'Silver Bells.'"

Silver bells, she thought illogically, as he pulled her up the stairs. Her lips still felt damp and swollen, and for an instant, she was sure the bells he meant were of the wedding variety.

When they reached the room, her parents, Amanda and the others—Evan, Bob, Clayton and the members of the marketing and promo departments—were all looking pointedly at her and Santa. So were the four little boys who shared the room.

"I think we're in trouble," Santa whispered. He gave her a surreptitious pat on her rear end that turned her cheeks scarlet.

She playfully slapped his hand. "If you don't quit, you really will be," she whispered back as she glanced around the room. The boys looked clean, neat and well fed but, even so, Cyn felt suddenly sad. Paxton held out a large sack of gifts, and Amanda bounced up to each boy and delivered wrapped copies of *Little Amanda's Perfect Christmas*. Each boy also received a second gift, which Cyn had wrapped—footballs, catcher's mitts, baseballs, hockey pucks.

She glanced at Santa. They hadn't talked about his childhood for years now. Still she knew that part of Jake Jackson's history also belonged to Santa. He'd lived in foster care and had been in homes that were probably very similar to this one. He caught her gaze, saw her sudden sadness and seemed to know what she was thinking. His smile looked a little wan. Then he winked.

"Ready to sing the next carol?" Paxton asked as he closed the gift sack.

Analise smiled. "Now that Santa and Cyn have finally come from wherever in the world they were..."

"Now, now, Analise—" Santa caught Cyn's hand and squeezed it. "Save your breath for the songs."

"Let's sing 'O Little Town of Bethlehem.'" Paxton leafed through his caroling book. "Will you please start us off, Santa?"

"'O Little Town of Bethlehem, how still we see thee lie...'"

Once again his voice swept Cyn away. The notes were so true and perfect that the very air of the room seemed to expand, as if to make space for them. Everything seemed fuller somehow, including her heart. Maybe that could expand, too, and make room for Santa. Everything—from the kids' smiles, to the wrapped packages they'd delivered, to Amanda's Kelly green dress—seemed suddenly brighter.

"'In thy dark streets shineth the everlasting Light.'"

Outside, the night sky was dark and cold and clear. Great puffs of white steam rose from grates in the sidewalks.

Across Central Park, twinkling stars nestled in clusters around the spires of skyscrapers, and all around her, the lights of Manhattan burned bright. Beneath the window in the Harrison House, a horse stamped its hooves and then, at the urging of a carriage driver, began its regular route around the park.

Just at that moment a light snow began to fall again, making the world seem fresh and clean and innocent. And yet, Cyn thought suddenly, if Santa was right, there was a kidnapper in their midst. Someone who knew Amanda. Someone who was pretending to be her friend.

Suddenly the words swam in front of Cyn's eyes. As if sensing it, Santa's arm gracefully nuzzled around her waist again. Her cheek brushed against his shirt as she gazed at his strong profile.

She wasn't sure but thought that Santa, who had no family of his own, might want one, even if he wasn't the sort of man to openly say it. She knew he wanted Amanda. But could she give him her whole family? Would she?

She raised her voice a notch. It wasn't nearly as good as his, but the two melded together as surely as their lips did when they kissed, or as their bodies did when they made love. They finished the song, gazing into each other's eyes. "'The hopes and fears of all the years are met in thee tonight....'"

"GOODBYE!" Cyn called repeatedly. "And thank you."

"See you soon." Santa waved with one hand and held Amanda's with the other.

"Merry Christmas and everything," Amanda murmured sleepily.

Outside, the air smelled like burning wood and freshly cut pine. A film of icy snow coated Fifty-ninth Street, and it shimmered under the white lamplights, as if the pavement had been strewn with diamonds. Just across the street, Central Park was blanketed in snow. Everything looked so clean and crisp and white that Cyn couldn't help but think of Santa's shirts. "Drive safely," she called again.

As the last caroler returned a final wave, she sucked in a deep breath—it was so cold it hurt her lungs—then blew it out, watching it cloud the air. For a moment, she, Amanda and Santa merely huddled together on the stoop of the Harrison House. Finally Cyn snuggled her hands deep into the pockets of her down coat and chuckled.

"Hmm?" Santa glanced at her, raising his brows.

"It actually smells clean out here," she said wryly. "For once."

"Not the usual in the city," he said smiling. "I'll grant you that."

"And cold."

"Then I guess we'd better hold hands," Santa said.

"We're holding hands." Amanda sounded as grouchy as she looked tired.

"I mean, your mother's hand."

"Oh," Amanda said. "Okay."

Santa chuckled as he sidled close and dipped a hand into Cyn's pocket. When she shot him a playful, censuring glance, Santa said, "Well, Amanda said it was okay."

Cyn smiled as he started to pull her down the steps. She realized he was headed across Fifty-ninth. "The car's over on Fifty-eighth!" she protested.

"True." Santa nodded just as they made it across the street. "But look at Central Park."

She laughed as she stepped onto the sidewalk. "What else *is* there to look at?"

"More virgin snow," he said persuasively.

"What's virgin, Mommy?" Amanda asked.

Cyn watched Santa bite back a grin. "Thank you, Mr. Santa Claus," she said.

Santa gazed over the top of Amanda's head and rolled his eyes. Then he looked at Amanda. "Virgin snow is the best kind for making snow angels, sweetheart."

Cyn never would have guessed it, but fatherhood suited the man. "Not a bad answer, Santa," she admitted. Looking at him, she knew he was suited for more than just parenthood. Under the streetlamp, his slicked-back hair gleamed with streaks of light. His seductive smile lifted the corners of his eyes, so they crinkled with tiny lines. His lack of concern about how his camel coat blew open with the wind made him look dangerously cavalier.

"What's snow angels?" Amanda asked.

At that, Cyn laughed outright. "I think you'll find the questions never end."

Santa swept Amanda into his arms, then headed down the stairs, leading into the park. "C'mon. I'll show you."

"It's dangerous out here!" Cyn exclaimed, scurrying after them. "And Amanda's pretty sleepy."

"I am not!" Amanda shrieked. The tone alone made it clear that it was hours past her bedtime.

"And we're not going to the reservoir or the pond," Santa reminded, over his shoulder. "Just to the first patch of snow." When he reached the bottom of the stairs, he swung Amanda around, then deposited her on the ground with a flourish.

"It may be virgin snow, but it's still New York City," Cyn protested. She glanced around, realizing with relief that they were still under a streetlight. "Are you two actually going to wallow around on the ground?"

Santa shot her a mock contemptuous grin. "Now, Amanda, the first thing you have to do is hold your nose."

Cyn's shoulders began to shake. "Don't listen to him! You don't have to hold your nose!"

"Sure she does," Santa said. "It's New York snow and all. Remember?"

Cyn rolled her eyes.

Amanda dutifully pinched her nose, and when she spoke, she sounded as if she had a cold. "Mommy don't do it right."

"I simply can't believe this," Cyn managed to say, but she obediently held her nose, too.

"Now, you fall flat on your back," Santa continued.

Santa sounded as if he were doing a commercial for cold medicines. Cyn giggled. *This,* she thought illogically, *is the father of my child.* In her wildest imagination she'd never have guessed that Jake Jackson would reenter her life. She certainly hadn't imagined him standing in Central Park on a snowy night, looking utterly dapper except for the fact that he was holding his nose. She clamped her chattering teeth together.

"Angels are serious business," Santa said in a low, lethal voice.

"Yeah, Mommy," Amanda said, looking like an angel herself. Her cheeks were rosy and a white knit cap pressed her curls against her forehead.

"Pay attention now," Santa said, as if he were about to present the world's greatest magic trick.

Cyn watched in astonishment as all six-foot-plus of Santa stood at rigid attention, then fell backward. If he weren't so handsome, he would have looked like an ironing board falling over.

Amanda was so awed that she quit holding her nose. Her brows knitted together as Santa began to sweep his arms in great, wide arcs. Finally she said, "That's fun."

Santa's belly laugh filled the air. "I think I broke my back."

Cyn laughed and strode toward him, feeling Amanda follow close on her heels. She stopped when her toes touched the flat soles of his shoes. "Told you so," she said.

He groaned. "Did you come to help me up or to gloat over my carcass?"

"Oh," she teased lightly. "I kind of like you that way." And she did. His hair had flattened at the back and lay against the snow, as if against a pillow.

"What?" he asked. "Completely out of commission?"

She grinned, stretched her hand down and made a show of pulling him up. "You could help!" she exclaimed breathlessly, backing up as he walked into her. He casually put his arm around her.

"Wow," Amanda whispered, staring at Santa's imprint in the snow.

"Make a few, Amanda," Santa said softly.

"Go ahead, honey." Cyn leaned against Santa's chest and glanced toward the stairs. "We've got to get you home soon."

As sleepy as Amanda was, she was suddenly whirling like a dervish from one clean spot to the next. Within a few moments the ground all around Santa's imprint was covered with tiny Amanda-sized angels.

"We better go," Santa called after a few minutes. "We an make some more on the roof tomorrow."

To Cyn's amazement, Amanda didn't even protest but ran nto her arms. She settled her daughter on her hip. As she scended the icy stairs, she glanced over her shoulder, won-ering why Santa had lagged behind. She realized he was ight behind her, and she was pretty sure he'd remained here in case she might fall. What a guy, she thought, sud-enly smiling.

At the top, they paused and surveyed the scene below. At east twenty tiny angels, with shining, glistening wings, took light around Santa's large one. "It's strange," Cyn found erself murmuring, "but I feel like we're looking down on eaven."

"Heaven's in the sky, Mommy," Amanda corrected im-atiently. "You said so."

"But sometimes, honey," Santa said gently, "you can ctually find little pieces of heaven on earth."

Cyn glanced quickly at Santa. He was gazing down at Amanda, with clear eyes that looked full of love. After a noment he turned and headed toward the street. She began o follow but the snow angels caught her eye again. They eemed to beg the question of whether she could share her wn angel, her baby.

"Santa's sleigh awaits, ladies!" Santa called.

Whatever emotion she'd just seen in Santa's eyes now eemed tempered by the humor in his voice. She whirled round and gasped. Santa was waving at her from inside one f the Central Park carriages. "We've got to go home!" *Home. Does he really want it to become both his and mine?*

"He'll take us," Santa yelled.

"But the car—" She lowered her voice as she neared him. 'And I'm not even sure it's legal to go..."

"It's not, but I gave the man a heap of money." Santa eaped down lithely, then helped her and Amanda inside. 'I'll get the car tomorrow," he continued as he climbed in next to her.

The driver called, "Go, Prancer!"

"Do you think his name's really Prancer?" Cyn whis-pered as the carriage moved forward.

Santa chuckled. "He looked more like Vixen to me."

"I want Rudolph," Amanda murmured, making Cy smile.

For New York, the snowy night was quiet, and when th horse neighed in the silence, Cyn felt as if she'd been tran ported to another century. Amanda nestled against her an her eyes drifted shut. She seemed to breathe in rhythm wit the steady clip-clop of the horse's hooves.

"Here, Santa," Cyn said softly. She disentangled Aman da's arms from her neck and shifted in the carriage sea "Why don't you hold her?" *Your daughter. Our daughte*

"I think she's asleep."

Their gazes met and held in the dark confines of the ca riage. Shadows flitted over Santa's face. "Are you sure?"

"She's a little heavy for me," Cyn lied.

He'd held Amanda many times, but this was differen Cyn wasn't giving her child to him because he was he bodyguard, but because he was her father. "C'mor Amanda." He carefully lifted her from Cyn's lap. Amand sighed deeply and curled against his shoulder.

The carriage seat was small—made for cuddling—an Cyn scooted next to Santa. She leaned against him an rested her cheek against his chest, feeling as comfortable a Amanda. She sighed softly as he put his arm around he "I've lived in New York all my life but I've never been i one of these carriages."

"First time for everything," he said. Cyn couldn't reall see but felt his arm curl around Amanda's back. His han appeared over the top of her knit cap, and he smoothed he bangs.

A first time for him to be a father, Cyn thought. Throug the carriage window she could see all the untouched snow i the park. Next to her, Santa's hand, which was so strong an yet so sensual, continued to smooth the hair over Amar da's forehead.

She had robbed him of their little girl. It was strange ironic, since for so long she'd thought of him as the thief. H had stolen from her family, as surely as he'd stolen he heart. And yet, she thought now, maybe it was Anton Sant she'd loved all along.

No doubt her younger self had wanted the wild rebel she'd been in Jake Jackson. But perhaps she'd sensed another man deep down inside. Perhaps she'd known there was a real man beneath—an Anton Santa inside Jake somewhere.

Thinking that, Cyn didn't feel like such a fool. Looking at Anton Santa now, it was becoming clear that she hadn't been one. This man made snow angels and said things about there being heaven on earth. He watched over her and her baby. And yet, for all that, she couldn't quite bring herself to invite him into her bed again or to let him tell Amanda he was her father.

If she did those things, her comfortably predictable world would become just like the virgin snow. Every day with Santa she'd take a thousand steps she'd never taken before. Mundane, routine things would seem as fresh and new as they did to Amanda. And her heart would feel so full...like it could break again.

"Still there?" he whispered. He leaned and found her lips, parting them in a soft, slow, heartfelt kiss.

"I'm just not sure I believe what's happened in the past week or so," she murmured when he drew away.

"Maybe this will convince you." He reached up and grazed his thumb and finger over her cheek, in what was more of a caress than a pinch. "It's real, Cyn. You, me, Amanda—everything that's happening to us is real."

*TWO DAYS TILL
CHRISTMAS...*

Chapter Eleven

Friday, December 23, 1994

"You didn't have to come with me to get the car." In the back seat of the cab Santa draped his arm around Cyn as if to indicate otherwise.

She tweaked his nose playfully as their driver pulled to a curb nearer the Fifty-ninth street entrance to The Plaza Hotel than to the Harrison House. "But we wanted to."

Amanda giggled. "Somebody's gotta protect Mr. Santa Claus."

"Oh, Giantelli's!" Cyn exclaimed, glancing across Fifth Avenue. One look, and her mouth started watering. She'd thought only Santa could make her drool like one of Pavlov's dogs, but she'd forgotten about Giantelli's. Stacked arrangements of cheesecakes, Key lime pies, tortes, tarts and bite-sized chocolate confections beckoned through the gleaming windows. "I'll make the diet my New Year's resolution," she murmured contritely.

Santa shifted his hips in the seat, dug into his pocket and peeled the cab fare from a money clip. "Hmm?"

"Why don't you get your morning papers while Amanda helps indulge my sweet tooth?"

"Why go across the street, when I'd be more than happy to indulge it right here?" Santa got out of the cab and offered her his hand.

"The day you're as sweet as Giantelli's," Cyn quipped, "is the day when you-know-where freezes over."

"Where?" Amanda asked as Cyn caught Santa's hand and stepped onto the sidewalk, pulling her daughter with her.

Cyn chuckled. "Just you-know-where."

Santa's eyes narrowed with sudden seriousness. "I should come with you."

"Mom and Dad'll be here any minute," Cyn said, hating the sudden reminder that they might be in danger. She nodded in the direction of the pastry store, where a policeman was mounted on his horse. "There's a cop right there."

"Well, it's just across the street," Santa conceded, glaring toward Giantelli's windows as if each cake were a villain in the flesh.

"You look so cute when you're concerned." Cyn cozied beside him and planted a solid smack on his cheek.

The kiss decided him. "I'll grab a paper and meet you."

Cyn caught Amanda's hand and headed across Fifth saying, "It's a beautiful day, isn't it, honey?"

"Why can't you marry Mr. Santa like Beauty and the Beast?" Amanda returned in a complete non sequitur.

Cyn would have stopped in her tracks if the traffic light hadn't been about to change. When they reached the opposite sidewalk, she considered voicing a denial that would end Amanda's train of thought. "Would you like that?" she asked, instead.

"If we went to a wedding, would Mr. Santa be my daddy?"

He is already. Cyn cleared her throat and held open Giantelli's door. "I suppose so."

Fortunately, the shining glass cases of scrumptious treats caught Amanda's eye and she raced forward. "Mommy! We gotta get these Santa Claus cookies, 'cause Mr. Santa can eat them all. Lots 'cause he don't share."

"Won't," Cyn corrected automatically. She glanced over the counter, into a clerk's sympathetic eyes. "It's okay," she said. "We'll take a dozen." Her eyes dipped down, past the cheesecakes, to a number of chocolate cakes decorated with red-and-green-icing poinsettias. "And I'll take one of those and—" She pressed a hand to her heart and smiled. "And one of those incredible marzipan Christmas trees, please."

"Can I get a baby pie?"

Cyn squinted at the tiny round crusts stuffed with lime filling. "Three baby Key lime pies," she continued.

The clerk hastily boxed their purchases and secured them with string, then handed the boxes to Cyn over the counter.

"Amanda," Cyn said, "I can't carry these and hold your hand, so grab my coat pocket. Okay?"

Amanda immediately did as she was asked, and the clerk was nice enough to step from behind the counter and open the door for them. Outside, the air smelled as clean as it had the previous night. The morning traffic had turned the snow in the street to slush, but the day was glorious.

"Look! There's Grandmama and Granddaddy!" Cyn nodded across Fifth, while she and Amanda waited for the light to change.

"Granddaddy!" Amanda screamed. There was no way he could have heard at this distance, but Paxton waved.

Cyn felt a rush of pure happiness. She wasn't exactly sure where she stood with Santa, but the past seemed ages away. Now they were headed into the frontier of the future. As hard as it was to reconcile herself to sharing Amanda, Cyn knew Amanda needed her daddy. The icing on the cake today was that her mother and father had both agreed to meet them for brunch at The Plaza.

And maybe if Santa were really in my life, things would be as perfect as this day, she thought. It was nearly impossible to imagine him leaving. "C'mon, Amanda, our light's green."

Cyn heaved the cake boxes up, pressing them against her chest, then started across the avenue, moving at Amanda's pace. The roads had been salted, but where the snow came only to the tops of Cyn's high heels, Amanda's boots were covered to the ankles.

"Grandmama!" Amanda yelled. This time when she waved, she nearly slipped.

"Easy there," Cyn murmured gently, glancing at the light.

Amanda came to a dead halt and stared down, to contemplate a pile of snow. "Can we wait till Santa comes and saves us?"

Cyn heard a nearby motorcycle rev its engine. "C'mon, Amanda, the light's going to—"

Suddenly Amanda tugged Cyn's coat with superhuman force.

My baby's not that strong!

"What the—" The cake boxes pitched violently from Cyn's arms as she whipped around, her body no longer moving of its own accord. *What's happening?* She wrenched in the opposite direction, and her fearful gaze darted to her coat pocket, just as a rider on a motorcycle lifted Amanda into the air.

"Mommy!" Amanda screamed.

He steered with one hand. Amanda was clutched beneath his free arm and her legs flailed madly above his handlebars.

But she still had Cyn's coat.

Her baby was holding on for dear life!

Cyn spun across the icy snow, out of control, with nothing between her and the kidnapper but Amanda's small, outstretched arm.

"Don't let go!" Cyn shrieked. She clawed at the air, reaching for the cycle, but when the man gunned the motor, Amanda lost her grip. As Cyn lost her footing one of her high heels flew off, spinning toe over heel. She tumbled across the snow in a ball of fur coat, like a round, fuzzy animal. Out of the corner of her eye she saw Santa emerge from the gold-framed revolving door of The Plaza and amble down the red-carpeted stairs.

Cyn scrambled to her feet just as the light changed. Cars and trucks bore down on her, horns blaring, showing no inclination of stopping.

Santa was now coming at a dead run.

Cyn bolted for Giantelli's, so fast that she lost her other shoe, and wound up slamming into the policeman's horse. "My daughter!" she screamed. "My daughter! My daughter!"

The cop dismounted and flipped open his notebook.

"Didn't you see? Didn't you see what just happened?"

"Ma'am, you'll have to calm down," he said gently.

But the cycle was fishtailing toward Fifty-ninth! Cyn shoved the policeman, threw her foot into the stirrup, then kicked the horse hard before she'd even fully mounted. She realized the cycle was taking a shortcut through the park, just as the horse reared on its hind legs and shook its massive head like the devil, trying to throw her. Somehow her flailing hands snatched the reins. Before the front hooves even hit the ground again, the horse was off at a sprint.

Cyn hunkered down in the saddle, galloped down Fifty-ninth, and when she saw a stretch of low guardrail, managed to jump it. Up ahead, the cycle hit a trail path. The man was headed uptown. Cyn reached around and slapped the horse's backside, screaming, "Faster!"

She hadn't ridden since high school and the freezing air and metal of the stirrups were painful against her stocking-clad feet. Her hat had flown from her head, her gloves were in her pockets, and her stinging eyes were tearing so much that she could barely see. She squinted against the sun and wind. Where was he going? The pond? The zoo? The Tavern on the Green, she thought illogically.

He headed for the reservoir. Cutting through a stand of trees, Cyn felt her heart soar. She was gaining on him. He had Amanda in front of him and he was steering with both hands, which gave him more control. She jerked the reins with all her might, forcing the horse onto the tree-lined jogging path around the reservoir.

"Get out of the way!" Cyn sat up long enough to yell, but terrified joggers were already diving off the track. Barren, snow-tipped tree branches dripped with icicles just inches above her head. She ducked again.

"You can't do this, lady!" an irate runner screamed.

"You're going to kill somebody," a woman shrieked.

"I've had it with this city!" a man yelled. "I'm going to move! I swear, I'm going to..."

Cyn barely heard them. She slunk so far down that her chest hugged the horse's neck. Even though his blowing mane and her own hair slapped against her cheeks in stinging strips, she hoped the horse's neck might protect her from the furious onslaught of the wind. "Amanda!" she screamed, wishing her little girl could hear her but knowing she couldn't. "Amanda!"

The cycle veered off, heading for the West Side. Good, she thought as he disappeared between trees. He was on fresh snow. She could see tracks. But where was he headed?

Just as the horse burst through a thicket, the cycle popped a wheelie and jumped a guardrail. By the time Cyn reached the spot, there was no sign of the motorcycle. And no sign of her daughter.

She kept moving. She was now trotting down a West Side sidewalk on a horse stolen from the police. Her eyes darted everywhere, but she didn't hear a motorcycle or see Amanda. Her stockings were in shreds and she could no longer feel her feet. When she looked down, she realized that one of them wasn't even in the stirrup.

She kicked the horse's belly, glancing down one street, then another, thinking that the motorcycle was blue and green. The man had been dressed in black and had worn a black helmet. On either side of him, she'd seen Amanda's two little legs kicking the thin air, as if seeking a foothold.

Over and over Cyn saw that blue and green bike pop its wheelie and jump the white guardrail, and she clung to the image. She'd just been thrown over a perilous cliff and that mental picture of Amanda was like the branch she'd caught to save her life. *I will see my baby again.*

Just as she darted down yet another street, the driver of a car slammed on the brakes. They squealed, then the vehicle hit a patch of ice and swerved in front of her. The horse reacted, leaping upward and resting his weight on his back legs. When he came down, his hooves missed the hood by a fraction.

Something inside Cyn snapped. "Get out of my way!" she screamed murderously at the driver.

The passenger door swung open. "Get in!"

It was Santa.

He didn't wait for her to dismount, but leapt out of the driver's side, then hauled her down into his embrace. Cyn's arms clung to his neck as he ran toward the car. She didn't know if minutes had passed or hours. But she suddenly felt something almost resembling relief.

"Don't worry." Santa reached across her and slammed her door. "No man escapes me for long."

"No woman, either," she murmured numbly.

"OFFICER BLANKENSHIP'S horse is at Fifth and Ninety-fourth." Santa clutched the car phone with one hand and the steering wheel with the other. Once he'd relayed the message, he hung up.

"The motorcycle was green and blue, and I think it was a man, but now I don't know—I just don't know," Cyn rambled. "He had black clothes and a black helmet and he jumped the guardrail."

"Where do you think he was going?" Santa demanded.

"New Jersey, maybe," Cyn said shakily. "But maybe uptown." Her voice wavered. "I don't know, anywhere."

"Okay." Santa tried to concentrate on driving, while his eyes darted down the side streets and alleyways. That was better than contemplating the murderous things he was going to do to whoever had taken his daughter. He didn't want to think about how Cyn had looked on that horse, either. Furious, terrified, numb, lost. Oh yes, he'd kill the man who had done that to her.

It was all his fault. He'd been hired to protect Amanda, and at the crucial moment he'd gone to buy newspapers. He'd known he was doing the wrong thing, but when Cyn kissed him, there was nothing he'd deny her. She'd wanted to go to Giantelli's while he'd bought the papers. So he'd let her. Now, unless he got Amanda back safe and sound and soon, he'd never forgive himself.

He reached across the seat and squeezed Cyn's knee. Beneath her ripped stockings, it was like a knob of ice. "Here." He cranked the heat and trained the vents on her hands and feet. "Your shoes are on the floor. Your daddy got them."

"What are we going to do?" she wailed. She leaned forward and stared through the windshield.

"We're going to find her." Santa wished he felt as convinced as he sounded. "And you're going to start rubbing your hands together. You won't be much help to me with frostbite."

That got her moving. She began to vigorously rub her feet together, too. Then she quickly stripped off her stockings and slipped her bare feet into her shoes. "But she could be anywhere...."

"Don't worry," he repeated. "I got the plate numbers."

"You got the plate numbers!" she echoed, her voice leaping as if for joy.

"The cops are running them. I gave them the number in the car, too, and they'll call as soon as they have something."

"Oh, thank you." Cyn pressed both her hands to her heart.

It was clear she was talking to God now, not Santa. Santa smiled reassuringly, praying he wasn't encouraging false hope. "There's more."

"You think you know who did it?" Her every word seemed to have "please" after it.

He shook his head. "But there was a guy from the *Daily News*, hanging out in front of The Plaza, looking for celebrities. He got a picture. Paxton bought the film, and he's taking it to an hour developer. He can get the results faster than the police."

"A photographer?" Cyn scooted beside him in the seat, her neck still craning in one direction, then another, as her eyes searched for the motorcycle. "If the story gets out—" Her voice suddenly caught, and she choked down a sob. "I mean, if there's a ransom— Oh no, if this hits the papers, somebody else could call in a ransom."

"The *Daily News* guy is the only one we saw."

"Where's my mom? What..." Her voice trailed off again, as if talking required too much energy.

Santa hoped Cyn could hang on and stay strong until they found Amanda. "With your father. As soon as they drop off the film, they're heading to your place. That way, if any calls come, they'll be there. They'll call us every half hour. If we haven't found her by the time we get the pictures, we'll get blowups. I'm sure it'll turn up something helpful."

He didn't really see, but felt Cyn cross her arms over her chest and hang her head. He knew exactly how she felt. "Cyn, it's way too early to give up."

"I'm not giving up!" Once again, she scooted next to the passenger-side window, her eyes scrutinizing the streets.

Good, he thought. He could handle anger better than despondency. As much as he wished he could take her into his arms, and that they could comfort each other, they had to keep looking.

"It's a motorcycle!" Cyn suddenly screamed. "Behind us!"

He jerked the wheel so quickly that the car fishtailed. Coming out of the spin, he did a U-turn in the middle of traffic, then laid on the horn and punched the gas. He'd passed two cars before he realized the cycle was silver.

He glanced at Cyn. Tears shimmered in her eyes and glistened on her lashes. "For weeks we've known this was a possibility," he managed to say. "It's why I'm here."

Cyn whirled on him. "Then why don't you do something about it?" she shrieked.

Her voice, so full of accusation, hit him like a blow. "She's my daughter, too," he said as he braked for a light. He turned in the seat and looked at her just as her mouth dropped open in astonishment and one of her hands flew up to cover it.

"I'm sorry. I am so sorry."

When she blinked, a tear fell, zigzagging a rivulet down her cheek. She slid next to him and pressed her face against his arm. "Aren't you scared?"

"Yeah," he said softly.

"How can you stay so calm?"

I have to be strong for you. "It's my job," he said.

And then Cyn began to sob, her fingers closing around his arm, as if she'd never let him go. He wished he were a better, smarter, tougher man. A man who could have kept her safe. Right now he would give his own life to place his daughter in her mother's arms again.

Yeah, this was his job, he thought. And he'd been in this position many times. He'd been forced to watch and wait, listen and investigate. But the object he sought had never been his own flesh and blood. Or the child of the woman he now knew he loved.

"ANGELO MAY HAVE TAKEN Amanda?" Cyn asked shakily, for the umpteenth time, as Santa pulled the car to a curb in Spanish Harlem.

Santa wanted to say that in such cases even one's best friend could be the culprit, but didn't. He surveyed the old tenement walk-up and shook out his fingers; they ached from clutching the wheel. He and Cyn had made loops through Queens, the Bronx and Jersey before a call had come. The motorcycle was a messenger bike from Too Sweet. And it was assigned to Angelo Garcia. "How well do you know him?"

"Just to look at."

Cyn's fury was barely contained. Her reddened eyelids were still puffy, but her eyes had regained a steely expression. The woman was nothing if not a survivor. From the look of her, Santa knew he'd have to kill Garcia pretty quickly, otherwise Cyn would beat him to the punch. "I want you to stay in the car," he said.

"No way," she snapped, pushing open her door.

He got out, then surveyed her over the hood. "Doesn't look like a great neighborhood," he said, glancing around. Down the block was a burned-out building. Across the street, a wheelless car had clearly been stripped. Graffiti marred every vertical surface.

"And so you're going to leave me in the car?" she shot back, almost sounding like her old self.

He circled the car and headed toward the steps. "C'mon—but stay behind me."

The outer and lobby doors were both wide open. In the hallways, paint peeled from the walls. All the way up to the fourth floor Santa kept wishing he had his gun. If Garcia had Amanda—which Santa hoped he did—all hell could break loose.

"Stand back." He paused at the apartment door and waited until Cyn was positioned behind him. Then he rang the bell.

After a moment a woman began calling questions through the door in rapid-fire Spanish. A twinge of pain touched Santa's heart; it had been years since he'd heard a voice so ike his mother's. The woman was looking through the peephole and not seeing him.

"Delivery," Santa called.

When the door swung open, an elderly woman peered up at him. She was dressed in black, wearing an apron, and her long silver hair was piled on her head. "Delivery?" she asked in English. "What delivery?"

"I'm looking for Angelo Garcia," Santa said.

The woman's face lit up in smiles. "Come in, come in," she said, pulling Santa into the room. Cyn followed. Sounds of happy, chattering children floated down from the farthest reaches of the apartment. Just as the door closed, a twentyish man wearing running pants and a hooded sweatshirt strode into the room. He stopped in his tracks. "Ms. Sweet?"

With a sinking heart, Santa realized that the scene was all wrong. Amanda wasn't here. The place smelled of ham and turkey and strong coffee. A tree was thoughtfully decorated with beautiful handmade ornaments. The head of a hiding child suddenly popped up from behind the sofa. Angelo Garcia was looking at them with watchful concern. To find so much homeyness in such a bad neighborhood reminded Santa of his own childhood and nearly broke his heart. These were people who struggled to love each other, and who did so, in spite of the odds against them.

"We're trying to locate your messenger bike," Cyn finally said. "It's missing from the garage."

Angelo's lips parted in worry. "I parked it and turned in the key, like I always do." He shrugged. "There are always more robberies around the holi—" His eyes narrowed. "You've been crying. What's wrong?"

"We have to find your bike," Santa said.

"What happened?" Angelo's eyes shot between Santa and Cyn.

"We just—" Cyn's voice caught, but she quickly steadied it. "Hoped you might know something."

Angelo stared at them, with his hands on his hips. Then he started yelling in Spanish as he pulled a leather jacket from the closet. He shrugged into it, then dug a pair of sneakers from under the sofa.

He was just tying his laces, when the elderly woman—
probably his grandmother, Santa thought—appeared again
now yelling at the top of her lungs and carrying two brown
paper bags and a thermos. Santa remembered enough
Spanish to get the gist. Without even knowing why they were
looking, Angelo was ducking out of a family dinner to help.
After some negotiation, the woman gave Angelo a set of car
keys.

Realizing what was happening, Cyn said, "You don't
have to do this. I mean, we appreciate it, but—"

"It's Christmas—" Angelo leaned and quickly kissed his
grandmother. "And one look at you guys tells me this ain't
about a lost bike."

At the door, the woman put her hand on Cyn's sleeve and
handed her a bag of food and the thermos. "Everything is
okay? No?"

Santa watched as those infernal tears shimmered in Cyn's
eyes again. "I hope it will be," she whispered.

"WANT TO SPLIT THE LAST of the coffee?" Cyn asked as she
squinted blindly through the windshield. Nearly all the lights
in all the houses in Paramus, New Jersey, had been extinguished, and Santa swerved in a wide arc on the curving
road with only the Christmas lights to guide him. The many
trees on one large lawn had been strung with tiny white
lights, but the trees themselves were invisible in the darkness. Looking at those lights, strewn like diamonds tossed
against the black sky, Cyn couldn't help but feel as if Santa
were driving through the air and above the chimney's..
right into the sky and the stars.

"Sure," Santa finally whispered. "Coffee might be
good."

Cyn nodded, then glanced at the digital clock as she
poured from the thermos Mrs. Garcia had given them.
Hours had passed. Each minute of each one had felt like
eternity. Her body ached from sitting at attention, the pain
in her shoulders was nearly unbearable, and her head was
throbbing.

"Here, Santa." After he'd taken the cup, her fingers lingered on his sleeve for comfort. Then she found a foam cup

and poured herself the dregs. She drank with one hand and kept the other on the car phone.

It was three in the morning. At nine it had been established that not even blowups of the photographs rendered anything useful. At ten, Santa had forced her to eat one of Mrs. Garcia's sandwiches. At eleven, convinced the person they sought was from Too Sweet, they'd staked out Bob Bingley's house. He'd arrived home in a cab, half-inebriated, with a tall redhead hanging from his arm like a stocking. Kidnapping had been the last thing on his mind. At midnight, it had officially become Christmas Eve. And at one, Analise had driven to Evan Morrissey's house to discuss what was happening.

It had been decided that only Evan would be told. Bob, ever the party animal, had been too full of holiday cheer to be of use. Clayton Woods already felt guilty enough. And Santa and the Sweets couldn't have cared less about how tomorrow's widely publicized promotion should be handled. They just wanted to keep the story out of the press and find Amanda.

When the phone rang, Cyn snatched the receiver to her ear. "Yes?"

"I'm calling from a pay phone off the West Side Highway."

She felt disappointment set in. "Angelo," she said to Santa. Pulling the mouthpiece closer, she said, "I want to thank you for all your help."

"No problem, but I've got to get my grandmother's car back to her now. She's working an early shift tomorrow...."

Cyn nodded as Angelo listed the territories he'd covered. He'd been down every street and alley in Brooklyn, Queens, the Bronx and Staten Island.

"Thank you so much, Angelo," she managed to say again before replacing the receiver. Somehow she swallowed the rest of her coffee. Just as she crumpled the cup, her bloodshot eyes met Santa's.

For hours neither one of them had wanted to say it. The unspoken words had hung in the air. "We've got to go home," Cyn whispered now. "We've got to sleep."

For sixteen hours Santa had remained as he was now—hunched over the wheel, his eyes roving from one side of the windshield to the other. *He loves her,* Cyn thought. *Why hadn't she let him tell Amanda that he was her father? What if he doesn't have the chance?* "Don't even think it," Cyn said aloud.

"What?"

Cyn shook her head. "Sorry, I'm just—"

"Beat," he finished.

"The police know what they're doing," Cyn said softly. "They're looking, too. They'll look all night."

After a long moment, Santa stopped the car, backed into a driveway, then turned around. He headed toward Manhattan again. As he did so, sheer defeat crossed his features. It vanished as quickly as it had appeared, but it made Cyn feel nearly as helpless as the fact that Amanda was gone. She slid next to him and rested her head against his shoulder. "Santa?"

"Hmm?"

Her mouth went dry and she swallowed around the lump in her throat. "No matter what happens," she said. "I know how much you love her and . . ."

"And?"

"And I love you, Santa."

He didn't say anything, just swallowed once himself. Good and hard.

SANTA COULDN'T BEAR to enter the apartment. Amanda wasn't there. Paxton was asleep in a reclining armchair, a plaid coverlet pulled over his suit. The phone was in his lap and his hand still rested on the receiver. Analise was asleep on the sofa.

Cyn nodded toward the hallway. Before tonight, Santa couldn't have imagined Cyn looking less than perfect. But she did. Her hair was stringy from where she'd raked her fingers through it all day, and her eyes were more red than green. Tension made her face look tight.

He'd never needed her more. He stopped beside his door, reached out and caught her hand. "Good night," he whispered.

He didn't know what her eyes said in return. That he was a fool, maybe. That tonight everything was different. That they were too old and too tired to play games. "I need you with me," she said simply.

He pulled her close and hugged her, squeezing her tight. When he released her, he merely nodded.

In her room they didn't turn on the light but fell across the bed. "I feel guilty sleeping," she murmured in the darkness. "I don't think I can."

"You can," he said softly. He sat and slipped her shoes from her feet. "Where is your nightgown?"

"My dress is fine." Her voice was little more than a croak.

He rolled off the bed and headed for her chest of drawers.

"Second drawer," she whispered. He found something flannel and warm. Behind him he could hear her undressing. "Here, Cyn." He tugged her sleeves free, then folded the garment and laid it over the arm of a chair. Then he pulled her gown over her head. He mechanically stripped to his boxers, then slid beneath the covers and wrapped her in his arms. Her own circled around his neck. She settled on top of him, burying her face in his chest.

"I feel as if . . ."

Her voice trailed off and her breathing steadied, becoming even. Santa was sure she had fallen asleep. He needed her more tonight than he'd ever thought he could need anyone. Even though she lay on top of him, she was the only thing anchoring him to the world.

"If . . ." she began again.

"What, Cyn?" His palms rubbed over the warm flannel of her gown, molding to the contours of her back.

"If I go to sleep," she murmured, "we won't find her."

"We'll find her." And they would. He would. He had to. "Can you sleep?"

"Yeah," he lied, knowing he couldn't. "I think I can."

"I've never felt so alone." Her voice was so low he could barely hear it. Any second she really would drift off.

"You're not alone," he said. *You'll never have to be alone if you don't want to be.* "I'm here. Right beside you."

She inched upward, and her lips sought his. He kissed her back slowly, feeling a comfort that transcended passion. Her lips said that bad things happened to good people, and that they were there for each other.

He wouldn't have thought it possible, but the kiss deepened, until that comfort only she could offer turned to passion. And yet, what he felt wasn't so much her lips and tongue, or how her belly curved against his aroused body, but her trust, her love, and her ability to give.

She moved slowly on top of him in the darkness and lifted her gown, while his hands slipped beneath it and slowly glided over her breasts. As she slid his shorts down his thighs, her nipples grew taut against his palms.

He kicked his shorts from his ankles, then pulled her fully on top of him. He shut his eyes, giving himself over to the sensations of her mouth on his. If their first kiss tonight had been of comfort only, this one was nearly feverish. Their tongues touched in an increasingly desperate desire to forget all that had happened.

Cyn moaned softly as her long legs opened and trailed down the sides of his thighs. His flattened palms curved around her waist and downward. Cupping her silken backside, he lifted her.

For just a heartbeat—when she touched him, to guide him inside her—his lips forgot how to kiss. As she sank slowly onto the length of him, he drew her closer and closer, inch by inch, until his arms tightly circled her waist.

He made love to her by barely moving. He nested inside the safe, warm haven she offered, until her breath became nothing more than catching sighs. He was sure he couldn't wait for her, but then she exhaled a soft sound of surprise that wasn't quite a moan, and rocked against him, over and over.

For the next minute all he could see was blackness. Then, in his mind, an arching stream of white-hot fire seemed to cut through the darkness. His muscles tensed until they were as hard and as rigid as steel. His hands gripped her backside and he drove her down on him, hard, as his hips thrust off the mattress to meet her. He exploded, feeling as if there could be no end to it. He so desperately wanted to savor this moment of forgetfulness.

"Oh, Cyn," he whispered, running his hands over her back.

She shuddered against him and brushed a hand over his head. She'd meant to smooth his hair but she was too tired, and her palm merely dropped onto his forehead. He wished he'd said something in the car when she'd said she loved him. All he'd been able to think was that he'd nearly had his family—only to lose Amanda.

"Cyn?"

He was sure she was asleep now. He said it anyway. "I love you, too."

CHRISTMAS EVE...

Chapter Twelve

"Just let her sleep," Santa muttered softly. It was 10 a.m. He hadn't slept at all until dawn. Now he was out of the shower and already in his trousers. As he buttoned the newly laundered shirt he'd brought in from the guest room, he watched Cyn's shoulders rise and fall.

The sleeves of her gown were pushed to her elbows, and the spread was bunched around her waist. One of her feet peeked out at the foot of the bed. He could see only half her face; the other was pressed into her pillow. The tightness around her eyes had vanished, and her lips were curled into a near smile. She looked so untroubled that Santa decided to let her sleep, at least until he'd called the police station and picked up the newspapers.

He tucked in his shirt, still watching her and wondering what would become of their relationship. Then he shrugged into his jacket and headed for the kitchen phone. In the living room, Analise and Paxton had barely moved. *Nothing like a heavy sleep to cure us of reality,* he thought, as he strode down the hallway. He wished he was the proverbial sandman, and that he could send them all to the land of dreams until he'd found Amanda.

He wasn't hungry, but he grabbed a knife from a drawer and a piece of fruit from a basket on the kitchen table. He was halfway through both dialing and peeling before he realized he'd gotten himself a pear rather than an apple.

"Officer O'Malley," he said when a receptionist came on the line. The man in charge of the case had the decency to answer on the first ring. *Good. He's been looking.* "This is Anton Santa. Any news?"

"We're still working on it. All we've got to go on is the bike, and it's so small it could be anywhere."

Santa wasn't surprised. If there'd been a break in the case, the ringing phone would have awakened the house by now. "I'm going back to Too Sweet," Santa said. "I'll start interviewing employees again."

"You'll find a Detective Black over there." O'Malley exhaled a cop's world-weary sigh. "He's been there all morning."

"Thanks. We appreciate all you're doing."

"This kind of thing's a real nightmare," O'Malley returned. "A shame on the holidays. We'll do everything we can to find the girl."

"She's my daughter," Santa found himself saying.

"I thought you were the body—"

"Yes. *And* she's my daughter."

"I understand, sir," O'Malley said gently, just before he hung up.

He didn't have a clue, Santa thought, trashing the pear core and silently heading down the hall. Just as quietly, he opened the front door and shut it behind him. As he waited for the elevator, his mind replayed the thousand times he'd looked into someone's eyes and said, "I understand."

Now the only one who understood was Cyn. They'd shared terror, grief and comfort. He'd never felt as close to anyone as he had to Cyn in the past twenty-four hours. But what had their lovemaking meant? Commitment or comfort?

He stepped into the elevator, without bothering to greet the operator, thinking that he'd been undercover, when he'd met her. He'd been so close to criminals that he could be mistaken for one. Hell, he'd even enjoyed pretending to be one. Four years ago, in the excitement of his undercover work, the only thing he'd regretted was not being able to tell Cyn the truth. But now, for the first time, he was truly on the other side of the law. The side where he was the parent of the victim.

"You okay, Santa?"

The doors opened. He glanced from the lobby to the operator. "Morning, Jim," he said gruffly. The man's concerned glance reminded him that he was usually more chatty. "I'm fine," he added as he stepped out. "And back in a second. I just need to get the papers."

"I'll hold the elevator."

Santa strode down the corridor and out the front doors. He dropped quarters into the machines at the corner and pulled out the papers: the *Times,* the *Daily News,* and *Newsday.* He shoved them under his arm and headed back inside. The temperature had dropped, and he found himself hoping that Amanda—wherever she was—wasn't outside. *Don't even think it.*

"You were quick this morning," Jim said jovially.

Santa nodded. "Yeah." As the elevator began its ascent, he pulled out the *Daily News.* He looked at the headlines and a familiar feeling of surety hit him so hard that he felt as if he'd been punched in the gut. It was more than a hunch. He'd found her. "Hurry up," he said.

Jim chuckled. "An elevator's only got one speed, Santa."

When the doors finally opened, Santa bolted down the hall. He pounded on the front door as he opened it. "Everybody up," he yelled. "Get up."

He bounded past Analise and Paxton, rushing straight for Cyn's room. "Cyn?" He leaned and shook her shoulder gently. "Cyn?" She rolled over and her green eyes opened in slits.

"I know where she is," he said quickly. "Get dressed."

She jerked upright. "Where?"

He was already halfway to the door. "Evan's, I think."

"Evan?" Analise yelled from the living room, sounding wide-awake. As Santa walked in, she jumped from the sofa and began wiggling her feet into her shoes. "But I was at Evan's last night. I didn't see anything that would—"

"Has either of you told anyone else she's missing?"

"No." Analise shook her head and brushed the skirt of her rumpled suit. "Maybe a policeman told someone."

"Of course I didn't tell anyone," Paxton said groggily. He squinted at Santa as if he couldn't quite remember what was happening.

Cyn scurried into the living room, her stockings trailing over her shoulders. Her eyes riveted on Santa's, she began to don her stockings, matter-of-factly and in front of everyone.

"It's in the paper," he said. He tossed the *Daily News* toward the coffee table, but Analise snatched it up before it even landed.

"That—that—*man.*" Analise's voice was so murderously hot it could have boiled water. Her head jerked up from the headlines and she stared at Paxton. "You never had an affair with Eileen, did you?" While she waited for a response, Analise staggered backward a pace, as if her mind were reeling and she couldn't quite keep her footing.

"Mother, we're trying to find Amanda!" Cyn shrieked.

"Eileen?" Paxton gasped. "My assistant? You think I had an affair with my—"

"Evan told me you—" Analise dropped the paper as if it had just scalded her skin. She reached over the back of the sofa and grabbed her coat. "I am going to go kill that man now," she announced with lethal calm.

"You're staying right here," Santa said smoothly. "Call the police. Tell them I'm at Evan's."

"Me, too!"

Cyn was shouting even though they weren't a foot apart. Santa was hardly going to argue. "Fine."

"He's the only one who could have told the media." Cyn ran back to her room and emerged with her and Santa's coats. "I don't know why he'd do this," she continued, her voice catching with relief. "But I don't think he'd hurt her."

"Why would he kidnap her?" Paxton asked, sounding confused.

"Because he wants to take over Too Sweet," Analise screeched. "That's why." She groaned. "And I'm the one who hired him! I thought his Wall Street background would—"

"Eileen?" Paxton asked again, clearly beginning to wake up. He shook his head. "I thought you were mad because

I'd finally decided to track down Jake Jackson. While I was trying to protect Cyn during the trial, you seemed so upset about all the lies I told ... and you said Jackson was Amanda's father, no matter what illegal activities he'd been involved in—''

"You knew!" Cyn gasped.

"Knew what?" Analise asked.

Paxton flushed guiltily. "You two better get going," he said. "We've got to find Amanda."

Santa grabbed Cyn's hand. "I suspected he knew," he muttered as he pulled her toward the door. "I asked you directly whether or not Jake was Amanda's father, Paxton," Santa called over his shoulder. "Why did you lie?"

"You two needed the chance to get to know each other again," Paxton replied.

Santa groaned. Under his breath, he muttered, "Your father is nuts."

"Call the cops," Cyn yelled at Analise as she went out into the hall. "You really think Evan has her?" she asked Santa.

"Sometimes I get a strong gut feeling," he drawled. "And I've never been wrong."

"So, you *know* he's got her?"

Santa put his arm around her, glad he wasn't lying this time. "I know he does, and she's just fine."

"THE BIKE'S RIGHT IN the damn driveway," Cyn seethed. Her eyes darted to the upper windows of the two-story house. If only she'd see Amanda's face peek out from behind the curtains...

"It's halfway behind a bush. Analise wouldn't have seen it in the dark." Santa pulled into a driveway two houses down.

Before they were even parked, Cyn pushed open her door and bolted. As soon as she saw Amanda safe and unharmed, she fully intended to commit her first murder. She didn't get far. Santa caught her elbow and she spun around.

"Keep your head," he chided softly.

A thousand protests shot to her lips, but she knew he was right. Looking into his eyes, she knew she could trust him.

She'd shared the best moments of her life with Santa, and he'd held her tightly during the worst. "I just want her back so bad," she said.

"So do I." He steered her around a hedge that separated the lawns. When they got next to the house, they circled around, staring into the windows one by one. Through the cracks in the curtains, it seemed that no one was home.

"Where is he?" Cyn murmured. "And where are we going?" she continued, when they'd reached the front door again.

"This time we'll see if one of the windows won't op—" Santa nearly grinned.

"What?" Cyn asked urgently.

He nodded in the direction of the porch. "The front door's open. C'mon."

She did a double take, then kept close to Santa as he cautiously approached the porch. "Looks closed to me," she murmured. But sure enough, it was open an inch; there was barely a crack between the door and the frame. *Does anything escape this man?* She watched his lips part.

"Get behind me," Cyn whispered before he could say it. She dutifully took the backup position. He nudged open the door, then went in. She followed. Just in front of the door were the stairs. The place felt empty.

"Hello," Santa called.

Cyn nearly jumped out of her skin.

"You here, Evan?" Santa sounded so jolly that he might have been delivering Evan's Christmas gift. He glanced at Cyn and shrugged.

"Let's check the downstairs." She was already moving toward the dining room, on her right.

Santa frowned when they reached the stairs again. He glanced up them. "He's hiding."

"After you," Cyn whispered.

They moved stealthily, hugging the wall. When they were halfway down the upper hall, they heard a scraping sound. Cyn jerked her head in the direction of the farthest room. Someone was moving around in a closet. Those were hangers scraping over the bar. She ran toward the sound, close on Santa's heels.

"Amanda!" Cyn exclaimed. She tore through the bedroom so quickly that she banged her hip on the side of an ornate brass bed. The room was empty, but the closet door was shut, and a key was in it! Cyn quickly twisted the key and flung open the door.

"Glad someone finally showed up," Evan said drolly. He was seated on a footstool, in the middle of the walk-in closet, with his feet propped on a typewriter. A silver tray, laden with the remains of someone's breakfast sat on the floor.

"He doesn't have her," Cyn murmured, barely aware that Santa charged past her. A moment later she realized he was dragging Evan from the closet by the scruff of the neck.

"Watch my suit," Evan protested. Santa cuffed him to one of the brass curlicues in the headboard, just as the phone on the nightstand began to ring.

"Where is she?" Santa demanded.

His drawl was so calmly menacing that Cyn figured Evan was about to die a slow, torturous death. "Spit it out, Evan," Cyn found herself saying, "or I'll kill you before he does. Where's my little girl?"

Evan's eyes narrowed. "I've heard the rumors about you and your burglar boyfriend, you know. And I'd like to inform you that your little girl clearly carries the genes of her criminal father." He smiled a sharklike smile. "Mind answering my phone?"

"Where?" Santa repeated. He advanced on his prisoner, murder in his eyes.

Either Santa's threat or the sudden wail of approaching sirens loosened Evan's tongue. "She was in the closet. This morning she kept yelling that she wanted breakfast. When I came in with the tray, she locked me in. The little creep took my wallet, too."

The phone was still ringing, and outside two cop cruisers squealed into Evan's driveway. Car doors slammed. "Why'd you do it?" Santa asked.

"Every time something bad happens to the Sweets, their stocks plummet." He flashed a grin at Cyn. "And I own more of them than you think I do."

The phone was driving her crazy. She snatched it up, pre
pared to say that the man of the house was under arrest
Then she realized that Evan might have a partner. She
clenched her jaw, waiting for the caller to speak first.

"Is someone there?" Analise finally asked.

"Mom?"

"She's here!" Analise exclaimed breathlessly. "She'
here!"

Cyn gasped. "Amanda?"

"Paxton just went to get her," Analise said in a rush
"She pulled right up to the store in a cab. After we called the
police, we realized that Evan wasn't handling things here
and— None of it matters. She's at the store!"

"Be right there." Cyn hung up, just as Officers O'Mal
ley and Blankenship charged into the room and began
reading Evan his rights.

"Is she okay?" Santa asked.

Cyn nodded. "She's at the store." Santa caught her in his
embrace and swung her around high in the air.

IT WASN'T AMANDA, but Bob Bingley who met them at the
door. A folded Santa suit, a wig and beard were piled in one
arm. He clasped his free hand tightly around Santa's bicep
as if he meant business.

"Where's Amanda?" Santa attempted to shake off Bob'
grasp.

"Third floor," Bob snapped.

Cyn ran toward the crowded escalators. "Bob, there are
things happening here that you don't know about."

Santa chased after Cyn. Since Bob wouldn't let go, he
simply dragged the poor man behind him. He knew he could
disengage himself, but he didn't exactly feel comfortable
belting Analise's right-hand man. He wanted to hurry
though. He wouldn't believe Amanda was safe until he saw
her. Up ahead, Cyn was already weaving through shoppers
and climbing the escalator stairs. She whirled around.

"Bob!" she screamed over the heads of the bystanders
"Let go of him!"

"Sorry! Some of us are trying to ensure that this pro
motion runs smoothly!" Bob tightened his grip on Santa as

they took the first stair. "But no one bothered to show up this morning—not you or Paxton or Analise or Evan—not even Santa Claus! He's sick again. Only Clayton came to work. So, Cyn dear," Bob railed, raising his voice to a shrill pitch, "I need your bodyguard in exactly two seconds."

"I can't believe this," Santa muttered. "You want me to be Santa Claus." To appease Bob, he began pulling the Santa garb over his suit while they jostled customers aside and ascended the moving steps.

"You can't go up!" Bob exclaimed, even though they'd already reached the second floor.

"Give me the pants." Without waiting, Santa jerked them from Bob's arms and stepped into them as he walked. Cyn was nearly to the top of the next escalator.

"Not upstairs! The promotion's down here! The kids are waiting beside Santa's chair!" When Santa grabbed the wig and beard, Bob wrung his empty hands nervously. "Oh, no, those pants are falling down. Padding. I've got to find extra padding!"

By the time the three of them reached the third floor, Santa found himself dressed from head to toe in the red velour suit.

Bob was still pawing at his sleeve. "Put on that beard. It's got elastic in the back!"

"Mommy!"

Santa forgot Bob entirely. His little girl shot out from behind a Barbie display and ran toward Cyn in a blur of green velvet. He watched Cyn drop to her knees and catch Amanda in her arms. She stood slowly, still clutching their daughter, and then turned around and around in circles.

Santa bounded toward Cyn and Amanda—his girls—and reached them just as Cyn collapsed in an armchair. "Are you all right?" Her hands roved over Amanda's arms, legs and back. "Are you?"

Santa was barely aware that Analise and Paxton were standing near the chair. He only had eyes for Amanda, who now wiggled in Cyn's lap. "I get to wear the same dress for two days," she said happily. "And Evan didn't make me get a bath or anything."

When Cyn glanced at Santa, tears were streaming down her cheeks. A wealth of understanding seemed to pass between them. Regardless of where they were all headed, their baby was safe. *Sand,* Santa thought illogically, his eyes stinging. *Must have sand in my eyes.*

He blinked just as Amanda looked at him. "You're not Santa Claus!"

He sank down beside the chair, squatting on his heels. He felt so relieved he could barely breathe. His little blond-haired, green-eyed girl was the most beautiful sight in the world. She really was his, too. Anton Santa had really brought that kind of beauty into the world. He cleared his throat. "There's only one Santa," he managed to say. "I'm just a representative."

Amanda's eyes narrowed. They seemed touched by more sadness than a child could know. "You can't hear what we want?"

"You mean, what you want for Christmas?" he asked softly.

Amanda's face became a mask of forced bravado, and Cyn began rocking her, as if sensing something was wrong. When Amanda blinked, one round tear rolled down her cheek. How could his daughter smile gleefully one minute, then cry the very next? Santa wondered.

"I gotta see Santa!" she suddenly wailed.

"You can talk to me," he said.

His little girl's arms stretched for his neck. As Amanda fell from Cyn's lap onto his knee, Cyn shook her head in worry. Her eyes said, *Please fix this, Santa.*

A lump lodged in his throat. "So, what do you want for Christmas?"

"I don't want nothing. I gotta get a daddy," Amanda said in a rush. Then the floodgates opened. One minute she'd been talking; now she was sobbing against him. His chest constricted, and he rubbed her back. "It's all right, sweetheart," he soothed.

Finally Amanda sniffed. "You're nice," she said weakly. "Right?" She looked at him as if his eyes might contain the answers to all the questions in the world.

He nodded. "Yeah."

Words suddenly poured from her lips so fast that he couldn't keep pace. "What about a girl whose daddy was so bad that he had to be a con-vic and then she stold money and didn't go where she was spose'd to—" Amanda stopped just as suddenly as she'd started and hiccuped.

Santa knew exactly which convict daddy she was talking about. He had half a mind to tell her the truth now, Cyn be damned. Instead he asked, "What money?"

Amanda hung her head and swiped at her cheek with the back of her hand. "The cab man counted, and he said he was spose'd to take fourteen to come home, and he said I took three hundred dollars 'cause it was at Mr. Mor'sey's house." A sob caught in her throat. "I still got the rest! I could give it back!"

"We know you took three hundred dollars from Evan's wallet, honey." The edge in Cyn's voice cut through Santa's heart like a razor. "But you had to, to come home. It's okay."

The words only sent Amanda into another fit of sobs. "He— he—"

"Who Amanda?" Cyn asked urgently.

"Mr. Mor'sey says—says I was mean..." Amanda sniffed.

"What, honey?" Santa ducked his head so he could hear her.

"'Cause my daddy is mean and me, too, like Little Amanda in our story and that's why I gotta get a new daddy," she whispered mournfully. "'Cause I steal stuff—" Amanda sucked in sharply. She pursed her lips, holding her breath, then exhaled shakily. "I steal Barneys and Barbies and Slinkys—and I'm a crim'nal!"

Santa had had about all he could take. He found himself glaring at Cyn. His eyes said, *let me tell her.* And Cyn wavered. He hated her for it. His little girl's heart was breaking, and he could do little more than have a staring contest with her mother. Even worse, Cyn won. He blinked first.

"Okay." Cyn sighed warily. "Go ahead."

He felt his heart drop to his feet. Did this mean Cyn would eventually be willing to let him into *her* life, too? "Amanda?"

"If I gotta go to jail, do I meet my daddy?" Amanda whispered.

Santa winced. "Amanda, this is going to be confusing but I want to tell you something very important." *How am I going to tell her this?*

"Listen to Santa," Cyn said softly.

He wasn't sure, but he thought he heard Analise and Paxton nearby, urging him on. Cyn's hand dropped onto his shoulder. She squeezed, in support. Amanda stared at him intently and his heart started to pound. "This is going to be a little confusing."

Amanda's eyes looked murderous. "You said that, Santa Claus."

He opened his mouth, then shut it again. Cyn squeezed his shoulder harder. *Hell, just say it.* "I'm your daddy, honey."

Amanda looked nonplussed.

"I used to be a policeman," Santa continued. "That's what I was when I first met your mother." He watched for a reaction, but Amanda looked baffled. He didn't blame her. He didn't know where he was headed with this, either. "I was working undercover, so your mother never really knew my real name. She thought my name was Jake Jackson."

Amanda's eyes widened.

"I'm your daddy," he said again.

"You're my daddy?" she asked in astonishment.

"That's the main point," Santa conceded. Amanda wrenched around in his arms and stared at Cyn.

"It's true, Amanda." Glistening tears caught in Cyn's lashes. "He really is."

Amanda's mouth formed a round, perfect O. She turned around again and stared at Santa, as if she'd never seen him before. "When I went to Mr. Mor'sey's, you got married and had a wedding?" she asked slowly.

Santa was beginning to feel as if he were going to collapse. He glanced at Cyn, who averted her gaze. "No," he said.

"So, you gotta get a wedding now?"

His throat was so dry it was beginning to ache. "I suppose we *could,*" he said gently.

Amanda wiggled in his lap. "You gotta, to be a daddy."

When Cyn looked at him, he wished he could read her mind. Tears shimmered in her eyes, as if she might start sobbing. Her lips were twitching, almost as if she might laugh. Her eyes had widened in surprise. He was a master at reading people, but he couldn't have second-guessed her if his life depended on it. And maybe it did, he suddenly thought.

Santa became conscious of the fact that they were in a corner of a crowded toy store. People milled around them, casting curious glances their way. Even so, they remained a blur. He'd found his inner circle—his family. He belonged with Cyn and Amanda. *Yeah,* he thought, *suddenly Christmas doesn't seem so lonely, after all.* "Cyn?"

She looked as if she'd guessed what he was about to say, but couldn't quite believe it. "What?"

"Will you marry me?"

She gasped. "Are you serious, Santa?"

"He's serious, Mommy." A pleading tone crept into Amanda's voice. "I can tell."

"Marriage is a lifelong commitment," she murmured, as if that might not have crossed his mind.

Was Cyn going to turn him down? Somehow he managed to smile. "That's the general idea."

Amanda tugged on his sleeve. "If we get married, do we all live in our house?"

He chuckled softly, his gaze never leaving Cyn's. "We do."

"Cyn!" Bob wailed. "There are a hundred kids downstairs!"

Santa glanced toward Bob. He was hovering nearby, holding two pillows and a belt. Santa sighed and looked at Cyn again. "I'd tell you to think it over, but I don't really want to wait until tomorrow."

"But who could say no on Christmas?" Cyn whispered.

"Exactly," Santa returned.

"It's not that I don't want—" She squirmed in the armchair, straightening her posture. "I mean, I do want to marry you. It's just—so many things have happened. I haven't really thought too much..."

He squinted at her. "But you want to marry me?"

"Oh, yes." She sounded shocked.

Amanda flung her arms around his neck. "You're my daddy!"

"She just said yes!" Bob exclaimed. Amanda scurried to the floor as Bob gripped Santa's elbow and jerked him to his feet. Cyn rose gracefully from the armchair. She was smiling, even though her eyes were misty. If she'd really said yes, it was the most convoluted yes he'd ever heard, he thought.

"I just said I was going to marry you, Santa," Cyn said, huskily. "Aren't you going to kiss me or something?" She reached across the space that separated them and gave him one of her trademark pokes in the chest. "Scared, Santa?"

"Oh, terrified," he drawled, catching her finger. He pulled her close, his lips hovering above hers.

"You're not really, are you?" she asked, snuggling against his chest.

"Me? Never." His lips grazed hers as he spoke and his arms tightened around her waist. "You want to know why?"

"Why?" she returned raspily.

"Remember that gut feeling I was telling you about?"

She gazed deeply into his eyes. "The one that's never wrong?"

"Yeah," he whispered. "I've got it right now."

"Mind telling me what it's saying?" Cyn murmured.

"That you're a sure thing, Mrs. Santa Claus." She smiled against his lips when he kissed her, just the way he meant to keep her smiling for the rest of their lives.

CHRISTMAS DAY...

Epilogue

Sunday, December 25, 1994

"Get up."

Santa bit back a smile and kept his eyes squeezed shut. He'd meant to return to the guest room but had fallen asleep in Cyn's arms. Not that Amanda cared. She was now wetting her fingers, presumably by sticking them in her mouth, and then repeatedly wiggling them in his ears. When he suddenly opened his eyes, catching her in the act, she giggled naughtily. He smiled. "Merry Christmas, Amanda."

His daughter hovered over him. "You gotta get up, so maybe it will be," she crooned. Santa glanced down at his bride-to-be, who nuzzled against his shoulder and opened her eyes.

Cyn squinted at him, then at Amanda. Was it really Christmas morning? she wondered. And was she really lying here with Santa? It all seemed like a dream. "Merry Christmas," she murmured.

"Santa came," Amanda announced. She shifted from one foot to another in excitement, and fidgeted with her gown, tugging the front of it. "I know, 'cause he ate those cookies we left on the stool by the chimney."

Somehow Santa managed not to smile. They'd been chocolate chip. His favorite. "Why don't you go sit on the sofa? And your mom and I will be out in a minute."

Amanda bugged her eyes and pursed her lips, in an exaggerated show of pique. "Don't be a fem'nist."

Santa arched a brow.

Cyn giggled, feeling comfortably cozy nestled against Santa's rock-hard chest. "She means an annoyance, remember?"

"Ah." Santa grinned. "Your mother and I may be feminists, but the sooner you go, Amanda, the sooner we get up."

Amanda flew from the room. Over her shoulder, she called, "Okay, but hurry."

Once she was gone, Cyn squirmed upward and kissed Santa, still not quite believing she'd said she would marry him. Not that she had reservations. All she was mulling over was the date. She grinned. "Since you're such a feminist, Santa, why don't you go start my shower?"

He chuckled. "I'll even wash your nooks and crannies."

Cyn's whole left side turned a little colder when he rose from the bed. She rolled to her stomach, so she could soak up the warmth from where he'd lain. "Santa," she murmured sleepily. She told herself she had to get up, but shut her eyes and drifted for a moment. She just felt too cozy for a shower, even if it *was* warm.

It was thinking about Santa *in* the shower that finally got her moving. Just as she dragged herself into the bathroom, he emerged. "Hmm," she said. "Stark naked and dripping wet. It sure looks like I got what I wanted for Christmas."

He laughed and grabbed her, hugging her tight, thinking he had a whole lot more to give. "Just wait till I put that bow on my head."

"Oh!" she exclaimed, leaping back, just as the water from his dripping hair splashed her cheeks. She realized her gown had soaked clear through, and that they were standing in a puddle.

He grinned, hauled her into his arms again and playfully swatted her backside. His hand lingered for a moment, grabbing a palmful of her soft flesh. "Last one to the Christmas tree's a rotten egg," he said as she slipped by him, pulling off her gown. He couldn't take his eyes off her. Cyn really was magnificent. When she coyly tossed her gown at him, he caught it. Even though she snapped the curtain across the rod and disappeared, he remained on the other side for a moment, smiling.

Then he went into overdrive. By the time Analise and Paxton rang the bell, Amanda was dressed and breakfast was in the oven. Usually Cyn made a full-scale brunch, but this year, she hadn't had time. The previous night, before they'd put out the remainder of Amanda's gifts and stuffed the stockings, the two of them had picked up scones, *beignets,* bagels and fruit. They'd made an omelet casserole from a recipe he'd found in one of her cookbooks. And it had been his first taste of relaxed, domestic bliss.

"Merry Christmas!" he called, emerging from the kitchen and heading down the hallway.

"Merry Christmas!" Paxton boomed.

"Morning, son-in-law." Analise hugged him and planted a smack on his cheek just as Paxton clapped a hand on his shoulder.

From her doorway, Cyn took in the scene. It was the homiest she'd seen in a long time. Her parents were back together. Apparently Evan had manipulatively tried to drive a wedge between them. And because her parents had their differences at the time, it had worked. Paxton had explained the whole story about Santa's past to Analise, too.

Where Analise didn't believe in keeping secrets and would have accepted Jake Jackson as Amanda's father—jewel thief and all—Paxton had wanted to protect Cyn. Later, thinking his lies about Cyn's marriage to Harry were the reason Analise had left, Paxton had done what he could to track down Jake. Instead, he'd found Anton Santa. Of course, Paxton had known Cyn wouldn't take kindly to the truth... at first. So, when the opportunity arose, he'd decided to both protect Amanda *and* play matchmaker. He'd hired Santa. And the rest was now history.

They were together again. A family. As her soon-to-be husband fiddled with the CD player, "It's Beginning to Look a Lot Like Christmas" began to play. Cyn grinned at Amanda, who was standing in front of the package-laden tree, with her hands on her hips. She was wearing her new appliquéd sweatshirt and, for once, it wasn't on backward.

Santa Claus was in front, just the way he was supposed to be. Analise was madly snapping pictures.

"Mommy! Can I open them now?"

Analise and Paxton headed for the sofa, and Santa placed a cup of hot coffee in Cyn's hand. "Sure, honey." She'd nearly reached the sofa herself when Santa pulled her into an armchair and onto his lap. "My coffee," she murmured as it splashed.

"That's what saucers are for," he returned absently, his gaze riveted on Amanda. The sound of tearing wrapping paper filled the room, and the first bow flew through the air.

The adults sipped their coffee, snapped photos and listened to carols, while Amanda gasped and oohed and aahed. When she'd opened half her presents, Cyn noticed Amanda stacking some of them by the front door. "Honey, why are you carrying them over there?"

Amanda whirled around. "I'm gonna give lots of them to that Harrison House where we Christmas caroled," she said breathlessly. "Just like in our story."

Santa glanced from Amanda to Cyn and back again. It was such a sweet thing to do. But didn't his daughter want her toys? Just because the girl in *Little Amanda's Perfect Christmas* gave her gifts away didn't mean his Amanda needed to do so. "You don't have to," he reminded.

Amanda charged toward him and Cyn. "I got what I want." She giggled, wet her fingers again and stuck them in his ear.

"You did?" he asked in surprise, suddenly realizing he'd left his present for her in the guest room.

"A daddy for Christmas!" she squealed. She hopped up, kissed him on the cheek, then ran back to the tree, just as Analise snapped another picture.

Cyn chuckled. "Oh!" she exclaimed. "Your present's in my room, Santa."

He rubbed her hip. "You better go get it," he drawled. "Or else."

As soon as Cyn hopped off his lap, Santa rose and headed for the guest room. He and Cyn emerged at the same time, and within seconds they were ensconced in the chair again.

"Is that for me, Daddy?" Amanda asked, eyeing the three-foot-tall box in front of the armchair.

"Sure is," he said as she walked over slowly and plopped down in front of it.

"But first, you gotta do this." Amanda nervously handed Santa a flat, square box.

He smiled and gingerly opened his gift. When he saw it, he had to fight back a belly laugh. He should have known what she'd get him. It was an eight-by-ten green frame, with a red mat. Inside, was a glamour photograph of Amanda. Her dress was slinky, her hair was topped by a rhinestone tiara, and she had on enough makeup that she could have passed for thirty.

"She insisted we go for the glamour shot," Cyn whispered.

"I'm a knockout," Amanda announced. Even though she'd seen the picture before, she looked stunned at seeing herself so dolled up.

"You sure are," he said with a chuckle. He knew it wasn't in his best interest to tell his little knockout that he loved her just the way she was. Nevertheless, his fingers curled possessively around the frame, and he sighed, already dreading her teen years. No doubt, he'd be running off her countless suitors with his shotgun.

"Why don't you open yours, sweetheart?" he asked. This time, Amanda unwrapped slowly, running her small fingers beneath the paper folds and disengaging the tape. She solemnly folded the wrapping neatly when she was finished, too. Cyn leaned and helped her with the cardboard lid.

"Oh, Daddy!" Amanda murmured in awe, scrambling onto a footstool and staring inside.

Santa leaned around Cyn and pulled the gift from the box. It was a hand carved, delicately painted nutcracker soldier that was as tall as Amanda. Santa realized his daughter was staring at him with wide-eyed wonder, as if he'd discovered her innermost secrets. She gasped. "When I grow up, I was gonna get me a prince." She averted her gaze and stared into the nutcracker's eyes. "How'd you find out?"

"Just a lucky guess," he said softly.

Amanda inched toward the armchair, stood on her tip toes again and kissed his cheek. "Thank you, Daddy."

"You're welcome." He smiled as Amanda seated herself next to her nutcracker.

"Analise," Paxton said. He sounded nearly as solemn as Amanda as he placed a box in his wife's hands.

"I bet I know what this is," she whispered happily, slowly opening the gift. Inside was a black velvet jeweler's box. Analise snapped open the lid and held up the contents for all to see. Sure enough, it was another red and green link for her lucky Christmas necklace.

She smiled at everyone. "Christmas, our wedding anniversary, and an engagement all rolled into one."

"It could have happened sooner if Paxton had just told me the truth when I asked him," Santa chided. He winked at Paxton.

"For all I knew at that point, you would have been on the next plane out of town!" Paxton chuckled.

Analise hugged her husband and reached into the pocketbook at her feet. She handed him a tiny box.

"Cuff links!" he exclaimed after a moment. "I've been such a mess without you, darling."

"But I'm back now," Analise whispered as he kissed her.

"For good?" Paxton asked.

"For good," Analise returned.

"Well, aren't you going to open it, Santa?" Cyn asked, poking Santa's chest. While he was watching Analise and Paxton, she'd surreptitiously put his gift in the very lap where she now found herself squirming. Santa glanced down.

"This looks promising." He picked up the small box, then gazed into her eyes.

Cyn smiled and wiggled her brows. She felt her heart beat double time as she watched him open her little package. The second she'd seen it, she'd known it was the perfect thing.

"A pocket watch." He gazed downward, feeling the heavy weight of the gold in his palm.

"I had it engraved yesterday," Cyn nearly whispered.

Santa unlatched it, his eyes roving over the tiny cursive letters of the inscription. "For My Husband," he read loud. "In Memory Of The Time We've Lost—In Happiness For The Future We've Found." His voice suddenly caught. "Love Cynthia."

His hand closed tightly around it; he was still holding it when he handed Cyn her gift. "This looks pretty promising, too," she said huskily. Somehow Santa found it difficult to smile. He realized Cyn's hands were shaking.

"Tiffany's—" She stared into her lap and laid the shining gold wrapping paper aside. It had been days since she'd seen Santa inside Tiffany's. Had he already decided to ask her to marry him? *No. It couldn't be a ring.* She turned in Santa's lap and gazed into his eyes.

"Open it," he said.

"Open it, Mommy," Amanda whispered.

Cyn swallowed around the lump in her throat. *He was thinking about proposing before yesterday afternoon. But then, I've been thinking about marrying him since the day was born.* With trembling fingers, she managed to open the box, then the jeweler's box inside.

"It's lovely." She cocked her head and gazed at her engagement ring. She was barely conscious of the fact that Amanda was now standing, and that Paxton and Analise were craning their necks. "Somehow, it looks like me," she murmured as Santa lifted it and nestled it on her finger. "Guess this makes it official?"

"Sure does." His arms tightened around her waist and he pulled her as close as he could.

Cyn's eyes roved over his heavily lidded, changeable brown eyes and his soft expressive mouth. *I'm looking at the man with whom I'm going to spend the rest of my life.* She ran a hand through his hair, then stretched upward. "Merry Christmas, Santa."

"Merry Christmas, Cyn," he murmured. Their lips met in such a soulful kiss that both knew their love was fated, and that nothing could ever come between them again.

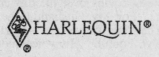 **HARLEQUIN®**

The proprietors of Weddings, Inc. hope you
have enjoyed visiting Eternity, Massachusetts.
And if you missed any of the exciting Weddings,
Inc. titles, here is your opportunity to complete
your collection:

Harlequin Superromance	#598	*Wedding Invitation* by Marisa Carroll	$3.50 U.S. ☐ $3.99 CAN. ☐
Harlequin Romance	#3319	*Expectations* by Shannon Waverly	$2.99 U.S. ☐ $3.50 CAN. ☐
Harlequin Temptation	#502	*Wedding Song* by Vicki Lewis Thompson	$2.99 U.S. ☐ $3.50 CAN. ☐
Harlequin American Romance	#549	*The Wedding Gamble* by Muriel Jensen	$3.50 U.S. ☐ $3.99 CAN. ☐
Harlequin Presents	#1692	*The Vengeful Groom* by Sara Wood	$2.99 U.S. ☐ $3.50 CAN. ☐
Harlequin Intrigue	#298	*Edge of Eternity* by Jasmine Cresswell	$2.99 U.S. ☐ $3.50 CAN. ☐
Harlequin Historical	#248	*Vows* by Margaret Moore	$3.99 U.S. ☐ $4.50 CAN. ☐

HARLEQUIN BOOKS…
NOT THE SAME OLD STORY

TOTAL AMOUNT	$
POSTAGE & HANDLING	$
($1.00 for one book, 50¢ for each additional)	
APPLICABLE TAXES*	$ _____
TOTAL PAYABLE	$ _____
(check or money order—please do not send cash)	

To order, complete this form and send it, along with a check or money order for the
total above, payable to Harlequin Books, to: **In the U.S.:** 3010 Walden Avenue,
P.O. Box 9047, Buffalo, NY 14269-9047; **In Canada:** P.O. Box 613, Fort Erie, Ontario,
L2A 5X3.

Name: _____

Address: _____ City: _____

State/Prov.: _____ Zip/Postal Code: _____

*New York residents remit applicable sales taxes.
  Canadian residents remit applicable GST and provincial taxes.   WED-F

Take 4 bestselling love stories FREE

Plus get a FREE surprise gift!

He's at home in denim; she's bathed in diamonds...
Her tastes run to peanut butter; his to pâté...
They're bound to be together...

for Richer, for Poorer

We're delighted to bring you more of the kinds of stories you love
in FOR RICHER, FOR POORER—a miniseries in which lovers
are drawn together by passion but separated by price.

Don't miss any of the FOR RICHER, FOR POORER
books, coming to you in the months ahead—only from
American Romance!

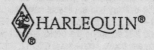

CHRISTMAS STALKINGS

All wrapped up in spine-tingling packages, here are three books guaranteed to chill your spine...and warm your hearts this holiday season!

#302 THE KID WHO STOLE CHRISTMAS
Linda Stevens

#303 I'LL BE HOME FOR CHRISTMAS
Dawn Stewardson

#304 BEARING GIFTS
Aimée Thurlo

This December, fill your stockings with the "Christmas Stalkings"—for the best in romantic suspense. Only from

HARLEQUIN®

INTRIGUE®

HARLEQUIN®

AMERICAN ◆ ROMANCE®

Four sexy hunks who vowed they'd never take "the vow" of marriage...

What happens to this Bachelor Club when, one by one, they find the right bachelorette?

Meet four of the most perfect men:

Steve: **THE MARRYING TYPE**
Judith Arnold
(October)

Tripp: **ONCE UPON A HONEYMOON**
Julie Kistler
(November)

Ukiah: **HE'S A REBEL**
Linda Randall Wisdom
(December)

Deke: **THE WORLD'S LAST BACHELOR**
Pamela Browning
(January)

STUDS

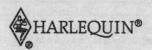

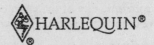

HARLEQUIN®

Don't miss these Harlequin favorites by some of our most distinguished authors!
And now you can receive a discount by ordering two or more titles!

HT#25483	BABYCAKES by Glenda Sanders	$2.99	☐
HT#25559	JUST ANOTHER PRETTY FACE by Candace Schuler	$2.99	☐
HP#11608	SUMMER STORMS by Emma Goldrick	$2.99	☐
HP#11632	THE SHINING OF LOVE by Emma Darcy	$2.99	☐
HR#03265	HERO ON THE LOOSE by Rebecca Winters	$2.89	☐
HR#03268	THE BAD PENNY by Susan Fox	$2.99	☐
HS#70532	TOUCH THE DAWN by Karen Young	$3.39	☐
HS#70576	ANGELS IN THE LIGHT by Margot Dalton	$3.50	☐
HI#22249	MUSIC OF THE MIST by Laura Pender	$2.99	☐
HI#22267	CUTTING EDGE by Caroline Burnes	$2.99	☐
HAR#16489	DADDY'S LITTLE DIVIDEND by Elda Minger	$3.50	☐
HAR#16525	CINDERMAN by Anne Stuart	$3.50	☐
HH#28801	PROVIDENCE by Miranda Jarrett	$3.99	☐
HH#28775	A WARRIOR'S QUEST by Margaret Moore	$3.99	☐

(limited quantities available on certain titles)

TOTAL AMOUNT	$
DEDUCT: 10% DISCOUNT FOR 2+ BOOKS	$
POSTAGE & HANDLING	$
($1.00 for one book, 50¢ for each additional)	
APPLICABLE TAXES*	$_____
TOTAL PAYABLE	$_____

(check or money order—please do not send cash)

To order, complete this form and send it, along with a check or money order for the total above, payable to Harlequin Books, to: **In the U.S.:** 3010 Walden Avenue, P.O. Box 9047, Buffalo, NY 14269-9047; **In Canada:** P.O. Box 613, Fort Erie, Ontario, L2A 5X3.

Name: _____

Address:_____City: _____

State/Prov.: _____ Zip/Postal Code: _____

*New York residents remit applicable sales taxes.
 Canadian residents remit applicable GST and provincial taxes.

HBACK-OD